Journey to Gettysburg

A NOVEL

Mark L. Hopkins

MARK L. HOPKINS

Copyright © 2014 Mark L. Hopkins
All rights reserved
First Edition

PAGE PUBLISHING, INC.
New York, NY

First originally published by Page Publishing, Inc. 2014

ISBN 978-1-63417-299-8 (pbk)
ISBN 978-1-63417-300-1 (digital)

Printed in the United States of America

CONTENTS

Preface..5

Prologue..7

Making the Home Fires Burn...11

North to Virginia..25

Uninvited Guests..41

Looking for a Doctor..49

The Ladies' Relief Hospital...59

Moving On..69

Charlottesville and North...79

Fighting the Good Fight...90

Glory Hallelujah in the Land of Cotton 101

On the Road to Winchester..111

A Home Away from Home 127

The Army of Northern Virginia...134

Sharing the Story..145

Shopping for Shoes in Gettysburg 154

Meeting the Yankees..159

Everyone Goes to Battle 170

Retreat 178

Williamsport 189

Heading to a New Home 200

The Ravages of War 210

The Mutual Defense Agreement 221

Epilogue: David Picks Up the Story 231

Author's Notes: The History Behind Journey to Gettysburg 235

Afterword..243

About the Author...244

PREFACE

The Battle of Gettysburg holds a special place in my heart. I was eleven years old when my father first took our family to visit that famous battlefield. We wandered that hallowed ground from Devil's Den to the site of Pickett's Charge. In the Visitor's Center there was a raised relief map of the battlefield that filled a lower floor room. It was so large that one had to look at it over a railing from the floor above. It had lights on it in all of the various places and a ranger told the story of the battle while turning on the lights in the strategic locations of the story. The battle came alive to me with that presentation. That next spring the Battle of Gettysburg became my year-end report in American History class. Each student was required to make a fifteen minute report to close out the year. I started my report on Monday and was still on my feet on Wednesday telling the story with a chalk board full of battlefield diagrams and breathing heavy with excitement. Thus, I had my first experience telling a story from history in front of a class of students. It was the beginning of what later became a labor of love for me, teaching history.

In July of 2013 I attended the Reenactment of the Battle of Gettysburg. It was the fourth time I visited the battlefield near that small city in southern Pennsylvania. More than 170,000 soldiers laid their lives on the line there in what became the pivotal battle of the Civil War. Fifty-Seven thousand became causalities. Twelve of my ancestors fought in that battle, four for the union and eight for the south. Most historians believe The Battle of Gettysburg was the most important battle in American history. In no battle before or since has so much been at stake and so many given their lives for a cause.

A number of people have helped me write this book. These include editor and writing consultant Kathryn Smith who cleaned up my writing style and played the role of muse. Each time I seemed to get bogged down she had a question or a comment that created the needed motivation. Kathryn continually challenged me to be more descriptive and to paint pictures with words so the reader could not only see what was on the page but, also, could envision what was in my mind. My wife, Ruth, always a first editor in my writing, encouraged me to attend the 150th Reenactment of the Battle of Gettysburg in July of 2013 where the story of Matthew Mason and his journey to Gettysburg begin to form in my mind. Even Granddaughter Madeline played a role. She was the first of the young adults, the target audience for the book, who read the story as it was being completed and promptly pronounced it the best book she ever read. Despite any possible bias she might have had, with comments like that the book just had to be published.

PROLOGUE

※

July 3, 1863

"Son, do you have a gun?" the officer asked.

"No, sir. I had one, but the firing pin blew up and burned my face," Matt said.

"Well, I can't have you going into battle without a gun," the officer said. He left the line, and in a moment, he was back with a flag in his hand. "Do you know anything about using a signal flag?"

"No, sir. I've seen them used, but I don't know what the signals are," Matt responded.

The officer said, "Well, you stay close to me when we get into action, and I will tell you what to do with the flag. I swear, if you run, I will shoot you in the back. Do you hear?"

"I understand, sir. I won't run," Matt responded. The officer left, and Matt began marching down the road with the rest of the men, his mind spinning. How in the world did he get into such a mess? He wasn't in the army. He had come here looking for his Pa. Less than an hour ago he had left the battle lines to escape the mayhem that was about to occur. They had caught him, thinking he was a deserter. Now he was marching right back into it.

He looked over at the man to his left. "What outfit is this, sir?" he asked.

The man responded, " This is General Isaac Trimble's brigade, but it don't make no difference because we are all going to be dead in a little while anyway."

Matt started to respond to the man, but he was looking away. Matt could see tears in his eyes.

The marching column came to a halt, and all of the men turned and walked off the road into the woods. Matt soon became aware that there were many other men already in the woods. His unit kept moving down the hill until bright sunlight began filtering in between the trees. As the woods opened up, he could see the cannons of General Heth's artillery lined up toward the south of his position. He knew his Pa was with the artillery, and he strained his eyes to see if his Pa was with the cannons, but it was hard to make out any individual while looking out into the bright sunlight.

On the ridge off in the distance more than a half mile away, there was an endless sea of men dressed in blue stretched as far as he could see from left to right. Matt could also see their cannons lined up along the ridge facing the ones of the Confederate forces, and he began to feel a tightness in his chest that slid all the way down to his stomach. He began feeling sick, but fought the nausea by taking very deep and slow breaths. His thoughts were interrupted by the bleat of a bugle followed by a voice yelling something he couldn't distinguish in the distance. Suddenly, there was a deafening roar as all of the cannons fired at once. The air was so full of smoke that he could no longer see the ridge where the Yankees were. In a matter of minutes, the Yankee big guns answered shot for shot. He heard the Yankee cannonballs landing in the woods all around. When one hit, he heard the yells and cries of injured men, quickly followed by the sounds of medics rushing to help them.

After two hours of the big guns firing over and over, silence fell. Matt heard the bugle call again, and the men around him stood up and moved forward to the edge of the trees like sleepwalkers. Almost as a single man, they left the shelter of the trees and lined up side by side. They stood there for what seemed to be the longest time, their coats forming a long gray line. The officer who had given Matt the flag arrived just as the order came to move out.

Matt was at the far right of the second line of Trimble's unit, a line stretching a quarter of a mile up the line of trees along the edge of the ridge. To Matt's right was a long double line of men that a man he had talked with earlier identified as General Pickett's brigade. They stretched out of sight to the south. All were moving forward purposefully, marching in one great double line.

As they moved forward, the Yankee cannons started up again, but the sound they were making was different, and they were not lobbing cannonballs up into the woods. He heard the man beside him curse and say the dreaded words: "Grape shot." He knew from listening to conversations between the soldiers that grape shot was composed of riprap, metal, chains, rocks—anything hard and destructive that could be fitted into the muzzle of a cannon. When it blasted out, the grape shot scattered and cut down the marching men in a swath several feet wide. As quick as a gap opened in the line, men moved up to fill it, and the wave of soldiers continued walking toward the ridge where the Yankees were waiting, leaving the wounded and dead men behind them.

All around Matt, men were falling, and blood was everywhere. Not far ahead he saw a stone fence with dead and dying men lying behind it. When he was a few feet from the fence, he felt something hit him hard, and he felt his body falling toward the ground. He looked down, and his heart jumped. His bare feet and legs were covered with blood. He wondered if he had been shot. Matt turned over and looked toward the blue-coated soldiers on the ridge one last time as he closed his eyes and lay still.

His body was quiet, but his mind was still moving forward. His thoughts raced back to the chain of events that brought him to this point. His Ma's face appeared to him over and over. Sometimes she was like she used to be before the illness. But sometimes he could see the pain of sad resolution in her face. His life of the past several weeks was moving through his mind like pictures in a book with a narrative that included the voices of his Ma, the banker from Mt. Airy, and even the braying of his mule, Ol' Mose, who had been a part of his family since before he was born. He had heard that before death, your life passes before your eyes, and he wondered if he was dying. The pictures seemed alive. In his mind they were.

MAKING THE HOME FIRES BURN

"Hey, boy, are you Matt Mason?"

"Yes sir," Matt answered. He put down the small hatchet he had been using to chop kindling and strained through the bright sunlight to see into the back of the buggy that had pulled up in front of their gate.

He had heard the horses' hooves a few seconds before the buggy appeared around the edge of the barn. The black driver had halted the horses in front of the gate and nodded in Matt's direction. The voice from the buggy was familiar to Matt, and he recognized the face of the big man who took up most of the backseat. Matt knew the man was the bank president from Mt. Airy. He had been there with his Pa in years past. His coat was draped over the back of the seat, and his bow tie was untied and hanging down the front of his shirt like the ears of a basset hound. There was another man in the back of the buggy with the bank president, but he couldn't make out his face in the shadow.

The deep voice again came from the buggy. "How old are you now, son?"

"I'll be sixteen in August, sir," Matt responded politely.

"You are a good-sized fifteen-year-old," the man replied. "I'm sure you will make a big man like your father."

Matt knew he was big for his age. Everybody said so. He had grown almost a full foot over the past two years. His pants were tight on his hips and were short on his legs. Ma said he looked like high water was coming. Today he had on an underwear shirt with no sleeves. Most of the time he didn't wear a shirt at all, but it had been cool for a May morning when he got out of bed and headed for the barn to do his chores. He again responded politely to the bank president, "Yes sir, I hope so."

"Is your mama home?" the man asked, leaning out of the buggy and peering more closely at Matt.

"Yes, sir. She is inside, but she is sick."

"I heard she was still sick," said the man. "She's been down quite a spell now. Is she getting better?"

"Some days are better than others," Matt said. "She is not up today."

"Too bad. Do you know where your Pa is?" the man questioned.

"No, sir. He went off to join the Army of Virginia just after the war started two years ago in '61. We have heard from him from time to time, but right now we aren't sure where he is."

The bank man said something Matt couldn't hear to the man in the shadow and then directed another question to Matt. This time his voice came up stronger and sounded a bit more directive. "Son, why didn't your Pa enlist with the army here in North Carolina instead of in Virginia? We would know exactly where he is if he was with our boys."

"I don't know, sir," Matt responded. "Raleigh is way over there, and he could enlist in Big Lick, Virginia, and be a day's ride closer to home. At least that is what he told Ma when he left."

Matt didn't tell the man that his Pa was an admirer of General Robert E. Lee, who headed up the Army of Virginia, and he had more confidence in Lee's leadership than that of any of the generals in North Carolina.

"Okay, son. Tell your mama I came by and was asking about her health. I will come back in a week or two to talk to her about some business," he concluded.

"I'll be sure to tell her, sir. I'm sure she will be better by then," Matt replied.

Matt pretended ignorance, but he knew exactly what the banker wanted to talk to Ma about. They had not paid their mortgage on the little farm now for several months. Without his Pa at home, it had been very difficult to even keep food on the table, never mind having enough crops or livestock to sell to pay a mortgage. The only thing they had that would draw any real money was the two cows. Selling them both wouldn't generate enough to pay the back mortgage. The little farm didn't need Ol' Mose to help with planting. They hadn't planted anything since his father left. The old mule was too feeble to sell anyway. He wouldn't bring a dollar. Ma was really worried about their situation and thought that they might lose their home like so many others whose men had gone off to war.

Matt watched the buggy until it was out of sight, all the time hoping that he had told the truth, that his mother would be better next week.

He finished cutting the wood, carried the kindling inside, and set it down next to the fireplace. Their little house had two rooms, a bedroom where his Ma and Pa slept, and a bigger room that served as kitchen, parlor, and everything else. The fireplace was made out of rocks his Pa had dug out of the ground when he cleared the first ten acres for crops years ago. It was a big fireplace, and there were several cook pots and kettles sitting on the floor close by. Matt glanced over to the ladder that was leaning against the side of the bedroom. That room was constructed like a room within a larger room. He slept in the loft above the bedroom. The only way up and down was the ladder that his Pa had made out of two saplings and several cross pieces.

When his Pa was home, Matt could often hear his folks talking just below him in their bedroom late at night. Sometimes the sound of their voices put him to sleep. Other times he learned things about their life that parents did not talk about in the presence of their children. That mostly had to do with illnesses, family problems, and financial matters. Matt didn't ask many questions, but he did absorb everything he heard and kept it stored in his mind for future reference.

He heard his mother's voice from the other room. "Matt, who was that at the gate?"

Matt went into the bedroom. Ma was lying on the bed. He had pushed it over to the wall where she could look out the window. "It was the man from the bank, Ma," he told her.

His mother lifted herself up off the pillow and balanced on her elbow. "Oh my," she said. "What did he want?"

Matt sat down on the edge of the bed and responded in a low voice, "I don't know, Ma. He said he would come back in a week or two when you are better. He said he needs to talk to you."

She nodded but didn't say anything.

He looked at his Ma. She had been such a strong lady, fair with long blond hair. She always said that Quakers were mostly Dutch and English, and they were big people, blond and blue-eyed. His Ma was always tall and thin, tall but not thick like many of the other women Matt knew from the other farms around. Everyone had always said Matt looked like his Ma. He was tall and thin like she was before she got sick, with her blond hair and blue eyes. Over the past two years, during his growth spurt, he had begun to develop arms and shoulders like his Pa. He doubted he would ever be as big as his Pa, but he was still growing. Maybe he would. He knew he would never have his Pa's dark hair and olive skin, though over the past two years his hair had begun to darken, and working on the farm out in the sun had given him a well-tanned face. Even with those changes, Matt's face was still his Ma's made over. Anyone who knew her back when she was feeling good could pick him out of a crowd as her son.

Now, after months of illness, she was a shadow of her former self. Her hair didn't appear blond anymore. It was more the color of long grass in the wintertime, tan and dry looking. Her skin had lost its color and was almost white, and her eyes were so deep set that he could hardly see any color in them at all.

"Son, we have some serious talking to do," Ma said. "When you finish your chores, I want you to come back and spend some time with me."

"Okay, Ma." He grinned suddenly. "You know I already know about the birds and the bees, don't you?" Matt expected to see a smile, and he wasn't disappointed, but it was a small one, almost a grimace.

"Yes, son. Your Pa took good care of getting your head ready to be a man before he left," his mother said softly. "You and I need to talk about this farm, the animals, and some things about our neighbors. So come back by suppertime so we can just sit and talk a bit. Don't forget."

JOURNEY TO GETTYSBURG

Matt left through the back door and headed for the barn. He needed to get Ol' Mose inside and see about feed for Bossy and Bess. It didn't take long to feed the cows and lead Ol' Mose into the barn and fill up his oat bag. Back in the house, Matt went to the fireplace and swung the kettle out. It always had enough grits for a couple of bowls. He dipped himself a bowl and walked over to the window box and cut himself a slice of butter to flavor it. The window box sat on the sill just outside the window across from the fireplace. In the summer they could put tins of water in it for drinking, but the water also served to keep things cooler than summer heat would allow without the box.

"Do you want a bowl of grits, Ma?" he called out.

The voice came back from the bedroom, low but audible. "No, son, I'm not hungry."

Matt walked into the bedroom. "Ma, I don't think you have had anything to eat all day. Have you?"

"I'm just not hungry, son. The pain in my stomach gets worse when I try to eat anything," she replied.

Matt was immediately concerned. "Ma, we need to get the doctor out to see you again. Why don't I go in to town and get him tomorrow?"

Ma leaned back on her pillow. "We might do that, son, but I have some things for you to do first. Let's talk."

Matt pulled up a stool and sat next to the bed. The stool was low, and his knees were almost to his chest. When he was smaller, the stool was just the right height for him. His Pa had made it to fit him then, but Matt had long ago outgrown the stool. Still, it was the only other piece of furniture in the bedroom, and it was handy.

The conversation was long and wandering. Ma talked about the early days when she met his father, Isaac Mason. He was on a trip up into Pennsylvania to buy some livestock. She was the seventeen-year-old daughter of a Quaker elder who lived on a farm near Lancaster with her parents and her two younger sisters. It was on a Saturday when they met by accident in a store in town. Her father had gone to the bank, and she was shopping with her mother and sisters. She turned around when she heard heavy footsteps entering the store.

"He was so big he filled up the doorway," she said.

Matt had heard this story many times before, how his folks met and how she was immediately fascinated by the big country boy from North Carolina, and how Isaac couldn't take his eyes off her. She could feel his eyes following her around the store and was flattered by the attention.

Suddenly, she changed course. "Matthew, we haven't done right by you with your religious instruction. I was raised a member of the Society of Friends. My father was an elder in the church. We didn't believe in slavery or in war. And for sure, we were not to marry anyone who was not of our religious persuasion. We called those who were not members of the Society of Friends the English."

Ma continued. "When your Pa and I met, it was on a Saturday. The next day when we arrived at our meeting house for services, your father was there. He was dressed totally in black and with the traditional Society of Friends hat on. He sat in the back of the men's section during the worship service while I sat with the women on our side of the little sanctuary. I could feel his eyes on me through the entire service. When it was over, he asked if he could drive me home. Mother gave her consent. It was a good thing my father was elsewhere talking with several of the men because for sure, he would have said no," she said.

"When I married your father, I thought he was a member of the Society of Friends. My whole family thought so. When I found out he wasn't, I was in a state of shock."

The story was very familiar to Matt. By the time they were at the house, she was hopelessly in love with Isaac Mason. She invited him to stay for lunch without even asking her mother. Afterward, they walked in the vineyard and talked. Isaac was still there at supper time and spent an hour afterward talking to her father.

"When they finished talking," she said, "he came to me on the porch and asked me to marry him. I was so overcome with emotion. He said my father would give his consent, if I wanted to. Oh, did I ever."

Ma paused as she always did at that point in the story. She took a couple of deep breaths and started again.

"Your Pa and I were married in the minister's home behind a Quaker meeting house just across the Virginia border. Your Pa had been wearing the black coat and his Society of Friends hat every time I saw him after we met at the store. Somewhere down the road after we were married, he confessed that after we met, he realized that I was a member of the Friends, so he found a store in Lancaster where they handled clothing for members of our group. He asked the owner how he should dress to fit in with a group of Quakers. The store owner fixed him up for a price, of course. We were already married and riding south through Virginia when he told me what he had done. When he told me, he smiled, took off his black coat and his hat, and stowed them in the back of the wagon. It was then that it dawned on me that I was now married to an 'English.'"

Ma's voice came up louder, and she obviously felt a wave of emotion. "That realization hit me like a ton of bricks, and for a moment, I wondered if I would go to hell because I had married an English."

Ma stopped for a moment as if she was thinking. She said, "If the English were different, as I had always been taught, I couldn't tell it with Isaac Mason, except for the fact that he didn't go to church much. Of course, we don't have a Quaker church close to us. The only church of any kind is the little Methodist Church down in Mt. Airy. It doesn't have a permanent pastor, only a circuit rider who comes by about once a month."

Matt had heard all of the stories before. He kept waiting on something new, but he knew his Ma would get to it in her own time. There was no sense in trying to hurry her. Sure enough, the conversation eventually turned to the problems they were facing with the farm and her health. She told him that some morning soon, he would come into her bedroom and she would not be there.

"Where are you going, Ma?" he broke in.

"Matthew, at the end of my last visit with the doctor, he told me there was nothing else he could do for me. He predicted that the pain would get worse, and it has. Eventually, the good Lord will come and take me," she explained.

Matt broke in again. "Ma, you must not talk like that. You have to eat and get out in the sun some. The fresh air would help you. You can't give up."

"When I say I will be gone, I mean that my body will be here, but my spirit, the real me, will be gone," she said calmly. "When that happens, you have to accept that the good Lord has spoken, and it is for the best."

Matt held his tongue, knowing that it would do little good to argue with his mother. He let it go and resolved to see that she ate something and decided he would create a makeshift bed out on the porch so she would get some sun and feel the breezes.

Ma went on with her one-sided conversation. She told Matt that he was to do several things over the next couple of days, and she began a list of chores for him.

"Son, we are going to get you ready for a trip," she said. "I want you to go and find your father, wherever he is. It will take you several days to find the Army of Virginia, but your father needs to know what has happened here, and he can tell you what you need to do for your future. That future is not here on this farm. Without him, this farm isn't ever going to be a successful venture."

Ma continued. "Take one of the cows to the Martin family over by the ridge. I understand that Mrs. Martin is having trouble with her milk for the baby, and having a cow would be a big help to her. You tell her it is only a loan, or she won't take it. Then don't worry about it. They need a cow, and they will take good care of it. Take Ol' Mose to ride, but go slow and don't overtax him. He can carry your weight but can't run or even trot. Take the four chickens and the other cow down to the store in Mt. Airy. The cow should bring fifteen dollars. Lots of people need the milk for their children. You tell Mr. Williams at the store that you need Union money for the cow. Lots of people come through on the stage with Union money, and he has it under the cash box. I've seen him put it there. Tell him you are going on a trip north where Confederate money may not work so well. You need Union money for the cow. You can trade the chickens for some beef jerky."

Ma paused for breath. He could almost see her forming the words in her mind. "On the way back, stop where the stream comes close to the road and look for some plants that grow by the stream. The plants are large, maybe head high, and the tops of the plants look like the Queen Anne's lace that grows in the field just up the hill from the house. Cut some of the sprouts from the plants and bring them home. I want to make some tea I've heard about but never made before."

With those words, Ma seemed exhausted. "Let's get some rest, Matthew," she said. "You've got a lot to do tomorrow."

Matt was up early the next morning. He ate his grits, checked to see that Ma was still sleeping, and headed for the barn. He milked the cows and put their halters on for the trip to the Martin farm and then down to Mt. Airy. He put some of the milk into the box on the window sill and drank the rest. He pumped the well to get water for the basin in the kitchen and to replace the water in the window box. Then he went back to the barn for Ol' Mose. The mule was a bit balky but finally came out of the stall. Matt needed him to help lead the two cows. They were easier to handle if their ropes were attached to Ol' Mose. Matt didn't know why it was that way, but it was.

It was midafternoon when Matt returned from the trip to Mt. Airy and the Martin farm. Ol' Mose was still a steady mount, and it was easier riding than it would have been walking the rock road in bare feet. In the house, he put the plant sprouts he had cut at the creek down on the table and went into the bedroom. Ma was asleep, so he went back out to the fireplace and dipped himself another bowl of grits. He sat down at the little table with the grits and a string of beef jerky. The combination of the warm corn porridge with the butter seasoning and the salty beef jerky were just enough to quell his hunger.

He heard Ma moving on the bed in the bedroom, and he took a bowl of the grits in to her.

She smiled at him. "Matthew, set the grits down on the table. I will eat them later. Did you bring the sprouts to make the tea?"

"Yes, ma'am. They are by the sink," Matt said.

"Matthew, add some water in the tea kettle and put it over by the fire. Don't put it over the fire yet. We aren't ready to make the tea. Go back to the sink and cut the sprouts in small stems and put them aside until we are ready to bring the water in the kettle to a boil."

Matt went back into the other room, filled the kettle, and cut the sprouts.

He heard Ma's voice from the bedroom. She wanted to talk again, so Matt went back in and sat down on the stool at the edge of the bed. She was almost melancholy as she began to talk to him this time, not nearly as spirited and positive as she had been the night before.

"Matthew, tonight I want you to pack up whatever you want for your trip to find your father. You can put it by the front door, ready to pack on Ol' Mose. Be sure to pack light. Don't take anything you aren't sure you will need. I want you to take along your father's old gun. I know it is heavy and I hope you never have to use it, but you are going to be traveling north across the mountains, and that is bear country. That gun probably won't kill a bear, but the noise and the pain of the rifle ball might turn him away or, at least, give you time to get up a tree. When you have everything ready, I want you to bring in the two horse blankets we have in the barn and hang them over the rail on the porch."

"Yes, ma'am," Matt said.

Ma seemed to drift away for a moment, and then she was back. "Do you remember the well your father began to dig before he left for the war?"

Matt nodded that he remembered.

"It is by the fence he built to separate the north ten acres from the back road. There are lots of big rocks in that fence. I want you to go up to that old well and move about thirty rocks from that wall and put them over next to the well. That will probably take you until dark. Go on now."

Matt went out the door and walked quickly up to the old well. It was about four feet deep. Pa said it would need to reach about twelve feet before it would begin to seep water. The rock fence was about twenty feet away, and Matt began hauling the rocks over to the edge of the well. Thirty rocks were plenty to bring that well back up to ground level, which he thought was what Ma intended. He wondered why she had assigned this task, but it didn't come to him.

That night after washing off in the outside trough, he came in the house again and sat down next to his mother's bed. She was sleeping but was moving and speaking out loud from time to time. Then as if she realized he was there, she came awake.

"I did what you asked," Matt said. "The rocks are beside the well."

"That's good, son," she said. "Matthew, if you come in anytime and find my spirit gone and only a body here, I don't want you to be sad. My pain is so bad that I can hardly stand it. There is no reason in God's earth that I would choose to leave you, but before long, God is going to spare me this pain. He is going to take my spirit home to heaven. When that happens, there are some things I want you to do for me."

Matt felt the tears coming at the edge of his eyes as he listened to his mother.

Ma continued. "I want you to take the two blankets from the porch. Put one of them in the bottom of the well your father dug. Then come back to the house for me. Wrap me in the second blanket and carry me up to the well. I am not as heavy as a yearling, so you shouldn't have any trouble. Lay me on the blanket in the bottom of the well with the second blanket on top. Then take the rocks that you have stacked near the well and place them over my body in the bottom of the well. Stack them up until they are just above ground level. That will serve as a grave for me where your father can find me if he is ever able to come back here. Then take the cross with the eight point star on it that is there against the wall and wedge it into the rocks so anyone who ever sees this grave will know that I was a Christian lady. The star will tell them I was a member of the Society of Friends."

Matt looked at the cross with the star etched into the wood. He hadn't noticed it before there against the wall. Ma must have been working on it for a while; maybe she had kept it under the bed. Matt recognized the wood from the barn, and the star was the like the ones he had seen on Quaker farms painted on the side of the barns.

Matt was crying by this point, and he started to talk to Ma, assuring her that everything would be all right. Ma shushed him and said, "You are right, everything will be all right. The good Lord will see to it."

Then she said, "Now, one more thing, Matthew. When you have finished placing the rocks and the cross, I want you to come back down to the house, and be sure you have Ol' Mose packed the way you want him. Lead him over to the fence near the road and tie him there while you take care of the house and the barn. Remember, when you leave to find your father, you cannot ride Ol' Mose uphill as you head for Fancy Gap. You can ride him downhill, but only for an hour at a time. Ride him for a bit and then let him walk with you and rest for a while before you ride him again. He is near his time and will serve you until he can't do it anymore. When that time comes, you will have to do what you need to do to put him out of his misery. Do you understand?"

Matt responded, "Yes, Ma. I understand." Matt had watched his Pa put one of the cows out of its misery once before. It had stepped in a hole and broken a leg. Pa took his rifle and put a bullet right between its eyes. Pa said trying to fix the leg and keep the cow off its feet would be just too much pain for the animal. Pa dressed the cow out, dried the meat in the barn, and they had meat on the table for supper for several weeks.

"Once you are ready to leave, take a heavy piece of wood and dip it in the pitch that your father used to patch the roof," Ma said. "Bring it in the house and stick it in the fireplace. It will catch fire and burn for a long time. Take it to the barn and light everything you see that will burn. Then bring it back to the house and light the curtains and the beds. That will pretty well take the house down before too long.

"When you find your father, you tell him that I did what he always said he would do when the bank vultures were trying to take the land he cut out of the trees, the land he sweated over. He always said he would burn it to the ground before he would let them take it from him. You tell him we burned it to the ground." Ma's voice was very firm and forceful as she finished. The phrase "burned it to the ground" would resonate with Matt for a long time.

Matt listened in disbelief. He had heard his Pa say they would burn the place down before they would let the vultures take it. That was not new to him. He had thought about that before, but then it was make-believe. This was real. This was his Ma planning for him to burn the place down if he came in and found her gone!

Matt pondered his response. He could tell her none of that was going to happen, that she was going to get better, and all would be fine in a few weeks. He could just agree with her, though he really couldn't envision any of what she said actually happening. In the end, he thought better of responding at all. Really, what could he say that would make sense? Instead, he let it go. He couldn't grasp even the possibility that he would come in some morning and find her "gone" as she put it, that he would be doing all of the things she had directed.

His mother spoke again, and her voice was very soft now. "Now, Matthew, let's make that special tea you brought me."

Matt went back into the other room and pushed the kettle over the fire. When the water came to a boil, he put the stems he had cut up earlier into the water, watching as the water took on a rich brown color. When he brought the kettle back out, he could smell the tea. It was a strange smell and not one he could remember from another time. He poured the tea into two cups and carried them back into the bedroom where his Ma was dozing.

When he came into the room, her head came up off the pillow, and she asked him about the two cups. He said he thought he would join her. "Have you tasted it?" she asked sharply. He assured him he had not. She said, "Good. This is old people's tea and not for you. I may need two cups for myself."

Old people's tea, he thought. He remembered once several years ago when he was in town with his father that a friend gave his father something to drink. The man had asked Matt if he wanted a taste. His father broke in and said, "Matt is too young. This is old people's drink." Matt assumed that it was some kind of alcoholic beverage that kids his age shouldn't drink. So now Ma had some old people's drink too. He didn't think about it more because his mother was beginning to talk again.

"Matthew, when we finish here, I want you to go back to the sink and throw out the sprouts and anything that is left over from the tea you just made. It isn't good left over. And I want you to wash the kettle with soap."

Matt nodded that he would do it.

"Now, come over here and lie down on the bed with me while I drink my tea. Stay with me until I go to sleep," she said. Matt did as his mother requested. The bed felt soft. He was tired after his day of errands and hauling rocks. He listened as she hummed the tune of "Amazing Grace" softly and sipped her old people's tea. He worried about what tomorrow would bring but somehow couldn't believe that someday, soon both his mother and the farm might be gone and he would be alone. Soon he was asleep.

NORTH TO VIRGINIA

Matt was about a half mile from home before he allowed himself to look back. His tears were falling heavy now, but through them he could still see that the smoke was black and filled the sky. He knew the neighbors would be coming, attracted by the smoke, but it would take them a while to get there since the closest one lived almost two miles away. Matt was surprised by how fast everything went up in flames and would like to have stayed to watch, but his mother had warned him to leave as soon as the fires were set. Neighbors coming meant questions that he shouldn't have to answer.

He turned again to the road ahead. He was riding Ol' Mose, but shortly, he would have to begin walking as the road turned upward toward Fancy Gap at the top of the Appalachian Mountain ridge. There was a trading post at the Gap, right on top of the ridge. He had been there once before with his father and remembered that from the Gap he could see nothing but mountains in all directions.

The road was covered with rock down on the flat land when he headed toward Mr. Airy, but as the road began to climb the ridge in the other direction, it became packed dirt. Like all dirt roads, in rainy times it became all mud. Most of the time there was room for only one wagon on the road at a time, but that wasn't a problem since very few wagons were on the road these days. Always, the ruts could be seen in the road, and from time to time, they were deep where wagons had battled the mud and sunk, making twelve- and fifteen-inch indentions in the soft ground.

Matt's mind was racing. He fought the urge to think back over the details of the last two days, knowing that despair was just below the surface. Instead, he had to think ahead. His father had always told him, "Today and tomorrow are the most important days of your life. If you do the best you can today and concentrate on planning tomorrow so that it will be the best that it can be, your life will be good, and you won't have to worry about what has gone before." Still, his mother's face kept creeping into his consciousness. When it did, the tears came again and again.

He was about three miles up the road when he crested a ridge, and there he allowed himself one more look back at the farm. He could not make it out from where he stood, but the black smoke was still coming up from the burning buildings.

Ma's words came into his mind then: "When you find your Pa, you tell him that we burned it to the ground."

For sure, no one would be taking their farm, the place that his father and mother had poured their lives into with so little return.

Then he heard his father's voice in his head again: "Matt, I don't expect to ever be a rich man. The only wealth I will ever create is in your life and your future. We brought you into this world and watched you grow into a fine young man. Your mother and I expect that you will be the expression of the value of our lives." Matt fought back the tears again.

As he walked, Matt thought more and more about his father off with the Army of Virginia fighting the Yankees. They hadn't heard from him in several months. He hoped that at the end of this journey he would find his father and he would be able to tell him about Ma, about the banker coming to visit and about the farm. He hoped that his father would be able to tell him what to do next. He hoped that he would find his father. He hoped that he would find his father…alive.

It was a hard day's walk up to Fancy Gap, and Matt was tired when he arrived just after dark. His feet were heavy, and they had a few sore spots on them from the sharp rocks. He found the going harder as the climb up the ridge began, but it was a relief to get off the rocks and onto the soft dirt of the hill road. Ol' Mose had balked several times along the way, and Matt stopped to let him rest. The old mule labored with every step at the steepest spots, but in the end, he made it across every ridge.

When he arrived at the trading post, Matt tied Ol' Mose where he could eat some grass, and then he went inside. The proprietor was in the process of closing the store but was obviously glad to see a potential customer come in the door. Matt introduced himself and told the man he was on the road and, with his permission, would sleep under the trees across the road that night. The proprietor told Matt his name was Diggins. Matt knew he would never address him as just "Diggins"; he had been taught to show proper respect, and the man would be Mr. Diggins when Matt talked to him.

"Son, you can bed down anywhere you want to. No rain is expected for tonight, but we have been having some fog, and the dew is pretty heavy in the mornings this time of year," Mr. Diggins responded.

Matt was busy looking at the shelf behind the counter, and he settled on something to supplement his regular fare of beef jerky.

"Mr. Diggins, I think I would like a loaf of bread and a tin of honey," Matt said.

Mr. Diggins smiled and said, "Those are good choices, son. My wife baked the bread this morning, and the honey is fresh. A man brings it to me about once a week. He was just here this morning too. What size tin of honey would you like?"

Matt knew that he would get a better price if he bought a larger tin, but he knew he would have to carry whatever he bought. He responded, "Just the smaller one, Mr. Diggins. How much do I owe you?"

Mr. Diggins looked at the two items. "That is fifteen cents, son. What kind of money are you carrying?"

Matt answered, "I have Union money, sir. Is that all right with you?"

Mr. Diggins was obviously pleased. "That is just fine. We have people from both sides of the Mason-Dixon Line come through here. It is good to have some change in both Union and Confederate money. It is good for business."

Matt was almost out the door when Mr. Diggins cautioned him, "If you have food with you, it will attract bears. They can smell food from a couple of miles away. You don't want to have any food close to you. I have an old ice box on the porch that is made of reinforced metal. You should take any food you have and put it in there. The latch on it is pretty tight, and even if the smell escapes, they probably won't be able to get in there. If you hear bears moving in the night, it is not likely they will approach you. That is, if you don't have any food on you. If you do keep even a piece of bread, they will take it right out of your pocket."

After supper, Matt followed Mr. Diggins's directions and put his beef jerky, honey, and leftover bread in the box on the porch. He went back into the trading post to ask Mr. Diggins about the best route to get north to Big Lick. He listened to the proprietor's best advice and told him he would give it some thought.

He moved back across the road to his makeshift campsite and built a small fire. He laid out his blanket on the soft grass and checked on Ol' Mose to be sure he was tied up tight. He didn't want the old mule to be spooked by any bears and head back down the road for home. The last thing Matt did was to lift the old rifle out of the harness that held it in place along the mule's side. That gun seemed to weigh a ton, and he was immediately glad that he had Ol' Mose to carry it. He took the rifle and placed it by his blanket in case he needed it in the night. He remembered Ma's words: "It might not stop a bear, but the sound and the sting of a musket ball might scare him away or, at least, slow him down a bit."

Matt looked around for a tree he could climb in case a bear came calling. There was one about ten feet away that had low-hanging branches. Then he thought, *Can't bears climb trees?* That thought didn't give him much comfort.

It was a restless night. His ears were alert to every noise coming from the woods, and more than once he felt his hand move toward the rifle hidden just under the edge of his blanket. His mind kept going back to the events of the morning. He had to stop thinking about his mother and the little farm and concentrate on the journey ahead.

Matt knew he would be on the road at least a couple of weeks and maybe longer and tried to view it all as an adventure. His past was a blur until just a week ago. Now everything was crystal clear in his mind, every happening a major event. From Fancy Gap north, every step was into unfamiliar territory. Where would he be tomorrow night this time? Finally, rest came.

Matt was up with first light and went across the road to retrieve his food. The trading post would not be open for a couple of hours, so there was no one to talk to. Within minutes he was off down the road. Yesterday he had walked up the hill for almost eight miles to the trading post on the Fancy Gap ridge, but now, going downhill, he could ride Ol' Mose without worrying about overtiring the old mule. Today was going to be a better day.

Mr. Diggins had given him two alternatives for his trip north that made sense. He could head up the ridge road, a path that was passable for a man riding a horse but not a wagon. Or he could go down the ridge to Hillsville and then turn north on a better road through the little settlements of Dugspur and Jacksonville. The ridge route was a bit shorter, but there was some advantage in going through the little towns where people lived and where he could get food and perhaps find a place to sleep indoors if the weather turned bad. The ridge path did not go through any towns, though there were some small settlements not too far off the ridge. The goal at the end was the same. He was headed for Big Lick, a good-sized town at the edge of the Shenandoah Valley. Once he arrived there, he could travel the rest of the way north on the flat land of the valley between the two mountain ranges.

He decided on traveling through Hillsville and the other little towns. It was an easier road, easier on Ol' Mose, and if he had trouble of some kind, he was closer to finding help if he needed it. So Hillsville it was.

Riding Ol' Mose made the traveling much easier. They weren't moving very fast, but they were moving at a steady pace, and his feet were healing up from the sore spots caused by the rocks in the flat land road. Hillsville was a small village with about ten buildings, a little store, and a station for the stage coach. The stage came through about once a week, according to a man who was sitting on the porch of the livery stable where it stopped. It was the largest building on the main street.

It was about two o'clock in the afternoon, and there were still five or six good travel hours in the day. Matt went around to the back of the stable and sat down on a bale of hay where he broke out his beef jerky, the loaf of bread, and tin of honey. There was a blacksmith shop in the back of the livery stable, and the man who was just inside swinging a sledge hammer was almost as big as Matt's Pa. He watched the man for a while as he ate his lunch.

A boy about his age appeared around the edge of the blacksmith shop and stood looking at him from the corner. Matt looked back at the boy and smiled. "Hello," he said.

The boy walked over to Matt. It was immediately apparent that he only had one arm. His right arm was gone, cut off above the elbow. The boy sat down a few feet away on a hay bale.

He seemed a bit shy, so Matt opened a conversation. "My name is Matt Mason. What's yours?"

The boy responded, "I'm Hop. My real name is Harold, but everyone calls me Hop. I'm Hop Hopkins. I don't much like the name Harold, so I don't use it." Once warmed up, Hop had a lot to say. "Are you traveling through or planning to stay a while?" he asked.

Matt responded, "I'm coming from Mt. Airy, North Carolina. I'm on the way north to find the Army of Virginia. My Pa is with them. We haven't heard from him for several months, but I think he is all right. His name hasn't appeared on any of the casualty lists."

Hop was obviously interested in his travels and his search for the army. "I wish I could go along," he said. "I don't have much to do here. I live in the loft of the livery stable. My mother died, and my stepmother is busy with her new baby and doesn't want me around. I would sure like to see northern Virginia and the military camps."

Matt thought about Hop's veiled query and the possibility of having a traveling buddy along for the trip north. "I wouldn't be heading toward the war if I had alternatives," he said. "I need to find my Pa. If I had a place to call home and food on the table, I would certainly stay close by my people, at least until the fighting is over." He looked at the boy with open curiosity. "How did you lose your arm?"

Hop glanced down at the stub on the right side of his body. He said, "I lost it about a year back in a hunting accident. My friend and I were hunting rabbits, and he accidently shot me in the elbow. The shot took the arm right off, and the scatter shot went into my side." Hop lifted his shirt to show the scar where the doctor had gone in to clean out the lead pellets that had been lodged there.

He continued, "Getting shot hurt something fierce, but by the time the doctor was working on me, I was out of it. I didn't wake up for a couple of days. By then my arm was gone, and I had some big adjustments to make to just get through each day. I was right-handed, and learning to write left-handed was a real chore. I have been at it a year and haven't made much improvement."

Hop laughed. "It is a good thing I don't have any shoes because I don't think I would ever learn to tie shoe laces with one hand. Still, a few years ago, hardly anyone in this town had a stump, but today, after two years of war, there are several who have lost an arm and three or four who use crutches to walk, so I am not the only one."

Matt was soon finished with his lunch. "Hop, where could I get a drink of water?" he asked. "And I need to water my mule. Do you think it is all right if I water him at the trough at the back of the livery stable?"

Hop answered, "My Pa won't mind if you water the mule there, and I'll get you a drink of something good."

In a few minutes, Hop was back with a tin cup of cider. Matt thought it tasted wonderful. "Can I pay you for this?" he asked, handing the empty cup back to Hop. "How about a nickel?"

Hop said, "No, I'm glad to be of help. It is good cider, isn't it? The lady at the café has kind of taken me on to raise, and she gives it to me when I ask."

After thanking Hop and bidding him good-bye, Matt climbed on Ol' Mose, and they headed north toward Dugspur, which Hop told him was just six or seven miles away. That distance was about right for the final five hours of their travel for the day. As he rode north, he thought about Harold "Hop" Hopkins. He hadn't thought about the people he might meet as he traveled north to find his father, but it felt good to meet what he considered to be a new friend along the way. He might never see Hop again, but he would not forget the boy he met behind the stable in Hillsville. Matt wondered if he would have such a positive outlook on life if he had lost his arm and had to live in the loft of a livery stable.

That night, camped just north of Dugspur, Matt looked back on his day. It had been an easier travel day with the road going mostly downhill and on flat land. The road was primarily dirt with some rock in a few of the low places where it was obvious there was difficulty getting through when it rained. Ol' Mose was doing fine, and he was riding on most of the downhill roads and walking up the hills on the other side. It was a pattern that worked, and he resolved to keep it up as they worked their way north.

He counted his money in his mind. He had only spent the fifteen cents of his fifteen dollars in the trading post at Fancy Gap. Tomorrow he would need to find some oats for Ol' Mose. The mule could make it fine for a few days on grass, but every two or three days he would need some oats too.

That night he rolled his blanket out on a bed of grass next to a small stream just off the road. He was careful to keep his rifle close by his side in case some bears came calling. Before he lay down, he hung his pack with his dwindling supply of food on a rope from a tree limb across the road well away from where he set up his camp. If bears did come calling, he would rather they be across the road, away from him and Ol' Mose.

Matt was awakened by a light rain while it was still dark. He tried to roll up in the blanket, but after a while, the rain began coming down harder, and he knew he needed to find shelter. He was up and moving fast. He retrieved his pack and hooked it on the old mule. Soon he was headed up the road looking for a place to get in out of the rain.

Twenty minutes passed and then an hour. By then he was soaked to the skin, and the road was a quagmire. He decided that since he was already wet, he might just as well just go on as if it were not raining. It wasn't a cold rain. After all, it was early June, and this was southern Virginia. It didn't get cold here in June. His reasoning made sense as he repeated it over and over to himself. *It isn't a cold rain. It isn't a cold rain.* Unfortunately, he was getting both wet and cold, and every little breeze made him feel colder.

Matt came around a turn, and there on the side of the road was an old buggy with a top on it. It wasn't much and it wasn't in out of the weather, but the top would at least get him out of the rain. He tied Ol' Mose next to a tree for some cover and climbed into the back of the buggy. Obviously, someone had gotten stuck trying to maneuver around a muddy spot in the road. They had unhitched the horse and left the buggy behind, intending to come back and pick it up when the weather dried up.

The rain kept up for about an hour, then it began to slow, then it stopped altogether. Matt's clothes were still sopping wet, but he took his heavy rubbing brush and began to rub the water out of Ol' Mose's coat. That old mule had enough trouble without getting sick, and if he was sick, he wouldn't be able to carry Matt. In fifteen minutes, he had Ol' Mose dry, and he could climb on his back and head up the road. He rode on toward the little village of Jacksonville. Unfortunately, Matt was still wet. From time to time he felt a sprinkle, and he hoped it was not getting ready to rain hard again. He had hoped for some sunshine that would allow him to lay out his clothes and get them dry, but that was not to be.

Matt arrived in Jacksonville late in the afternoon and tied up his mule outside the one store in the little village. He went inside and asked the proprietor if there was a place he could stay the night out of the weather. He didn't realize it until he stopped walking, but his clothes were dripping water. He could feel the drops of cold water on his feet and saw that he was making the floor wet. When Matt saw the man's eyes looking down at his wet floor, he realized that he had created a problem. He began to apologize and back out toward the entrance door when he heard a female voice coming from the back of the store.

"Where you from, boy?" she asked.

Matt responded, "I'm from the Mt. Airy area in North Carolina, ma'am."

"Now, don't you go back out of that door with those wet clothes," she ordered. "You will catch your death. You come back here where I can get a look at you."

Matt said the only thing he could think of at the time. "Yes, ma'am."

Matt walked through a swinging door at the back of the store toward the female voice. When he entered the back room, it was obvious he was in the living quarters of the proprietor and his wife. The lady with the big voice had a body to match. She was both tall and heavy, with iron-gray hair pulled into a knot on top of her head that made her look even taller. Matt surmised that she was in her late forties or early fifties, and she had a pleasant look about her, like he imagined his grandmother in Pennsylvania that his Ma often talked about would look.

The sneeze he had been stifling ever since he came into the store exploded right as he found himself standing in front of her. It came so fast he could hardly get his hand up to his face. The lady began to laugh, and her big voice carried all the way through the store and probably out into the street.

"You must have been holding that one for a while. It was a big one. Okay, son, you are already halfway to being sick with your wet clothes and a cold coming on. How long has it been since you had a good meal?" she asked.

Matt thought for a moment. "It has been quite a while, ma'am," he said. "I had some hot grits a couple of days ago, but beef jerky and bread have been my staple since I have been on the road."

Her voice came up in an authoritative tone. "Son, I want you to get those wet clothes off and into a bath right away. We will get you cleaned up and warmed up at the same time."

Matt was expecting that maybe he could leave the store with something to eat other than his beef jerky, but he didn't anticipate having a bath right in the middle of the proprietor's living quarters. Sure enough, there was a big tub there with water in it, and there was hot water boiling in a kettle in the fireplace. Someone had planned to have a bath before he came in, and now it was Matt who was going to be in the hot water.

"Son, what is your name? You aren't my son, so I need to call you something," the big lady said.

"Ma'am, I'm Matt Mason from Mt. Airy, North Carolina," he responded.

"My name is Pearl Gunn, but everyone just calls me Pearl. All right, Matt. Now we are on a first-name basis and have been properly introduced, but I don't see you taking your clothes off. Do you intend to get into that bathtub fully clothed?" she asked.

Matt had been uneasy but was more so now. "Ma'am, it doesn't hardly feel right to be taking my clothes off right here in the daylight with a lady in the room."

Pearl laughed. "Okay, the lady—and I am glad you noticed I am a lady—is leaving the room. I'm going to pick some things out from the store for supper. When I come back, I expect you to be in that tub and your clothes piled over there on the bench."

Matt had heard that tone of voice from his Ma more times than he cared to remember. He knew when he had been ordered to do something, and he needed to do exactly what the lady said.

Pearl walked over to him again. This time she handed him a bar of soap and a small linen cloth. She said, "I suspect you know what to do with these."

He said, "Yes, ma'am."

She turned to the fireplace and took the kettle with the boiling water off the stand, walked over to the bathtub, and poured the water in. She reached her other hand into the tub to test the water and pronounced, "That is about right." With that she set the kettle down, turned, and walked through the swinging doors and was gone.

Matt began pulling off his wet clothes. He got down to his underwear and climbed into the tub with his shorts still on. The bath was hot and felt wonderful. He luxuriated in the warmth of it all and wondered how he had happened on such good fortune.

In a few minutes, Pearl was back in the room carrying several items from the store that would eventually end up on the supper table. Then she went over and picked up his clothes. She said, "I am going to hang these outside on the line to dry, and we will see if we can get you a change of clothes for your trip. I notice that you have no underwear in this stack. Is it because you weren't wearing any, or do you still have them on in the bathtub?"

Matt was immediately embarrassed. "Yes, ma'am. I still have them on."

Pearl responded. "Matt, I will have them now." The last word, *now*, came up in tone in such a way that he could not mistake the spoken authority.

Matt heard himself say, "Yes, ma'am" for the third time.

He reached down and pulled off his undershorts, lifted them up, wrung them out, then handed them to Pearl. She smiled, added them to the pile, and took the entire stack out the back door. He continued to sit in the warm water, and shortly, she came back in.

She began to busy herself around the kitchen, and things began to smell good. Matt wasn't sure what she was cooking over the open fireplace, but whatever it was certainly beat having another supper of beef jerky and dry bread, and he was sure he would like it. He watched as she put plates on the table, and one by one the finished food dishes were placed there as well.

Then she walked over to the bathtub where Matt was still enjoying the warm water. She said, "Okay, time to get out." He didn't move right away, and she smiled. She turned around and picked up a blanket off the chair and held it out. She said, "You stand up, and we are going to wrap you in this blanket until after supper." With that, Matt was up, the blanket was wrapped around him, and he found himself sitting at the small table.

When she sat down with him, Matt asked, "Isn't your husband coming?"

She responded, "No, he will keep the store, and when we have finished, I will go and relieve him, and he will come and eat. He likes to eat a little later."

Matt's eyes took in the bowls on the table, each filled with something good. There were mashed potatoes, gravy, and a meat dish he couldn't quite make out because of the onions and mushrooms on top of it. There were carrots and tomatoes. The best smell came from a platter of muffins that still sat over by the fire. He couldn't tell exactly what they were, but they looked like the blueberry muffins his Ma used to make. It was just the right time of year for blueberries, and Matt was glad he wouldn't have to fight the bears to get some!

Eating supper with Pearl was not all that different from being home when his mother was able to fix the meals. Matt ate and the lady talked, and occasionally, she ate. She wanted to know all about him, his home near Mt. Airy, his mother and father. Matt answered each question carefully, avoiding any mention of the circumstances of his mother's death and the burning buildings as he left home. Where did he think his father was? He didn't know, but he thought he could find the Army of Virginia, and when he did, he knew his father would be with them.

All too soon supper was over, and Pearl was cleaning off the table. Matt was a bit uncomfortable in his blanket and wondered out loud about his clothes on the line. Pearl said it was doubtful that they would be dry yet, and she would get him some things to wear.

She left the room through the swinging doors, and in a few minutes, she returned. She had several shirts, pants, socks, underwear, some suspenders, and shoes. She suggested that he try them on. He slipped on the underwear behind his blanket and stood up to try the pants. When he did, the blanket fell to the floor and left Matt standing there in his new underwear. Pearl began to laugh.

She said, "Don't worry, Matt. The men around here work in less than you have on. Let's see what fits and what doesn't. You are a big young man. I would say you are over six feet tall and around 160 pounds. How close am I?"

Matt responded, "Pretty close, ma'am. My Pa is six-feet-five and 250 pounds. He is thirty-six years old this year, and before he left for the war, he was the biggest man in Surrey County. Some think I am going to be as big as he is when I stop growing."

"Matt, how old are you?" She asked curiously. Matt told her he would be sixteen in August. He heard a low whistle from the doorway. Pearl's husband was looking across the swinging doors. He said, "Boy, you are a big one for only fifteen. I'll bet you can do a full day of man's work right now."

Matt responded. "Yes, sir. My daddy said I could do a man's work when I was only thirteen."

Matt heard a bell ring from the front of the store. The proprietor's face disappeared from the doorway, and Matt sat down to try on the shoes. He looked at the size of the shoes and saw that they were tens. He knew that wouldn't work. The last time he had a pair of shoes they were elevens, and that had been way last winter. He had grown a couple of inches since then. Matt normally had a new pair of shoes each year late in the fall. Those did him well until spring when it was always a relief to get them off. By the end of February, they were always too tight to be comfortable.

When Matt couldn't get the shoes on, Pearl turned the sole of the shoe upside down on the bottom of his foot. She said, "I've seen full-grown bears that didn't have feet that big. You need thirteens for sure." Pearl went through the swinging doors and back into the store.

In a few minutes she came back. She said, "Matt, the tens are the biggest size we have left. If you could stay with us for three or four days until the stage comes through, they should have a new shipment on board. There might be a thirteen in that shipment."

Matt said, "I don't think I can wait that long. I need to get on up the road north."

"Well, think about it," Pearl responded. "You can stay here with us." She urged him toward a cot in the corner. I know you must be tired. Why don't you lie down?"

Matt told her he needed to take care of his mule. She asked him where the mule was, and he told her he tied him to the hitching post out front. Pearl told him she would go out and bring the mule around back and see that he got some oats. Matt objected weakly but sat down on the cot. Before he knew it, the light of sunrise was coming in the back window.

He moved quietly around the small room. He could hear competing snores from the bedroom, and he didn't want to wake his hosts. He did, however, want to get out into the morning and on down the road before everyone woke up and began talking about breakfast. He felt the urgency of moving north and finding his father. Matt dressed in his new clothes and headed for the back door. There on a table, he saw a pencil and a few pieces of paper. He sat down at the table and quickly wrote a short note.

Dear Friends,

Every traveler should meet people along the road like you. I could not have felt more welcome. The gifts of clothing were wonderful, and every time I look in a mirror and see this striped shirt, I will think of you.

I do appreciate the wonderful meal and have taken the liberty of taking along two of the muffins you fixed last night for dessert. They will be eaten down the road and will add to the fond thoughts I have of you. I apologize for leaving and not saying good-bye face-to-face. Perhaps there will be another time when I can express my feelings in person. If I can route myself this way on the way back, I will certainly do so. If not, I'm sure God will reward such kindness.

I will always be in your debt.

*Sincerely,
Matt Mason*

He reread the note and was pleased that he didn't detect any mistakes in the written English. He had gone through the eighth grade at the little school down close to Mr. Airy, but his real education took place at the little table by the window with his mother standing over his shoulder. She had told him more than once that she was educated at home by her mother. In a Quaker family, the mother was responsible for the education of the children, both boys and girls, until they turned thirteen. Then the boys were turned over to their fathers, and the girls stayed with their mothers to learn the finer points of running a household.

His Ma's mother had been a stern taskmaster. She taught Ma to read from the Bible and made her practice her penmanship by the hour. Ma was determined that Matt would have the same upbringing and the same education. Matt could remember doing and redoing his writing assignments until they were letter-perfect. Whether the subject was English, history, or arithmetic, when it was written down the writing had to be perfect. If it wasn't, he could be sure he would be doing it again.

Looking at the note, he was pleased that his Ma was also a stern taskmaster. In truth, if it hadn't been written properly, Matt would have done it again and again, if necessary.

Matt put the note on the table where just a few hours ago he had sat down with Pearl for supper. He quietly went out the door and looked for Ol' Mose, who was tied up next to a shed with the feed bag still on his head. He saw his clothes hanging on the line and retrieved them, put them all in his pack, and unbuckled the feed bag from the mule's head. He hung the bag on a nail by the door of the shed. In a few minutes he was headed north up the road toward Bent Mountain and Big Lick.

UNINVITED GUESTS

Matt was well into his fourth day of traveling when he ran into his first difficult stream crossing. He and Ol' Mose had followed their pattern of riding downhill and on the level and walking uphill whenever the road started to rise. Streams came regularly down from the ridges on both sides of the road, but all had been relatively easy to cross. Most were not very deep, and wading across had not been a problem.

Late in the day they were still south of Bent Mountain when Matt led the old mule over a rise, and there in front of him was a stream obviously swollen by the rains of the previous day. It was not so wide but it was deep, and both would have to swim if they were to cross to the other side. Matt did not doubt his ability to swim the stream but wasn't sure about Ol' Mose. He tied the mule to a bush at the side of the road and walked upstream a couple of hundred yards, looking for a place to ford the water. No luck. He came back and did the same thing the other way. Still no luck. The road they were on ran right into the stream and came out the other side. It was obvious that other travelers who came this way were used to just driving straight through. Unfortunately, with the rain yesterday and the evening before, the water was too high to wade through it. They would have to swim.

Matt stripped off his clothes and put them in the pack with the rest of his things. He tied the pack to the mule's harness just at the back of his head. Ol' Mose, for sure, would keep his head out of water. He led the old mule down to the edge of the water and walked in up to his waist. Ol' Mose took a couple of steps into the water and then stopped. No amount of soft talking or pulling the reins would get him to move.

Then Matt hit on an idea that he thought might work. He had seen his Pa urge the mule on with an apple several years ago. He had no apple, but he did have the jar of honey, and there was lots of high grass near the bank. He walked Ol' Mose back out of the water and retrieved the honey from the pack. Then he took a big handful of the grass and poured some honey on it. He let the mule taste the honey with his big tongue. With each extension of the tongue, Matt moved back so the mule followed him. Soon they were in the water moving deeper and deeper. So far his plan was working. By then Matt was hanging onto the reins to hold himself up in the water. There was a current moving right to left, but it wasn't strong. Matt was swimming, and soon, the old mule was too. When his feet were no longer in contact with the bottom of the stream, Ol' Mose began to bray. He was obviously distressed and kept pulling to go back. Matt pulled harder to get him to come forward with him. After what seemed like an eternity, Matt felt the bottom of the stream on the other bank, which allowed him the traction he needed to pull Ol' Mose out of the deeper water. When the old mule felt the stream bottom under his feet, he stopped braying and followed Matt up the rise to the bank. They were across!

Matt sat down on the bank to rest with his clothes laid out before him. He slipped off his wet shorts and put on the dry ones he had taken off Pearl's clothesline that morning. It felt good to be across and doubly good to be back in his clothes again. He took out his curry brush and began to rub Ol' Mose dry. In a few minutes both were ready to head up the road again.

It was nearing dark when the road took him past some cliffs. Matt looked up at the rocky tops about a hundred feet above the road level. He thought to himself that this would be a good spot for an Indian ambush if this was still Indian country. The road turned sharply around the edge of the cliff, and he looked ahead to a high ridge in front of him that seemed to climb straight up. It was going to be another hard climb, and he was not sure either he or his mule could make that climb today. He began to look for a place to camp for the night and found a clearing about twenty yards off the road. He set about gathering some wood and dried leaves for a fire and put hobbles on Ol' Mose so he could graze freely but not wander too far away.

It was totally dark, and he had just spread his blanket and laid down next to the fire when he heard noises on the road. In a few minutes he could clearly hear voices. He didn't move, just listened. The voices stopped, and he heard the sounds of footsteps moving toward his camp. Then he saw a gun barrel poke through the bushes into the clearing. Matt sat up straight.

A man's voice said, "It's just a kid, Jess. He has a fire going." Two men appeared in the clearing wearing gray Confederate Army uniforms. The insignia on their shoulders identified them as members of the Army of Virginia. "Hey, son, can we sit a spell with you?" said the man pointing the gun.

Matt would have been pleased to have some company, but these two guys didn't look like his notion of soldiers at all. Both had beards and looked and smelled as if they had not bathed in weeks. Still, he didn't feel in a position to say no to them. After all, the men were obviously members of the same army his Pa was in, so maybe they could tell him where the army was and how to find them. They might even know his Pa.

"I'm pleased to have your company," he said. "I'm sorry I have no food to offer you. My name is Matt Mason. I'm from Mt. Airy, North Carolina."

"Thanks, son, we've got some food. I'm Jess, and this here is Tom," said the first man. The men came over and sat down. Matt noted the rifles they were carrying. The guns reminded him more of the guns farmers used to shoot rabbits and squirrels than anything that would work in a war with the Yankees.

Tom said, "What are you doing here, boy?"

Matt explained that he was looking for the Army of Virginia to find his father. "My Pa's name is Isaac Mason. People call him Zeke. He is with General Henry Heth's artillery unit. Do you know him?"

Jess said, "We wouldn't know your Pa, but Heth is a name we have heard from time to time. We are in the cavalry with JEB Stuart. We don't spent much time with the army units. We are mostly on the road looking for the Yankees and bringing back information to General Lee and General Stonewall Jackson."

"Can you tell me where the army is and how I can find them?" Matt asked.

"When we left they were at Culpepper, resting up after the big battle," Tom responded. "Do you know about Chancellorsville?"

"No, I haven't heard of Chancellorsville," said Matt. "What happened?"

Jess picked up the story. "We just routed the Yankees in our biggest battle yet. Chancellorsville is way up the road north of Richmond, toward Washington. They had more men and more cannons than we did, but Old Man Lee sent Stonewall Jackson's bunch along with Stuart's cavalry around behind the Yankees, and we had 'em in a cross fire. Before long they withdrew."

Tom said, "We rode across the battlefield after it was over, and I never saw so many dead people. It will take the burial detail weeks to get them all in the ground."

Matt asked, "So the army moved off to Culpepper after the battle?"

"Yes, but we weren't with the army," Jess said. "Stuart took us about five miles up the road to Brandy Station."

"Can you tell me how to find Culpepper?" Matt asked.

"Oh yes, it is on the east side of the mountains, about two days north of Charlottesville," said Tom.

Matt was anxious to find out more about the army and where it was. These fellows seemed willing to talk, and he didn't want to lose his opportunity. "Why aren't you guys with your unit?" he asked.

The two men looked at each other, and then Jess responded, "Like I said, we are in the cavalry under JEB Stuart. We were at Brandy Station with our unit when the Yankees came on us by surprise. They had followed us after Chancellorsville, and old JEB was either too tired or too drunk to put out sentries. They came down off the hill at us while we were still sleeping. They ran us back into the woods and ran off our horses. They took most of our equipment, all the horses they could catch, and captured several of our men. Tom and I were sent home to get some fresh horses."

Tom declared, "If we were in the Yankee cavalry, they would furnish our horses, and we wouldn't have go find our own."

"Yes," Jess agreed, "and we would have a decent rifle that would shoot more than a time or two without jamming. I can't count the number of times I have pulled the trigger on this old blunderbuss and had it just go 'click.' You are better off just getting out your sword and going hand-to-hand rather than counting on a gun that won't work."

Tom said, "Matt, if you are going to find your Pa, you may have to go to Culpepper and follow their trail. Rumor has it that the army is going to cross the Mason-Dixon Line into Pennsylvania next, but we don't know which way they are going, whether it is toward Philadelphia, Harrisburg, or somewhere else."

Jess boasted, "Yeah, we have had the Yankees on the run everywhere we have met them. We don't have the uniforms, guns, or cannons the Yankees do. Half of our men don't even have shoes. But we do have generals who know how to win a war. Lee and Jackson are both genuine fighting men."

Tom added soberly, "We heard a rumor that General Jackson had been wounded after Chancellorsville, but we don't know if it's true. We heard he had been shot in the arm. An arm shot wouldn't get old Jackson. He's too tough an old bird."

After a moment, Jess said, "It's getting late, son. Do you mind if we just bunk here by the fire with you tonight? It is too dark now to find another spot."

Matt was enjoying the company of the men and their stories. "Sure," he said. "It's fine with me."

The men laid out their blankets on the ground, and before long, everything quieted down. Matt could hear the crickets from the stream bed and the gurgle of water. Soon he was asleep.

Matt woke up to the noise of movement in the camp. The sun was just coming up, and the two men were already up and breaking camp. Ol' Mose was in the camp with them, and Matt saw that his hobbles had been cut.

Jess realized that Matt was awake, and he said, "Son, I know you want to do your part for the Confederacy, so we are taking your mule. We will get home, get our horses, and get back much faster if we can ride your mule." With that Jess, and the other man both climbed up on Ol' Mose.

Matt was on his feet in no time and moving toward the mule and the two men. He said, "Hold on a minute. That old mule is on his last legs, and he can't carry both of you." Then he realized Tom was pointing his gun at him. He stopped moving but objected again about their riding Ol' Mose. "You'll kill him!"

Jess responded, "Well, I guess if he can't carry us, he will have given his all for the cause. We bid you a fond adieu and wish you well."

With that, he pulled Ol' Mose's head around, and both of them began to kick the old mule in the sides to get him to move. Ol' Mose was doing the best he could to walk where they were directing him, but the weight was obviously more than he could handle. Still, he took them through the brush, and Matt heard his hoofbeats as he made it to the packed dirt of the road.

Matt turned back to his blanket and uncovered his old rifle. He had brought it along more as a menace than as a weapon, but he was not about to let them get away with his mule. For sure, he was not going to have his mule mistreated. Matt knew the gun was loaded, and he began to run down the road, looking for a path up the ridge to his left. He knew the road turned around the ridge less than a half mile down the road. If he could get to the top of the ridge and find his way to the cliff before they got there, he might have a clear shot at the mule thieves. There it was. The pathway led up the hill to the left. He started up the hillside at a run. Before long his legs and lungs were rebelling at the fast pace he had set up the side of the ridge. It was a relief when he made it to the top and could run on relatively level ground down to the rock face of the ridge that overlooked the road.

He was there for just a few seconds before he heard the hoofbeats of the mule and the voices of the men yelling at him to go faster. Matt laid out on the rock at the edge of the cliff and put the old rifle out in front of him. He had only one shot in the gun and knew he would not have a chance for a second shot even if he had another rifle ball he could load before these two experienced soldiers located him and returned fire. He would have to make it count.

Matt took aim at the first rider on the old mule. He heard his father's voice in his ear: "Aim small and squeeze slowly." Matt had a bead on the man called Jess. He was aiming about shoulder high where he had the most margin for error. He was about to pull the trigger when he realized that he just could not shoot a man, no matter what he had done. Taking his mule was a hanging offense in some counties of North Carolina, so killing him would be justice. But he couldn't do it. He moved his aim forward and focused on Ol' Mose's eye. He knew his old mule did not have many days left in him, and with the two men on his back, he would not last out the morning. Before he thought more about it, he squeezed the trigger.

Immediately, there was a loud noise, and he felt a sharp pain in his right eye. He dropped the gun and reached his hand up to his face. When he touched the right side of his face, he felt immense pain, and worse, he couldn't see out of that eye. He rolled over and looked back down on the road with his good eye. His bullet had found a kill spot on Ol' Mose. The mule was lying still in the middle of the road. He could not see the two men. He knew he had to get out of there fast.

Before he realized it, Matt was on his feet and running back down the ridge toward the road. He couldn't see out of his right eye, and making his way through the bushes and staying on a path was difficult at best. As for the men, he did not know if they had climbed the cliff where the shot came from or assumed he was the shooter and headed back down the road to cut him off.

Matt made it to the road and retraced his steps to the small camp and scooped up his gear. It was at this point that he realized he was still carrying the old rifle. A glance down at the firing mechanism told him that the firing pin was gone. When he pulled the trigger, the old gun had enough firepower to blow the musket ball out the muzzle, but the powder had blown up through the firing pin as well. There was no need to reload even if he had another shot. This rifle would not be firing again.

He headed into the woods away from the road. He knew if the two men were coming after him, they would look for him on the road. He though his best chance for escape was to climb the ridge on the other side of the road and to make his way along the ridgetop until he was sure he was not being followed.

Matt found a path on the top of the ridge and headed north, stopping from time to time to listen for sounds of the men. He didn't hear anything, but he didn't feel safe. He went on that way for a good two hours before making his way back down to the road that headed ever northward toward Bent Mountain and Big Lick. His thoughts continued to race about what had happened, about Ol' Mose, and about the two men who had taken advantage of him.

Matt was sorry that his old friend who had served so well on their little farm had to meet such a tragic end and that he had to be the one to take the mule's life. Matt thought, *I hope Ol' Mose knew that I did the best I could for him. I knew he would never make it long with those two men on top of him, and for sure he would never make it across that stream that had been so much trouble yesterday.*

Mostly, as the thoughts stirred in his mind, he thought of his mother's words: "Ol' Mose is near his time and will serve you until he can't do it anymore. When that time comes, you will have to do what is necessary to put him out of his misery." Those men had stolen Ol' Mose's last few days and hours. Matt had done what was necessary to save the old mule from the misery of being ridden to death with two men kicking his sides. He did wonder about his decision to shoot Ol' Mose rather than one of the men who was causing the misery. Maybe that was in his makeup, an expression of the Quaker side of his family. That would require some additional thought at another time.

Matt's major problem now was what to do about the burns on his face and an eye that would not open. He wasn't sure if he could see even if he could get the eye to open. He needed a doctor, and he was close to the little village of Bent Mountain but a longer way from the larger town of Big Lick. He decided he could ask about a doctor in Bent Mountain but would probably have to leave his wounds untended until he could make his way down the ridge to Big Lick.

LOOKING FOR A DOCTOR

Bent Mountain was just a little village with one store. Matt counted eight buildings on the main street, and in the distance he could see a small church with a steeple. He walked into the only store in town and found himself face-to-face with a boy about his own age, but a good head shorter. "Is there a doctor in town?" he asked.

The clerk pursed his lips and gave a low whistle. "Man, that is some mess on your face," the clerk said. "We don't have a doctor here in Bent Mountain. One comes up from Big Lick a couple of times a month. He sets up his office in the church down the street."

"Do you know when he is coming?" Matt asked.

"We never know for sure. They ring the church bell when he is in town," the clerk said, continuing to stare intently at Matt's face. "That is some wound," he said with a soft voice. "How did you get it?"

"I was hoping to have rabbit for supper, and the gun misfired," Matt responded. He did not tell the clerk about the two men and his mule. Matt felt lucky to have had the confrontation with the two soldiers and lived to tell about it, but he wouldn't tell it here; maybe to his Pa when he found him. He was also feeling some real pain in his heart about Ol' Mose. How could he have let that happen, let the two men take advantage of him and steal his mule? It was all a tragedy that he couldn't talk about yet. Maybe later.

Matt saw a mirror in the clothing section of the one-room store and walked over to it, almost afraid to look at his face. When he did, it looked worse than he could have imagined. The skin was black. He assumed that to be from the powder burn. He could see under the coating of the soot that the skin was red and burned. That was especially true around his right eye, which was still swollen shut. He couldn't get a good look until he cleaned off some of the powder residue that covered the right side of his face.

"Could I have a washcloth and some water?" Matt asked the young man.

The clerk took him over to a table that had linens it. "The washcloth is five cents. I will get you some water," the young man said.

Matt took the basin of water and the cloth back to the mirror and began trying to clean the wound. Each movement of the cloth on his face brought sharp pains. He finally settled for just wetting the cloth and holding it on his face. When he had soaked some of the black soot off, he was able to get a better look at the state of his skin and eye. It was an ugly wound and, most likely, would leave a scar. The real problem was his eye though. Would it heal itself and be okay, or would he forever carry that legacy along with the memory of those men and the death of Ol' Mose?

The clerk brought him over a small tin of salve that he said was good for burns. "This costs ten cents," he told Matt.

Matt thought the clerk was certainly taking advantage of his problem to make a little money. Still, he didn't have much choice, so he reached in his pocket and produced the Union dime.

He hoped his face would feel better when he put the salve on. He took a corner of the washcloth and dipped it in the salve and applied it gently on the burned skin. The pressure of the washcloth made it hurt more, and the salve also had a stinging effect. He had hoped it would make the burn feel better, but it didn't. Maybe later it would.

"Is there someplace I can stay the night?" he asked the clerk.

"We have a bunkhouse across the street. It costs a quarter to stay there, but it is inside and warm. We are expecting rain tonight," the clerk said helpfully.

Matt bedded down that night in the bunkhouse. It was a stay-for-pay place, and his twenty-five cents gave him access to a bunk in the corner with a naked mattress on it. Matt spread his blanket on the mattress and lay down to test it out. He hated to part with the twenty-five cents, but he felt he needed to be inside and did not want to go looking for a place out in the open. He had not spent but a little of his money, and he felt it was worth the quarter to be under a roof where he could better take care of his wound.

Even so, Matt had difficulty sleeping that night. Every time he turned over, he felt the pain of the burn on his face. When the pain hit, he woke up. Getting back to sleep was an exercise in thinking back through all that had happened the day before. He felt like crying, but there were three other men in the room, and crying just wouldn't do. By the next morning, the salve had made the burned skin feel better, but when he touched it, he felt the same pain as the day before.

Matt woke up hungry and went back to the store to buy a muffin, and that, along with a string of beef jerky, became his breakfast. As he was eating the muffin, he asked the same clerk who had helped him the day before how far it was to Big Lick.

"Big Lick is about twelve miles," the clerk said. "The road is mostly downhill, but it is all rock between Bent Mountain and the city." He looked at Matt's bare feet. "You may want to consider buying some shoes."

Matt wondered what the cost would be but asked instead, "What are the biggest sizes you have?"

The clerk walked over to the display of shoes and looked at the outside of the stacked boxes. "We have them all the way up to twelves," he said.

"I would take at least a thirteen and maybe a fourteen, depending on the style," Matt responded. "Just out of curiosity, what does a pair of shoes cost?"

"These are eight dollars," the clerk responded. "There are some others that are cheaper, but these are the good ones."

"I'll pass on the shoes. You don't have my size anyway," Matt said. He wiped the muffin crumbs off his chin, thinking that Pearl's blueberry muffins had been much better tasting. "Big Lick is a funny name for a town. Where did that name come from?"

"These hills are full of salt deposits, and the animals come from all over to lick the salt," the clerk explained. "Many of the men in the area make their living by hunting. We have deer, elk, beaver, and black bears in the area. There used to be bigger brown bear around, but these days you don't see them anymore. It isn't unusual to see a big black bear walking right down the main street just like he owns the place. It is usually in the early morning or around dusk when they come looking for food in the trash dump out at the edge of town."

Matt made note of the story about the bear and hoped he didn't meet up with any on the road to Big Lick. He thanked the clerk and headed north. Immediately, he missed his old mule. He was walking on a rock road that connected Bent Mountain on the ridge to the city at the edge of the Shenandoah Valley, which was supposed to be mostly flat land. He was trying to be careful with his steps, but every now and then he would misstep and feel the pain of a sharp rock on his bare feet. Yes, he was going to miss Ol' Mose every step for the rest of this journey.

Twelve miles was a pretty long hike, and he hoped he would be able to make it by dark. Fortunately, the road was well made, and he didn't have to do much walking on the road bed itself. He could walk down the edge of the road in the grass most of the way. The worst thing on the trip down to Big Lick was carrying the gun. More than once he thought of throwing it away. Something that heavy was going to be a major hindrance as he made his way northward. He reasoned, however, that even if the gun was useless without a firing pin, it could still appear to be a menace to those who were more than a few feet away from him and couldn't see the firing mechanism.

On one of his rest stops, he got in his pack and pulled out the undershirt that Pearl had given him back in Dugspur. He devised a firing pin cover that would mask the state of the gun. He had seen his Pa do that a few years back. It served to keep the powder and the pin dry when the days were damp and rainy. Hunters and soldiers would know what it was and wouldn't question why it was wrapped around the gun. With a cover on it, you could not tell if the gun was operational or not.

By late afternoon, Matt had reached the edge of Big Lick. A man on the street told him where the doctor's office was and then remarked, "Son, you really need a doctor with that face."

Matt didn't need the prompting. He knew it looked bad, but he was still hoping that it looked worse than it was.

Matt went to the doctor's office, but he could see the closed sign hanging on the door as he approached it. The office was like a storefront with benches on both sides of the door outside to serve as a waiting area. There would probably be quite a line waiting to see the doctor when the office reopened. He made note of the sign on the door that morning office hours began at 7:30 a.m. and resolved to arrive well before that time to get a place close to the door.

There was a small park in the middle of the town. He walked back there, seeing several men lying out on the ground here and there, bunking in the open as he intended to do. He laid his blanket on the ground near the closest tree to the doctor's office and was careful to leave his rifle in plain sight at the edge of his blanket. He intended to sleep with his good eye open tonight, but having the big gun in plain sight might inhibit any who thought they could take advantage of him. What was it his Ma used to say? "Fool me once, shame on you. Fool me twice, shame on me." Matt didn't intend to have a second bad experience, at least not if he could help it.

Matt was up the next morning well before the sun. He packed up his gear and the big gun and headed for the doctor's office. Several patients were already waiting outside the office for the door to open. When they opened the door, he was among the small group that came inside and sat down in the waiting room. He counted four people in front of him and two more who had followed him into the office.

The lady in charge of admissions kept coming in and out checking out the prospective patients. She looked each injury over and wrote some notes in her book. Matt wondered what she wrote in her book when she examined him. One thing was obvious. Those who had more serious injuries would be taken first. One man with a gunshot wound in his hand came in after Matt, but he was ushered back through the doorway right away. There was nothing for Matt to do but wait.

Finally, it was his turn. He was in the back room for several minutes before the doctor came in. The nurse had given him a cloth with warm water on it to hold on the right side of his face. She said the doctor would have an easier time working with him if the skin was softened up a bit. When the doctor came in, Matt judged his age to be in his late sixties. He hoped that meant he had lots of experience and would have seen serious skin burns many times before. His eye was another problem. Matt didn't know how the doctor was going to be able to examine his eye since he still couldn't get it to open.

The doctor took away the cloth, and Matt heard him exhale slowly. "That's a bad one, son. How did you do that?" Matt told him that he was shooting at a rabbit, and the gun backfired. It wasn't what happened, but that story would suffice for the time being.

The doctor took one of his tools and told Matt to get ready for some pain. He took hold of a piece of the skin, now soft from the warm water, and began to gently pull on it. The pain was sharp and immediate. Matt stifled the sound that was coming out of his throat. The doctor pulled harder, and the pain became excruciating.

At last the doctor stopped. He said to Matt, "Son, that dead skin has to come off so we can treat the new skin that will grow underneath. You evidently had this accident a couple of days ago. Am I right?"

"Yes, sir," Matt responded. "It took me a couple of days to find a doctor in these parts."

The doctor backed away for a minute then said something to the nurse. She left the room and reappeared a minute later with a lantern. It had a reflector on it that directed the light and made it brighter. "Now, son, I'm going to see if I can examine your eye," the doctor said. Matt felt pressure on both sides of his eye. The doctor was trying to lift the swollen skin away so he could get to the eyeball.

After a few minutes of trying different approaches, the doctor said, "I don't think I can get the eye uncovered. There is just too much swelling around it. Let's see if you can see the light when I shine it directly on the eye socket."

Matt could immediately see the light. It came and went for a few seconds.

"Now, what did you see?" the doctor asked.

"I could see a light passing by my eye," Matt responded.

"Good." The doctor nodded. "That is a good sign. It means your eye can detect light and dark, but we are going to have to wait until the swelling goes down a bit before we can get a good look at that eye." The doctor regarded him for a moment. "Where are you from, Matt?" he asked.

"I am from North Carolina, sir," Matt responded.

"What are you doing way up here?" the doctor asked.

"Well, sir, my Ma died a couple of weeks back. I am on my way to find my Pa, who is with the Army of Virginia up north somewhere," Matt said.

The doctor asked the nurse to leave the room and told her he would call her back in a few minutes. He waited until the door was closed and then said to Matt, "Son, are you intending to join up with the Army of Virginia?"

"No, sir. My folks decided two years ago that no matter how long the war went on, I was not to be involved in it. My job was to stay at home and take care of the place. Unfortunately, we couldn't make the payments on the farm after Pa left, and the bank was ready to take it when Ma died. My Ma was a strong Quaker, and she did not believe in war, and we don't believe in slavery either. Pa didn't have Quaker leanings. I need to find him. When I find him, I will do whatever he tells me, to join the army or not join."

"Matt, that eye of yours needs attention that I can't give it," the doctor said.

"Even if you stayed around Big Lick for a week or so to let the swelling go down enough so I could examine it, I am not sure I could do you any good. They have several good doctors at the army hospitals in Lynchburg. The best one is the Ladies' Relief Hospital, which is on Main Street near the riverfront. If we could get you into that hospital, I'm sure one of the doctors would know how to help you. I think if we put you on the railroad when the train ran north, we could have you at the hospital in a day or so.

"There is one catch," the doctor continued. "They will not let you into a military hospital unless you are in the army. They have way more patients than they can handle. To get one of those doctors to examine you, you will need to tell them that you are in the Army of Virginia."

Matt thought about the prospect of masquerading as a soldier, but he didn't say anything for a few minutes. He had never considered such. He felt immediately that doing as the doctor was suggesting would be dishonest. "I don't think so, sir," he said. "I don't know anything about being a soldier. If they asked me any questions at all, I would give myself away."

"Son, these are hectic times," the doctor replied. "You aren't on the farm in North Carolina anymore. You don't have anyone to take care of you. You have to do what is best for yourself, and I'm telling you what is best for you is to see a doctor at a military hospital in Lynchburg. You may have to stretch the truth a bit to make that happen. It isn't too great a stretch when you consider that your father is in the army and you are headed into a war zone not knowing if you will soon be in the army too. Besides, you are a big boy. There are many in the army who are younger than you and certainly smaller. Most who meet you will not think twice about your being a soldier.

"You do what you want. You can stay around here for a week waiting for the swelling to go down if you want to. You will be seeing a doctor who is not experienced at dealing with eye problems. A military hospital is the place for you where you have the best chance of being able to see through that eye again. Otherwise, you might be blind in that eye for the rest of your life," he concluded.

The doctor walked over to a chest of drawers against the wall. "If you want to go to the Ladies' Relief Hospital or one of the others, take these, and it will help you get to Lynchburg and seen by a doctor there." With that, the doctor pitched some clothes to Matt.

Matt looked at what was lying in his lap. It was a Confederate jacket and cap.

"The insignia on the shoulder is for a unit that is off fighting with General Lee and not something local, so you aren't likely to run into anyone who is from that unit," the doctor said. "If you do meet someone who is suspicious, just tell them that you are a new recruit, and they gave you this uniform to wear. Most of the uniforms they are issuing now were worn by someone already dead."

The doctor continued. "Now, son, when you leave my office, put the jacket and cap on, turn left, and go down the street to the railroad station. The Virginia-Tennessee railroad comes through here once a day going each way. Just join the other soldiers on the platform and wait for the train headed to Lynchburg. You will be there in about a day's ride if the Yankee cavalry doesn't show up and disrupt things. The military hospital is about a block from the railroad station in Lynchburg. You can't miss it, but if you have trouble, ask someone for directions, and be specific about Ladies' Relief. It has the best reputation for keeping people alive and getting them well. You will see a big sign over a door in the building that says Admissions. They will look you over and get you to the right doctor."

Matt thanked the doctor and started to leave by the door he entered the room through, but the doctor motioned toward a second door. He said, "Now, you go out that door and head for the train station before my nurse comes back. She doesn't need to see that you now have a Confederate cap on your head. All right? Now go on."

Matt was soon out the door and on the street. He didn't have a plan of his own, and he certainly needed someone to look at his eye, so he did as the doctor said. He put on the jacket and cap and headed down the street toward the train station. On the way there, he passed several people on the street. Most of them stepped back and bowed to him as he went by. He was amazed at how much respect these people had for the uniform of the Confederacy. If they only knew who he really was, he knew it would be a different matter.

There were several uniformed men on the platform waiting on the train. Most were wounded and headed for a hospital in Lynchburg, but a few looked to be in pretty good shape and obviously were catching the train north to rejoin their outfits with the Army of Virginia.

Matt joined the group, and though two of the men nodded to him when he sat down, no one spoke to him. He could tell from the talk he overheard between the soldiers that the train was overdue. There was speculation that the Yankees had disrupted its passage again, and the group might be waiting on that platform for a very long time. One of the men pulled out a string of beef jerky, and it reminded Matt that he had not eaten yet today. The hunger pains were growing. He got in his pack and came up with his small bag of beef jerky and the rest of the loaf of bread and the tin of honey.

One of the men saw the bread and honey and came over to him. He had a bag in his hand. He said to Matt, "I'll trade you a tomato for a hunk of bread and a spread of honey." The man opened his sack and showed Matt several tomatoes.

Matt thought to himself that a tomato would certainly taste good, not only now but later that night or tomorrow. He heard himself responding to the man, "It is a deal for two tomatoes."

The man said, "Done." The man looked at his burned face and the bad eye. "You must have had it rough, kid. What unit are you with?"

Matt had previously looked at the arm patch on his jacket and made note of the number. "The Twenty-First," he responded.

"Was your unit at Chancellorsville?" the man asked.

Matt said that it wasn't. The man sat quietly after that short exchange. It appeared soldiers didn't generally want to talk about the war even with others who have been through the same thing. Later, Matt was glad for the trade. The tomato tasted good, and he had some variety in his lunch that didn't cost him any of his money. He still had just over fourteen dollars in his pack.

He had been on the platform for about an hour when he heard the unmistakable sound of a train coming. He looked down the track, and he could see the smoke from the steam engine. In a moment he could make out the engine about a half mile down the hill coming through the trees. When it pulled into the station, the soldiers piled onto a flatcar near the end of the train. There were some passengers who got on the caboose, but the soldiers all were out in the open air. Matt was expecting to pay something for the train ride to Lynchburg, but they didn't charge the soldiers. He felt a little guilt pain, but it passed quickly. After all, he might join up, and for sure, he needed someone to look at his eye.

THE LADIES' RELIEF HOSPITAL

As it was early June, riding the train outside was pleasant enough. By now the weather was warm even into the evening, and he had his blanket if it got cool. That would be fine as long as they didn't have some rain along the way.

The ride into Lynchburg was relatively easy. Matt was thankful for the noise from the engine as it kept anyone from talking to him. He was very pleased that he was riding rather than walking on the rock road, which he could see alongside of the tracks from time to time. Here and there someone had made repairs to the road with new rock. Walking on the roadway was not bad except for the repairs; that was where the new rock would cut into bare feet.

The train arrived at Lynchburg late in the afternoon. Matt saw a group of about twenty wounded soldiers. Some were hurt pretty badly and had difficulty walking, and some of these had crutches. Others like Matt were ambulatory but had other obvious injuries. He asked one of the men if they were going to the Ladies' Relief Hospital. He gave Matt a wry smile and said, "Sure am. I want to come out of this war alive." Matt didn't want to be at the end of the line, so he merged into the group about halfway toward the back.

They soon arrived at what looked like a hotel building on the Main Street. There were several nurses at the intake station under the Admissions sign. They were categorizing the patients and putting tags on their shirts. Matt had one that said simply, "Eye." Evidently, they had a doctor who specialized in eyes. The nurses were all women except one older man who was seemingly doing the same job as the women. Obviously, most of the men were off in the army. This man walked with a decided limp, and Matt thought he was either too old to be a soldier or had been so badly wounded he couldn't fight anymore.

Matt was impressed that the lady nurses, wearing plain dark dresses with long aprons, all seemed to know exactly what to do and were very efficient in doing it. Their voices were soft and sympathetic when they spoke to the soldiers. It was as if they held them all in reverence for what they had been through.

It was well into the evening when a nurse came out and called his name. He followed her through the doorway and down a short hall. The doctor was standing at the end of the hall talking to a patient. The nurse told Matt to sit on the table, and the doctor would be with him in a minute.

The doctor was a short man, slightly built, and probably about the age of Matt's Pa, thirty-six or thirty-seven. He looked weary, and he wore a heavily stained apron over his clothes. Some of the stains were obviously blood. He looked over at Matt and said something to the nurse, who left and returned a minute later with a basin and a washcloth. She put the cloth down in the water and wrung it out, leaving quite a bit of water in the cloth. She placed it over Matt's eye and told him to hold it there. The water was warm, and it felt good. He felt the water dripping down his hand onto his shirt. He had been applying the salve from the store in Bent Mountain to his burned skin, and it seemed to be feeling better. His eye, swollen as it was, was a different story. Matt knew he could see light and dark; what he didn't know was the extent of the injury under the swollen eyelid. Matt was still holding the cloth over his eye when the doctor approached.

"Well, what have we here?" the doctor asked. "How did you do this, son?"

"Sir, I was hoping to have rabbit for lunch, but the gun backfired and burned my face. I have not been able to see out of that eye now for three days. The swelling is still bad, but better than when it first occurred," Matt told him.

The doctor looked first at the burned skin. "Young man, you have a really bad burn on the side of your face. We will try to get some of that dead skin off so we can work on the new skin underneath, but it is going to hurt some. Before we start on that, I want to see if we can get that eye open and see what we have inside," he said.

Matt could feel the pressure on the skin close to his injured eye as the doctor's fingers probed the swollen tissue. The pain of the tissue parting was not as bad as when the doctor at Big Lick was looking at him. Little by little, the doctor got closer and closer to his eye. The pain was bearable, and he said as much to the doctor.

"We have seen much worse, haven't we, nurse?" the doctor responded. "The swelling will go down eventually, but the important thing is to learn how much damage there is to your eye. The explosion may have taken your eye, or it may just be trauma to the soft tissue around it. We won't know until we get inside where we can take a look."

The nurse held a lantern over the doctor's shoulder. Matt recognized it to be one with a reflector like the one the doctor and nurse in Big Lick had used. When the light hit his exposed eye, Matt felt a sharp pain. He couldn't see anything except the bright light. The doctor motioned, and the nurse moved the light away. When the bright light disappeared, Matt could see the doctor's face. Almost that quickly, the doctor let go of the swollen tissue, and it covered his eye again. The pain stopped, and Matt felt elation as he realized he could see.

"I saw your face, Doctor," Matt said, smiling through the pain.

"Good, I was hoping you could," the doctor said. He turned to the nurse. "That eye will keep for a few days. We should keep some cold compresses on it to help the swelling go down."

The doctor turned back to Matt. "Your eye will probably be fine when the swelling goes down, but you are not going to have a good time with what we have to do to work on your face. You have some badly burned skin, and it has to come off."

The doctor was right; Matt didn't like the feeling of having the skin peeled off his face, not one bit. The pain was excruciating, and it seemed to go on and on. Between each effort to get the dead skin off, the doctor and nurse put warm saltwater on the exposed flesh. Each application created a sting that was as painful as pulling on the skin. Finally, the doctor told him to get up off the table. Matt wasn't sure whether they were through, had cleaned the area, or if they just quit to let him rest until tomorrow to do it all over again. Either way he was grateful to get on his feet.

"Nurse, mix him up some linseed oil and lime water for the burn," the doctor said. "Son, I'll see you in a few days."

The nurse ushered him back up the hall to the waiting room. She asked the older man with the beard who had been helping register patients to take Matt to what she called the holding ward. They didn't offer Matt a bed. Instead, they let him bring his pack and blanket into a large room where a number of other men were staying, all outpatients needing further treatment.

Matt laid his blanket out in a corner and sat down. By now it was approaching ten o'clock, and people were beginning to settle down for the night. He had waited almost all day to see the doctor; it seemed like the doctor had worked on his face for hours. Matt's face hurt, but he also hurt all over from the tension in his muscles in reacting to the pain of the burn treatment. He soon fell asleep.

When Matt awoke the next morning, he looked around at the other men in the room. Most were just sitting on their blankets as if they were waiting on something to happen. He recognized one of the men against the other wall as the one he traded with for the tomatoes. Their eyes met, and the man nodded to him. Matt stood up and went to the door that led outside. It was open, and he stood there in the light breeze for a minute, enjoying the sunlight and the respite from the smell and the rustle of bodies inside the ward.

Outside, some ladies from a nearby church had set up a food line in the backyard behind the hospital. They had brought a huge kettle of soup and some bread. Matt was suddenly hungry, more hungry than he could ever remember. He had lost track of the last time he had anything other than his beef jerky and bread to eat, and his stomach growled. There were already men in line, and Matt moved to join the group. Soon he had a tin cup of soup and a big hunk of fresh bread in his hands as well as a mug of hot coffee. Soup never tasted so good, and he wondered if he could go back for seconds. He decided against it when he noted that there were now close to forty men standing in line for the soup. He sat for the longest time, sipping on the hot coffee. He never drank coffee at home, and tasting it without any sugar stirred in it made him remember why. He thought to himself that coffee must be an acquired taste.

As he sipped his coffee, he was joined by the man who had traded him the tomatoes. The man asked, "What outfit are you with again?" Matt answered that he was with the Twenty-First. The man said that he had not heard of a Twenty-First unit around here. "Have you seen some action?" he asked.

Matt thought for a moment about how he should respond to the man's query. He finally decided on responding honestly—to a point. "No, sir," he said. "I just signed up and was practicing with my gun on a rabbit when it blew up in my face. They sent me to a doctor in Big Lick, and he sent me over here to be treated by the military doctors. When I get this eye healed up, I am headed back up to join my unit with the Army of Virginia. I have heard that they are in Culpepper resting after the whipping they gave the Yankees at Chancellorsville. I'm not exactly sure where Culpepper is."

"Son, Culpepper is about three days' walk north of Charlottesville," the man responded. "That is home country for me. From here you take a boat up the James River to Scottsville, and from there it is an easy walk into Charlottesville. Going north to Culpepper is a bit harder walk, but you can make it in about three days. If you are lucky, you can catch a stage out of Charlottesville that will drop you at Culpepper. They stop there on the way to Fredericksburg. They make that trip to Culpepper in a long two days' ride."

The man reflected, "I suspect the army will not be at Culpepper when you get there, but their trail will not be hard to follow. They have about fifty thousand men with horses and cannons. That many men make lots of tracks."

Unlike the soldiers at the train station in Big Lick, this man seemed anxious to talk. "I've been off fighting this war ever since it started," he said. "In the beginning we thought it would be over in two months. We whipped them at Manassas and Bull Run. Then later we got them again at Antietam. I think we must have killed more than twenty thousand of them blue bellies at Antietam. We thought they would call it off and head for home. But they just keep on coming. They have more horses, more cannons, and more men than we have. They have the forces, but we have the generals. Lee and Jackson know how to win a war."

"Do you know of General Henry Heth?" Matt asked. "He has control of most of Lee's artillery."

"I can't rightly say I have heard of him, but we have lots of generals," the man responded.

Matt thought he should ask the man some questions so he could learn more about the war, but he couldn't think of anything to ask. It was not necessary. The man continued to talk.

"We are here in Lynchburg," he said. "This is the home of General Jubal Early and his Twenty-Fourth Battalion. Early is an old-timer. He must be seventy years old. He just took his men, six thousand of them, on a foray up into Pennsylvania. His men say they looked all over for some Yankees to fight but didn't find any. They were up there for more than three weeks and finally came home down the Shenandoah Valley. Some think he was scouting out the territory for General Lee. The two are good friends. Lee calls Early his bad old man. Lee is rumored to be heading for Harrisburg, Pennsylvania, next to make an impression on the Yankees in their own backyard. So far all of the battles have been fought here in Virginia. It is time we carried the fight to the Yankees in their own territory."

At that point, Matt felt nature's call and excused himself from the conversation. When he returned, the man was gone. The rest of the day was an exercise in "hurry up and wait," the lament of enlisted men in the military who spend most of their time waiting for something to happen. So far Matt had seen only the admissions waiting room, the hallway where the doctor examined him, and the ward where the outpatient men were mostly sitting and waiting. He decided he would go for a walk and see what he could see of the rest of the hospital.

The hospital building seemed to have hallways that went in all directions. It was obvious that it had been built in sections. Matt walked first down the hallway past the admissions area to see what was on the first floor. It mostly housed examining rooms. The halls were musty and dark. There were no lights in the hallways. Light was apparent only where the windows brought sunshine to the inner sanctums of the hospital. Evidently, they saved the lighted areas for the examining rooms.

There were many people moving up and down the hallways: patients, doctors, nurses, orderlies, and janitors. None paid much attention to Matt as he moved through on his self-guided tour. He stuck his head out the back door of the hospital and saw two men dumping trash into a big hole in the ground. Smoke came up from the depths of the hole, and Matt could smell something that he later identified as burning flesh.

Matt quickly closed the door and turned to the stairway that went up to the second floor. He could hear sounds from there, mostly men talking in loud voices and sounds of pain and resistance. He arrived at the top of the stairs and was greeted by two nurses rapidly walking his way. He thought they might send him back down the stairs as a person who was obviously out of place in the most serious of hospital areas, but they passed quickly by without even a second glance. He realized he was in the surgery section of the hospital. He heard raised voices coming from the room just a couple of doors down the hall.

"No, doctor," a man's voice said. "You can't take my arm!" The voice was loud, and the last few words were almost a scream.

Matt heard the doctor's voice responding in measured tones, "Now, soldier, you have gangrene in your hand and all the way up to your wrist, and it has to come off. If I don't take it off, you will be dead by morning,"

Matt looked around the corner through the door and saw a doctor holding a hacksaw, standing over a man who was lying on a table. A leather strap across the man's forehead held his head stationary. He was stripped to the waist, his arm and side shining gray with iodine. There were two other men in the room standing on both sides of the table. All three of the men standing had on aprons that were heavy with blood.

The man was screaming now. "You have to use some chloroform! The pain, Doctor, the pain!"

The doctor responded, "Now, son, we don't have any more anesthesia of any kind. The pain is going to be the worst you ever felt, but that arm has to come off. We have been watching the progress of the gangrene for two days now, hoping for a shipment of chloroform. We can't wait any longer. Now is the time." The doctor motioned to the two men standing on either side of the table. "Hold him still now, boys. Give him that leather belt to bite down on. We are going to get this done." The men moved in and held the man's arms and legs. The doctor put a heavy piece of wood under the man's elbow and placed the saw on the top of the joint.

Matt backed away from the door as the patient started screaming. The sound followed him down the hallway to the stairs. He was suddenly sick at his stomach and began to run down the stairs to the back door. He barely made it in time before he threw up off the back steps. At first he could hear the man screaming upstairs. Then suddenly, it stopped. He hoped the man had passed out; he didn't dwell on other possibilities.

There were no other tours in Matt's days or nights. He did not care to see more.

His time at the hospital passed too slowly. He slept in the room with the other soldiers each night. In the mornings the ladies from the church were back with their soup and bread. They appreciated Matt's offer to help, and he moved the tables in place for them. On the second morning, several of the ladies brought muffins, but Matt didn't get one. Despite his helping with the tables, he was too far back in line, and there weren't enough to go around.

In the late afternoon of the second day, Matt walked down the street to a little general store and brought back some more beef jerky and bread. They didn't have any honey, or he would have bought that as well. His money was now still above the thirteen-dollar mark, and he felt good that he was making it on his subsistence rations in between the generous offerings of the church ladies.

He took a couple of short walks down the main street in Lynchburg, but mostly he stayed close to the hospital. He didn't want to miss an opportunity if the doctor got a free minute and sent the nurse to find him. Finally, on the third day, Matt was called back into the hallway where the doctor did his examinations. Matt had tried to keep the cold packs on his face most of the time, and he had applied the solution of linseed oil and lime water the nurse made. It was working. His skin was feeling better, and the swelling was going down. He could now easily distinguish between light and dark. He was sure his eye would be all right considering that he had seen the doctor's face during the earlier examination. He hoped the doctor would confirm as much with this visit.

When his time with the doctor finally came, Matt sat back up on the table, and the doctor began to spread the swollen skin around his eye again. The pain wasn't as bad now as before. Finally, the doctor was touching the eyelid and the puffy skin just below the eye. "Okay, soldier, I am going to open the eyelid, and you are going to see a bright light, probably bright enough to cause you some pain. We have to do this to know what to do next to treat that eye," he said.

Matt steeled himself for the pain, and it did come with the light, but it wasn't as bad as before. The nurse was standing right behind the doctor, holding the lantern that had the reflector on it. The doctor was looking into his eye. He continued to study the eye for several seconds before he told the nurse to take the light away. He then watched the eye's reaction.

"Good, good," the doctor said. "Son, the iris of your eye is reacting to the light. That is a good sign. Your pupil gets larger and smaller, depending on whether or not that light is shining on your face. That is a very good. I think that your eye will adjust and you will be able to see again. We just have to wait for the swelling to go down, maybe another week or so. I am going to tell the nurse to bring you back to me in three days. In the meantime, you keep the cold compresses on your face, and that will help the swelling go down."

Matt was happy with the doctor's diagnosis. He had been able to make out the doctor's face when the nurse turned off the light. He could see! When the swelling was gone, it was likely that his eyesight would be back to normal. He didn't have that much hope for the side of his face. The skin there was still red as fire, despite his use of the liniment. The cold compresses were helping the swelling, but healing the skin was going to take some time, and there was no doubt he was going to have a scar on his face that was going to remind him of the unfortunate circumstances of his accident for a very long time.

Still, Matt felt good. The swelling was going down, and his eye appeared to be healing itself. The skin would grow back as time passed. Matt decided he didn't need to wait around Lynchburg for what he already knew in his heart was going to happen. Every day that passed put him in greater jeopardy of being found out as a pretender and was one more day that the Army of Virginia might be moving farther north away from him. He needed to move on, and perhaps tomorrow was the day to go find that northbound boat.

MOVING ON

Matt spent most of the evening debating in his own mind about staying in the hospital for another week or getting on with his trek north toward wherever he might find the Army of Virginia. His thoughts were interrupted when a nurse came to the doorway of the room and briefly looked inside. Matt came to his feet quickly and moved toward the door. She had already gone down the hall, but Matt caught her within a few steps. He smiled at her and asked, "Ma'am, could I have a bandage to put over my face and eye?"

"Give me a few minutes, and I will bring you something," she responded with a smile.

When she brought the gauze bandage, he put it in his pack. He took the cloth he had been using for a compress, dipped it in a bucket of cool water, and held it up to his face over his swollen eye. He retraced his steps and lay down on his blanket alongside the soldiers in the room. Matt listened to the sounds of men sleeping all around him. The ward was uncomfortably warm, but a breeze was coming in the window that faced east. He knew from his previous nights in the ward that he could detect the first rays of sunlight when daybreak was just minutes away.

The next morning he was up with the first signs of light and retrieved his bandage and the tin of salve from his pack. He looked into the shaving mirror hung over a pitcher and basin in one corner of the washroom and carefully spread the salve on the damaged skin on his face. His face was still a mess, red with skin still peeling, and the eye was still swollen shut, but it was better than it had been. He covered it with the bandage, and then he retrieved his pack, blanket, and the old rifle and quietly left by the open door.

Matt had a new plan, and it did not include staying at the Ladies' Relief Hospital for another week. He was sure he was on the road to recovery and could easily handle moving on up the road.

Leaving the hospital, he walked quickly up the wooden sidewalk in front of a row of stores toward the riverfront wharf. The James River was a major thoroughfare for commerce in central Virginia, and boats were traveling both ways on the river during the daylight hours. By contrast, nothing moved on the river at night except the log rafts that brought timber to the sawmills. They kept local communities supplied with lumber for the constant construction that was going on in all of the cities that bordered the river. It was Matt's plan to hitch a ride on one of the riverboats as far as Scottsville. He would then follow the directions given by the soldier with the tomatoes to travel north toward Culpepper and the Army of Virginia.

There were three boats lined up at the wharf when Matt arrived at the riverfront. There were also several soldiers standing and sitting along the wharf, waiting for the opportunity to hitch a ride. Matt fell in with a group of seven men who were preparing to board the first boat. It was not a large boat, and its cargo was piled in the center of the deck. It also had a large metal fireplace with a grill over it near the front of the boat. Obviously, they did cooking there as the boat moved downstream.

There were several passengers already on board, and the soldiers took positions around the gunwales at the edge of the boat on both sides. The captain of the boat was a burly red-haired fellow, probably about forty years of age, just a bit older than Matt's Pa. He came to the front of the deck and motioned the soldiers to come close around him. Matt joined the group to hear what the captain had to say.

The captain spoke in hushed tones, saying, "I don't intend to charge any of you for hitching a ride with me down river to Scottsville. I do want something in return. I hope it doesn't happen again, but a few weeks ago, we passed a troop of Union cavalry, and the Yankees decided to use us for target practice. Two of my passengers were hit,

JOURNEY TO GETTYSBURG

and one of them died. I need you to commit to me that you will play the role of guards if we run into such a problem again."

The group all responded by nodding their heads, and a few growled angrily about the "damn Yankees" and "innocent civilians getting hit." Matt wondered how he would be of help with his crippled gun and its disabled firing pin. He hoped such a circumstance didn't occur.

Before long, two black crew men cast off the ropes that were holding the boat to the wharf, and Matt could hear the steam engine running quietly. The current of the river moved them slowly downstream, and Matt again felt very fortunate that he was riding rather than walking on his trip north. He realized that he would not have this good fortune without the hat and jacket the doctor had given him back in Big Lick. Matt still felt guilty about pretending to be something he wasn't, but at least with the bandage on his face, he felt sure no one would question whether he was a soldier.

Matt could tell by the quick passage of the trees on the bank that they were picking up speed. He had never ridden on a boat, and he concluded that this was a wonderful way to travel. He leaned back on his pack and slipped back into a light sleep, and from time to time, he opened his good eye to see what was going on around him.

A woman in a large apron was busying herself around the grill in the front of the boat, and it was obvious that the passengers and crew were going to have lunch when the time was right. He slipped back into sleep. A couple of hours passed. The cook quietly told the men close by that the soup was ready, and they could come when they wanted. Lunch was vegetable soup and bread, with drinking water that could be dipped from a bucket and ladle close by. It wasn't luxury, but it surely beat beef jerky and also spared Matt from dipping into his cash to purchase more food.

One of the crew members stood at the front of the boat holding a long heavy string with a weight on it. Periodically, he would drop it into the water and would call out something to the captain, who was toward the back of the boat standing behind a big steering wheel. Matt didn't ask but was sure that the man with the string was checking the depth of the water. The boat was built shallow with what appeared to be a flat bottom. Being flat on the bottom must be necessary in order to navigate the sometimes shallow water without scraping the hull.

One of the oddities that Matt noticed was that when the captain wanted the boat to go to the right, he turned the wheel to the left. When he wanted it to go left, he turned it to the right. "Now, why do you suppose?" Matt wondered out loud.

It was early in the afternoon by now, and the weather was warming up. He moved to find a place on the east side of the boat where the shade from the trees on the right bank would supply some cover from the sun. Once he saw three or four deer grazing on a small meadow just off the bank of the river. Fish periodically jumped from the water, and he thought about fishing in the stream back home close to the little farm.

Matt noticed that the soldiers did not get far from their guns. They had taken the captain seriously and intended to hold up their end of the bargain. Matt was very concerned about this and hoped that they avoided any confrontation with the Yankees. He knew his old gun wouldn't fire, and not participating in defense of the boat would give him away for sure. He breathed a sigh of relief when the day neared dusk with no incidents.

The crew maneuvered the boat over to the right side of the river to a place where it was obvious boats had tied up before. They would wait out the night on the bank. There were places where the river was very shallow, and the captain and crew needed to be able to see the hazards under the water in order to avoid running aground; night was not the time to be on the river. It was obvious that the riverboat was being run by a captain and crew who were veterans of the river, and every movement of the group seemed purposeful. No one needed to tell anyone what to do. Matt admired their expertise.

In a few minutes, the boat was secured to the stakes that were buried in the riverbank. The crew lifted the gangplank off the side and connected the boat to the bank. Several people were making preparation to get off the boat to walk around on solid ground.

One of the soldiers came over to Matt and said, "We are going to set up a perimeter on shore. We don't know where the Yankees might be, but we will all be better off if we are on solid ground and under cover if an attack comes."

Matt watched their leader and several other soldiers move over the gangplank to shore. He gathered his pack and the big gun. It had the cover over the firing pin, so no one could see that it was useless. He carried his gear across the gangplank and approached the man who had taken charge of the small group of soldiers. "Is there someplace you want me, sir?" he asked.

The man looked around at the wooded area along the bank. He pointed toward a low-hanging tree about fifty feet down the bank and replied, "How about over there? If they come, most likely they will come across the meadow through those bushes. You can set up there, and we will have a semicircle around the edge of the meadow. Everyone will have a tree to get behind. In a bit, we will assign watches. Can you take the first one?"

"Yes, sir," said Matt. He didn't know what he would do if he were on watch and the Yankees attacked them. He guessed he would yell to the rest of the men and make sure everyone was up and ready to fight. The old rifle would not fire, but it would make a formidable club. That was all he would have to fight with. For a few seconds, he contemplated telling the man that his gun was defective but thought better of it. No, he would have to take his chances and hope the Yankees didn't come that night and certainly not on his watch.

He breathed a sigh of relief when he finished his hour and a half on watch without incident.

"Have you heard anything?" the man who came to relieve him asked.

"No," Matt responded.

The man said something else to him in a very low whisper that Matt didn't hear. Matt nodded and headed off to his assigned spot. He set his gun up against the tree and lay down on his blanket. It was a warm night, and the crickets were out in force. He imagined that if the Yankees came, the crickets would stop chirping, and that might be a sign someone was coming. Of course, he did not know if that was the case or not. Soon he was asleep.

Matt was awakened with the touch of a gun barrel. He looked up into the face of the man who had taken over leadership of the soldiers.

"There is something moving in the woods. There are several of them," he whispered. "Get your gun ready."

A chill ran up Matt's spine, and he felt the hairs on his neck stand up. He was about to be in a fight with the Yankees, and all he had was a useless gun! He stood up and hoisted his rifle. He leaned on the tree and peered out into the meadow. The streaks of sunlight were just making their way to the ground, and he could see the meadow clearly all the way to the woods a full fifty yards away. If the Yankees were coming at them, the soldiers with Matt were going to get several good shots before they got close. He hoped that they did not have those new carbine rifles he had heard about that could shoot five rounds a minute. The guns this group of Confederate soldiers held were single-shot and had to be reloaded. They were lucky to shoot one round a minute.

Time passed. It seemed like hours but must have been just a few minutes. Matt could hear sounds in the woods, but not way at the end of the meadow as the leader had suggested. They were closer and to the right side where the woods seemed thicker. His mouth was dry, and he could feel the tension in the back of his neck. He looked down the row of trees at the soldiers. All looked alert and ready for whatever was about to happen.

Suddenly, something at the edge of the woods moved, and everyone seemed to stop breathing. Something stuck out of the brush. In a few seconds, a full head stuck out. It had antlers on it. Then as if squeezed out of the brush, a huge bull elk emerged into the meadow. He came a few steps out into the clearing and stopped and looked both ways. He dipped his head as if to check the grass.

Matt could hear breathing start again. He was too far from the other men to hear them, so he realized it must have been his own breathing he heard. He was looking at a giant bull elk standing in the clearing, not a troop of Yankee cavalry. Whee! What a relief!

The big elk lifted his head and looked back toward the woods. As if on a signal, two more elk followed him into the clearing. These had small antlers and were obviously female. Now all three of them were standing side by side at the edge of the meadow. One more rustle from the brush at the edge of the woods, and a small yearling emerged. Now there were four elk in the meadow.

The silence was deafening—at least it seemed so. Then just to Matt's right there was a sound like a clap of thunder. He jerked around toward the sound and saw the captain standing there with his rifle up to his shoulder and smoke coming out of the barrel into the air. Matt turned his head back toward the four elk. He just caught sight of two of them disappearing into the brush at the edge of the clearing. One of the does was on the ground lying where she had stood just a few seconds before.

He heard the captain's voice. "There will be meat for lunch today."

Everyone seemed to breathe easier right away. He saw several of the men smiling where before that was only steely determination on their faces. They were not only safe from the Yankees for the time being, but they were going to have elk meat for lunch. That was reason to celebrate!

The captain shook hands with the leader of the soldiers, and both were smiling about this unexpected luck. Matt saw two of the crew members come down the gangplank with knives and several other pieces of equipment. They were obviously going to dress out the elk and get it ready for the grill. Matt sat down next to the tree and began to breathe normally again. One of the soldiers came by him, stopped, and smiled. "It didn't happen this time, but you would have done fine, boy. Don't let it worry you. God decides when it is our time to go, not the Yankees," he said.

Matt didn't respond but thought that was a good way to think about it. He still didn't know what he would have done if the Yankees had indeed shown up with guns blazing and him with a defective peashooter.

When the meat from the elk was on the boat, the captain finished his preparation to head on down the river. The others on the bank began to cross the gangplank and take their places along the gunwales of the boat. Matt joined them and located a place where, later, he would find some shade from the sun. It was going to be a hot one.

The boat pushed off, and they were again headed down the river north toward Steelville. Matt put his hand on the bandage that covered the side of this face. His face and eye felt better each day. He knew the swelling was down around his eye. In a few days, he thought he might take the bandage off and test out his eye. He was sure in his mind that everything was going to be all right. His face and eye just needed some time to heal, and he had plenty of that. His trip north was getting longer and longer.

Matt tried to count how many days he had been on the road headed north. He had lost count. What day was this? He couldn't remember. How far was he from Culpepper? He didn't know, three days, maybe five. One thing for sure, he liked the train and the boat better than walking alongside of the road on the sharp rocks.

Everyone was on edge as they traveled farther north. There had been reports of Yankees in the area, and this boat had that history of confrontation with an enemy cavalry unit not long ago. Matt had felt safe from the war when he began this journey. The farther north he traveled, the more he realized he was headed into the teeth of the storm. North was Yankee territory, and the farther north they traveled, the more likely they would be to end up faced off with a Yankee fighting unit. He didn't feel safe anymore. His experience last night and this morning had stripped away any façade of safety. One thing for sure, he had to get away from this and any other group of soldiers and get rid of this Confederate jacket and cap. And he had to get himself a rifle that would actually shoot. He wasn't going to begin feeling safe until he accomplished both of those goals. Unfortunately, he was going to need the jacket and cap at least until he was on the road north of Scottsville.

For lunch that day they had both soup and meat. The elk meat had smelled wonderful on the grill and tasted even better. The cook was obviously proud of the dinner she put on the plates for the passengers. Everyone was in a good mood except the soldiers. It seemed that the farther north they traveled, the more tension they felt. Matt watched them closely as each soldier intently surveyed the riverbank.

Matt noted that of the seven soldiers, four had shoes and three did not. Two were barefoot like Matt. But the third had his feet wrapped in cloth. Matt had not seen such before and was curious as to how he might do the same thing. As they were eating their meal, he went over and sat down by the man and asked about the wrap around his feet.

The man told him about the fabric he had purchased and how to wrap his feet for best effect. The material was called canvas and was used to make tents. The soldier told Matt that there were small cities of canvas tents in California back in '49 when they were prospecting for gold. Some guy named Levi even cut some of the tents up and made them into pants for the miners. That material made for some pretty tough pants. Matt wanted to ask him if he found any gold but thought better of it. If he had struck his fortune, it was not likely he would be here now. At any rate, Matt resolved to visit the first shop he could find to look for that heavy fabric.

The trip down the river was uneventful until late in the day. The boat had passed a little town called Howardsville that was not one of their stops. They had continued down the river for about thirty minutes toward Scottsville when one of the soldiers called attention to riders coming along a ridge from the west. One of the crew members pulled out a spyglass. In a few seconds he said grimly, "They are Yankees, all right."

The head of the soldiers called out to the captain telling him they had seen a troop of Yankee cavalry riding toward them from the west.

"How far away are they?" the captain asked.

"They are about a half mile away. They should be here in ten minutes or thereabouts," he responded.

"Well, we will try not to be here in ten minutes," the captain said. "There is a bend in the river that turns straight north in about a half mile. If we can reach that bend, they will never catch us. The woods along the river on that side are just too thick to ride through at faster than a walk. Get your guns ready, but let's hope you don't have to use them."

Matt felt the steam engine on the boat rev up and watched the men get ready to defend the boat. He did exactly what they did. His useless old gun barrel joined seven more almost like it that were stuck out over the rail toward the advancing Yankee cavalry unit. The river was wide at this point, and they could stay a good seventy-five yards out in the river away from the east bank. Even if the Yankees did catch them, they would just be wasting their rifle balls. It wasn't likely they could hit anything at this distance.

As it turned out, there wasn't a problem. It worked out exactly as the captain had said. They reached the bend in the river before the cavalry troop caught them and turned straight north away from the troop. Neither side fired a shot.

For the second time that day, Matt began to breathe again. Up ahead he could see the wharf at Scottsville. It was bigger than he expected, almost as big as the one in Lynchburg. Several boats were already tied up there, and soldiers were camped along the bank of the river. It wasn't likely the Yankees were coming to Scottsville. He felt almost safe again.

CHARLOTTESVILLE AND NORTH

Matt waited until most of the passengers had gone ashore before he headed across the gangplank. He looked up and down the riverbank and was delighted to see hundreds of Confederate soldiers in an encampment. Some were down on a meadow marching. Some were training with their rifles with bayonets fixed, practicing hand-to-hand combat. Others were resting near tents closer to the wharf. Everywhere he could hear the voices of the drill sergeants shouting orders and giving directions. Matt had not seen anything like this before. It was a fascinating sight. He felt safe from the Yankees here with all of these soldiers in gray.

The little town of Scottsville was overwhelmed by the encampment of soldiers. Matt thought it was a good thing the army had brought its own provisions because there wasn't enough food in the entire town to feed the several hundred troops who were camped along the riverbank.

Several of the soldiers who had traveled with Matt on the boat entered the camp, and a couple walked on into the little town. Matt followed the latter group across the railroad tracks and into the center of town. It was a mud-street town with a train station and several buildings. One of the buildings was a trading post. Matt resolved to shop for the wrappings he needed for his feet after he saw where the other soldiers were going. They stopped in front of a saloon where Matt could hear music playing. In a few seconds they disappeared inside.

Matt walked back across the street to the little trading post. Inside was a well-supplied general store. There were two other customers in the store, and a man and woman were standing behind the counter.

"Well, son, what can I help you with?" the woman asked. She was a big lady who wore a white apron over her dark blue cotton dress. Like Pearl from the store in Jacksonville, she had a big voice. Matt was sure anyone passing by in the street could hear her talking to him.

"Ma'am, I need some shoes, and if you don't have my size, I need some heavy cloth that I can wrap around my feet. Do you have shoes in a size 14?" he asked.

She shook her head. "We have up to size 12. Even our boots just run from eights to twelves. Let me see your feet."

Matt stepped back from the counter where the lady could see his feet. She whistled and said, "Boy, you got some big dogs hanging off your legs. I don't think I can help you with shoes. Now what was it you were asking about cloth?"

"There was a man on the boat with me who had his feet wrapped in something he called canvas. It was a really tough material that was used to make tents in California during the gold rush. He said he bought the material in Lynchburg," Matt responded.

The lady walked over to a counter where bolts of material were stacked. She looked at several and then turned to Matt. "I'm sorry, son, most of the material we have is used to make clothing. I don't think any of it is tough enough to last more than a short time wrapped around your feet. Can't you get shoes from the army?" she asked.

Matt thought quickly. "No, ma'am. I am not in this outfit," he said. "My group is up at Culpepper, and I am trying to get back to them. Evidently, I have to depend on my own feet for the next three or four days to get to Culpepper, if my unit is still there."

"So you intend to walk up to Charlottesville and then on to Culpepper?" she asked.

"Yes, ma'am," Matt responded.

"Do you know about the wagon transport?" the lady asked.

"No, ma'am, I don't," he said.

"When you leave here, if you will go just to the north of town, you will find a stagecoach station," she said. "The stage doesn't run through here but once a day, but there is a wagon there that transports soldiers back and forth to Charlottesville. If you walk it, you can do it in a good long day. It is about twelve miles. But if they have a wagon leaving before too long, they should get you there by nightfall."

Matt was disappointed that he couldn't find the canvas but pleased that there was a wagon for transport to Charlottesville. He wanted to try the wrappings on his feet, but finding wagon transportation was even better. He thanked the lady for her help.

The walk through town was a short one as it wasn't a very big town. However, there were certainly lots of people on the street, and there were several wagons filled with goods. Matt saw a young man sweeping the wooden walkway in front of a building. The sign on the building advertised church services on Sunday mornings at ten o'clock.

"You have picked a hot one for working out in the sun," Matt said to the boy.

The boy looked up at Matt and responded, "Yeah, I like to get this done early in the day before it gets too bad. Where are you going?"

"I'm on the way to Charlottesville and then on to Culpepper," Matt responded. "I have a curiosity. This is such a small town, but it looks like the military thinks it is worth putting an army unit here, and the streets are full of wagons. Why is that?"

The boy smiled. "You are right. We haven't had to worry about the Yankees coming here. The military is providing protection for one of the major supplies and materials stations for all of central Virginia. If I could show you a map, you would see that this is the farthest point north for the James River that connects Lynchburg to Richmond. We are also just east of Staunton, the largest city in the central Shenandoah Valley. There is a mountain pass that runs almost directly from Staunton to Scottsville, and we are almost at the halfway point between Richmond and Staunton. Goods come in by wagon and rail and go out by riverboat. It won't be long before we are larger than Charlottesville and Lynchburg put together, maybe the largest city in Virginia." He beamed with pride.

"I'll be interested to see how that works out," Matt said. As he walked toward the stagecoach station, he thought about the boy's comments. What an amazing little place. He had heard of Lynchburg and

Charlottesville but never Scottsville. This was a place he would remember for future reference. Roads, rivers, and railroads bring prosperity with them. Scottsville, or somewhere like it, might be a place he would want to live in a few years.

Matt soon arrived at the stagecoach station, and there was indeed a wagon waiting. Several soldiers were already sitting in the wagon bed, and Matt climbed in the back with them. Within a few minutes, the driver came out of the little station house and looked over the side of the wagon bed.

"I'm glad you arrived, son," he said. "It takes six men to make a trip to Charlottesville pay."

Matt immediately realized he was going to have to dig into his stash to pay for this trip, and he wondered how much it would cost. The wagon master saw the expression on his face and smiled. "Don't worry, son. The army pays me, and you guys ride free. That is little enough compensation for what you will experience up the road."

Matt relaxed and was again pleased that he could ride instead of walk as they headed up the road toward Culpepper and the Army of Virginia. If the army was still there, he might find his Pa in just a few more days.

The ride into Charlottesville was bumpy, and the wagon didn't arrive until after dark. The wagon master unloaded them in the center of town, and a couple of the men disappeared into a saloon across the street that was blaring music and had tobacco smoke coming out over the top of the swinging doors. The others, Matt included, walked on up the main street.

Matt laid his blanket and the old gun down under a tree at the north edge of town and opened up his stash of beef jerky and bread. He had just enough honey left in his tin to cover about half of the piece of bread, but that was enough to give him the feeling that he had dessert with the rest of his meager fare. He sighed, remembering the church ladies and their vegetable soup back in Lynchburg and the grilled elk meat on the boat. It might be a long time before he had such good hot meals again.

Matt was up at first light and headed up the road toward Culpepper. He anticipated that he would see Confederate troops moving on the road between Charlottesville and Culpepper as the day wore on. One of the soldiers on the wagon had told him that it was about fifty miles up to Culpepper, and it would take him three to four days to walk it. He knew he wouldn't be the only one walking to Culpepper, and for a moment, he thought about waiting for someone else who might be walking on the road so he would have company, but he decided to go it on his own. The others were not up and moving as early as he was, and he knew he could make better time on his own.

A couple of hours had passed, and Matt was missing the rides he had earlier in his trip. He was already tired of walking barefoot on the side of the road. His feet were beginning to hurt. He had taken off the gray uniform jacket and put it in his pack, but he was still wearing the Confederate cap. He thought there might be some advantage to being dressed both ways, and so he stayed kind of halfway where he could take the hat off or slip the jacket on, depending on how he thought it might benefit him. He had covered about five miles when he heard the sound of horses trotting on the road behind him. As they got closer, he slipped off the cap and put it in his pocket.

In a few seconds, a buggy came around the curve in the road. His mind immediately flashed back to the buggy that had stopped in front of his gate at the little farm just a few weeks back. Had it only been a few weeks? It seemed like a very long time ago. He stepped to the side of the road to watch it pass. As he did, it slowed and then stopped.

Matt turned to see a two-horse buggy with three passengers. A deep voice came from the backseat. "Son, would thee like to ride with us for a while?"

Matt made note of the man's distinctive wording. He had on a dark jacket and the sort of round-rimmed black hat that marked him as Amish. His beard ran around his face, but he had no moustache, which was also usual for an Amish man. There was a small boy on the seat beside him, about eight or nine years of age. The driver appeared to be about the same age as Matt, though not as tall or big. Matt gratefully responded, "Oh, yes sir, very much."

"Thee can climb up there next to the driver," the man said. In a few seconds, Matt had his gun stowed under the seat and took his place next to the driver. "Tell me thy name, son," the man asked.

Matt gave him his name and told him where he was from.

"Where are thou going?" he asked.

"I am headed for Culpepper," Matt replied. "I have been on the road now for about two weeks. My Ma died, and I am looking for my Pa. He is with the Army of Virginia in Culpepper."

"How did thee get that injury to thy face?" he asked.

Matt had almost forgotten that he still had the bandage on his face. It was obvious to anyone talking to him, but Matt was so used to it after several days that he barely noticed that it was there. He turned around to talk to the man as the driver moved the horses into a slow trot and told him about the gun backfiring. "I was at a hospital in Lynchburg for treatment," he added.

The man asked another question, one that put Matt in a quandary. "Are thee in the army, son?"

Matt thought for just a few seconds before answering, "No, sir, I'm not. My Pa is. The last time I heard about it, the army was at Culpepper. I hope they are still there."

The man seemed satisfied with his response and headed the conversation in another direction, one that Matt was not happy to hear. "Son, the army has moved north from Culpepper. I heard that they left a few days ago and headed toward the mountains, toward a place called Front Royal."

Matt felt sharp disappointment. He had come a long way to find the army, and now they were moving away from him. Evidently, his trip was going to get even longer. Matt turned around in his seat again to speak to the man. "Sir, shall I assume that you are Amish?"

The man smiled and responded, "Yes, we are Amish. There are lots of us in this area, and lots of Quakers too."

"We are Quakers," Matt said.

The question came back quickly. "How is it that thou are a Quaker and thy father is in the army?"

Matt told the man he had misspoken. "I should have said that my mother and I are Quakers. My father is an English and doesn't have Quaker leanings."

"Are there many Quakers in North Carolina?" the man asked.

"No, sir, we are the only ones in Surrey County that I know of. There is no church there, not for Quakers or the Amish. There are a few Amish not too far away. I think they have their weekly meetings in someone's home," Matt said.

His answers seemed to satisfy the man in the backseat. They rode along for several minutes before anyone spoke again. This time it was the young man who was driving the surrey who asked Matt a question.

"Where is North Carolina?" he asked.

Matt smiled and said, "It is the state just below Virginia. From here it is a pretty good hike. I'm been traveling, mostly walking, now for a couple of weeks just to get this far. I think there is about as much of Virginia north of here as south. I think we are right in the middle here, north of Charlottesville." He looked over at the young man, who apparently knew so little of the world. "Tell me your name."

"My name is Jacob," the boy said. "That is my father and little brother, Jonathan, in the backseat. We are on the way home to our farm near Madison."

"I grew up on a farm too," Matt said. "What kind of things do you grow at your place?"

"We have about everything: pigs and cows and horses and chickens. We also grow vegetables and wheat, and we have a vineyard," Jacob said.

Matt made note of the fact that the horses were moving along at an easy trot. They were covering ground four or five times as fast as he could have on foot. He wasn't sure how far their farm near Madison was but hoped it was close to Culpepper.

It was late afternoon when the boy brought the horses to a stop. They had just crossed a small stream, and Jacob had let the horses stop and drink their fill. Now they were at a crossroads where the road kept on north and a branch went off to the west.

The father's deep voice came from the back of the surrey. "Young man, this is where we turn off. Culpepper is about twelve miles straight ahead. Our farm is about a mile to the east. It is getting late in the day. We would be pleased to have thee come home with us for an overnight if thou would like a place to sleep under a roof. We have a room in the loft of the barn, and my wife is a very good cook. What does thou say?"

Matt couldn't believe his good fortune. He wasn't looking forward to sleeping outside again tonight and having another supper of beef jerky and dry bread. He turned around in the seat and nodded enthusiastically. "I'd be much obliged, sir. The room in the loft sounds just fine, and supper sounds mighty good too."

Jacob turned the surrey east, and in a very short mile, they pulled up to an Amish farm that looked like the cover of a picture book his Ma had kept on the front-room shelf. The house was white, and the barn was red. As they drove up, a woman and a young girl came out on the porch.

"That is my mother and my sister," Jacob said. His mother was a plump lady with her hair hidden under a dark bonnet. His sister was a smaller, slimmer version of the mother.

As they stepped down from the wagon, Matt heard the woman say, "Well, what have we here?'

The man introduced Matt to his wife. "Martha, I want thee to meet Matt Mason from North Carolina. His mother passed away recently, and he is traveling north to find his father, who is with the Army of Virginia. We happened on him along the way and were impressed with the courtesy of his speech and his warm conversation. We invited him to stay the night with us, and he accepted."

"Well, we are pleased to have thee," she said to Matt. "Is it Matt, or is it really Matthew?"

"My mother always called me Matthew. She said she named me after the first Gospel writer," Matt responded. Then he turned to his host. "Sir, I'm sorry, I know your sons' names, but I don't know yours or your daughter's."

The man smiled and said, "We are the Mullers, Claude and Martha, and this is our daughter Mary."

"Well, Mr. and Mrs. Muller, and Mary, I am proud to make your acquaintance," Matt said. "I am already in your debt and wonder if there is some work I can do for you while I am here to pay for your kindness."

"Everyone on a farm has chores to do. I'll ask Jacob to find thee something worthy of the size and strength thou would bring to the task," said Mr. Muller.

Mrs. Muller started to go into the house. She turned back around and said with a smile, "Supper will be ready in about an hour. We will ring the bell."

Jacob led Matt out to the barn and up the ladder into the makeshift room just to the left of the loft drop, the big window at the front of the barn. Matt made note of the rope pulley that hung just in front of the big open window. He could see how they moved things from the ground to the loft. The barn on their little farm near Mt. Airy did not have a loft, so Matt had never seen the rope pulley mechanism up close. He stowed his gun and his pack and followed Jacob back down the ladder to the floor of the barn.

"Well, thee offered, and my father said we would take thee up on it. Thou can help me move some hay into the barn. We normally have two cuts a year, and the first one is ready to put up in the dry," Jacob said.

There was a stack of hay piled on a wagon at the back door of the barn. Jacob handed Matt a pitchfork and speared the first forkful of hay. He walked the load into the barn and dumped it in the stall just to the left of the door. Matt watched him and mirrored his effort. Before long, Jacob and Matt had emptied the wagon, and the stall was filling up with hay. After a couple of loads, Matt slipped off his shirt. Matt could feel air moving on his skin, and he was thankful for the cooling effect of the soft breeze.

After the boys had the hay piled up to the top of the stall, Jacob suggested they wash off in the trough by the back door of the barn. The water felt refreshingly cool, and Matt was glad to wash the sweat and straw off, but he also lost the bandage from the combination of sweating and washing in the trough. He could feel that the swelling over his eye had gone down significantly. He could see a bit, but it was like looking through a slit between the swollen eyelid and the puffy skin under the eye. He wondered what his face looked like, but he didn't have a mirror.

Matt slipped his shirt back on. He noted that Jacob did not take his shirt off and wondered about it but didn't comment, deciding he would store that question away and ask it later if an opportunity presented itself. It was the kind of question he would have asked his mother, only now she was gone, and he didn't know who he might ask about that and about other things that puzzled him.

He felt the tears gather at the edge of his eyes. He hadn't thought about his mother for a few hours while his mind had been on other things. Now her face was back at the front of his mind.

Matt was amazed at the dinner that Mrs. Muller and Mary put on the table. It had every dish he had dreamed of during his days on the road—sliced ham, sweet potatoes, and green beans, to name a few. To top it off, she had made a cake. Spelled out in raisins on the top in big letters were the words WELCOME MATT. It had been such a long time since his mother had been able to scrape up enough sugar and flour to make a cake, and he had never had one with his name on it before.

He was on his good behavior throughout the dinner, keeping his left hand in his lap on top of his napkin. He watched to see what fork and spoon to use and when. The cake was delicious, and he learned the raisins on it had been made from grapes the Mullers grew and dried. At first he thought the Mullers were serving wine, but it turned out to be grape juice. From the time they sat down, he felt Mary's eyes on him. He finally stopped turning toward her because he kept catching her looking at him.

When dinner was over, Mrs. Muller said to Matt, "Young man, I have been looking at that wound on thy face and thy swollen eye. I think thee needs a new bandage and some salve on that burned skin. Sit there at the table, and I will get what is necessary to doctor thee up."

Matt asked for a mirror to look at the wound before she put the new bandage on. He was surprised at the reaction to his simple request. "Son, we don't have a mirror to share with thee," she said.

He started to ask why not but thought better of it. When Mrs. Muller returned, she gently rubbed fresh salve on his skin, and Matt made note of the fact that the pain to the touch was much easier now. Evidently, his skin was healing nicely. She wrapped a long piece of fresh gauze over his eye and around the top of his head, tying it neatly in place.

Later Jacob walked back to the barn with Matt, and they sat down in his little room at the top of the ladder to talk for a while. Matt asked Jacob about his request for the mirror and his mother's terse response.

"We Amish view mirrors as instruments of vanity," Jacob explained. "We believe that one should not be preoccupied with one's appearance."

Matt thought about Jacob's response but did not ask more about that or any other Amish practices. Instead he went in another direction. "Why did Mary keep looking at me during dinner?" he asked.

Jacob smiled and said, "I think thou are the only boy outside of the family she has ever seen up close. Mother has home taught all three of us, and there aren't any boys Mary's age in Madison. I think she has been into Culpepper a time or two, but she was much younger then. She is fourteen now, and marriage is only a few years away. It is time she saw someone other than me to begin to know what it might be like to be with someone as a life mate."

Matt and Jacob talked on into the night. He was glad to have made another friend on the road.

FIGHTING THE GOOD FIGHT

Matt and Jacob were still in the loft talking when they began to hear muffled sounds outside. Suddenly, there was the noise of horses' hooves galloping close by, and Matt could hear the voices of several men yelling. Jacob jumped up and started to the edge of the loft.

"What is it?" Matt said.

"It's the town boys come to pay us a call," Jacob said. "They come every week or two. They throw rotten eggs at the house and open the gates to the corrals and let the animals out. It takes us most of the night to get things back to normal, and the mess on the porch is really bad. Mother usually ends up crying, and as Amish, there is nothing we can do."

Jacob left the room and clambered down the ladder. Matt went to the window and looked out. There below him in the front yard of the house were three boys, all a little older than he. Just as Jacob had said, they were riding their horses around in the yard, running over the flower beds, chasing the livestock down the lane, and throwing rotten eggs at the house.

Before he had time to think about it, Matt jumped out the window and caught the rope that was hooked on a pulley for raising things to the loft. His weight took him quickly to the ground and made a sound that attracted the attention of the boys, drawing them away from the house. Matt landed on the ground in front of the barn and picked up a pitchfork that he had left there. In an instant, the boys dismounted their horses and started toward Matt.

One of the boys said, "Look at the brave one-eyed chucklehead walking right up to us. Let's see how tough he is."

Matt stopped about ten feet from the boys and spoke to them in measured tones. "You have no call to treat these folks this way. These are nice people, and you should leave them alone."

"So what are thou going to do about it, chucklehead?" jeered the tallest boy. "Thee are not a fighter, so are thee going to pray us to death?" He purposely used the respectful language of the Amish, but in his mouth the words sounded rude and ugly.

Matt stepped forward and swung the handle of the pitchfork. It caught the tall boy behind the knees and knocked his legs out from under him. He swung back, and the arc of the handle caught the second boy on the side of the head, knocking him sideways and to the ground. The third boy picked up a rock and threw it at Matt. It caught him a glancing blow on the shoulder. He shook it off and moved toward the boy, who was the only one standing. Using the butt end of the pitchfork handle, he jabbed the boy in the stomach, doubling him over and leaving him gasping for air. He started to hit the boy on the back of the head, but he was already on the ground and a second blow didn't seem necessary.

It was over in an instant. All three boys were on the ground. Matt moved back to the tall boy who seemed to be the leader of the group and placed the sharp end of the pitchfork on his chest. The boy started to move, but Matt pushed the pitchfork down enough so that the boy could feel the sharpness of the spikes. Everything had stopped as suddenly as it started.

The other two boys began getting up slowly and moving away from Matt toward their horses. The boy under the pitchfork started to move too, but Matt pushed down a little harder with the business end of the fork and held him still. In a few seconds, the other two boys were mounted and began to ride back out through the gate, abandoning their friend.

Matt looked down at the boy on the ground. He looked to be around seventeen, maybe eighteen, and though he was older than Matt, he was not bigger.

"Now that we are alone, let's talk," Matt said. "You and your friends will never come here again and harass these people. If you see them in town, you will walk the other way. If there is ever any more trouble, I will bring some of my brothers, and we will find you in town. There are five of us, and I am the smallest one. We will make sure you never bother anyone again, ever. Do you understand?"

"You can't do that! You are Amish," the young man sputtered.

"Yes, I can and I will. I haven't been baptized yet," Matt responded. He emphasized the word *baptized* so that the boy clearly got his meaning. He might or might not be Amish but until he had said his vows and been baptized, he was just like any other young man, free to act on his conscience.

With that, Matt lifted the pitchfork and let the young man up. In a few seconds, he was on his horse and gone into the darkness.

Matt had been occupied with the three town boys and hadn't looked toward the house. Now he realized that the entire Muller family was out on the porch, watching and listening to what had just happened.

Mr. Muller came down the steps and approached him in the yard. "Matt, that just isn't our way," he said soberly.

"I know, sir, and I'm sorry if I embarrassed you. I just couldn't let them get away with treating my new friends that way," Matt responded.

"Thee told me earlier thou was a Quaker. Are you or not?" asked Mr. Muller.

Matt looked down at his bare feet. "I don't rightly know what I am, sir. My mother was raised by a Quaker elder. She taught me Quaker ways. My Pa is as English as a man can be. I guess what you have just seen is my Pa's ways coming out in me. Actually, knowing my mother, I don't think she would have been disappointed in me."

Matt heard Mrs. Muller's voice from the porch. "I am not disappointed in thee, Matt. I'm proud to know thee. I felt proud watching thee take up for us when thou knew we were forbidden to take up for ourselves. God bless thee, boy. I don't even know thee, and I already love thee like one of my sons."

With that, Jacob and Johnathan were off the porch, and both were patting him on the back. They only needed their mother's approval to be able to show theirs. Matt saw Mary watching him from the porch. Her eyes told him volumes that he knew she would never say. He knew he would never get to know her, but he liked being admired, even from a distance. And who knows? He might come back that way some day.

Mrs. Muller offered a fitting ending to the short celebration. She said, "Let's leave the cleaning up until tomorrow and all go in and have another piece of cake. There is plenty to go around for a second helping."

Matt couldn't think of anything he would rather do.

The next morning, Matt was up early. He thought he might be the only one about, but he heard sounds in the kitchen as he was washing in the basin on the back porch. He looked through the window and saw Mary standing over the sink. She motioned for him to come in. When he walked through the door, she said, "Breakfast will be ready in a few minutes. Sit down, and I will get thee some tea."

Matt smiled and responded, "Tea would be fine, but I'd rather have some milk. Do you have any milk left over from yesterday?" Shortly, Matt had a big cup of milk in front of him.

Mary came over to the edge of the table and spoke softly to him. "Matt, I want to thank thee for what thee did last night. I know Father told thee it wasn't our way, and it isn't. But we don't have much of a way to deal with bullies like the town boys. About all we can do is suffer in silence and clean up the mess afterward. It lifts my heart and my spirits to see them put in their place in a righteous way. When I lay down in bed last night, I dreamed all night about Bible warriors like David, Gideon, and my personal favorite, Deborah. None of God's warriors were people who turned the other cheek. This morning I said a prayer for thee. I think thou are one of God's warriors."

Matt didn't know how to respond to her words, and it was just as well as Jacob and Johnathan came in the door to the kitchen at that moment. Both boys sat down, and in a few minutes, Mr. and Mrs. Muller were at the table as well.

When breakfast was over, Mr. Muller spoke to Matt. "Thou are welcome to stay with us for a few days if rest would be of benefit," he said pleasantly. "We would be pleased to have thee as our guest."

Matt was surprised by Mr. Muller's offer. He had planned to get on up the road this morning as soon as he could gracefully leave. "That is a wonderful invitation, and I would like to accept," he said sincerely, "but every day I take off from getting to the Army of Virginia is one more day they move farther away. I need to move as fast as I can if I am to catch them and find my Pa."

"I thought that might be thy answer. I have asked Jacob to take thee on into Culpepper in the buggy," Mr. Muller said. "It will get thee up the road much faster, and thou should have no trouble picking up the army's trail from there."

Matt was almost overwhelmed by the gesture. He said softly, "I don't know how to thank you. Everything here and all of you have been just wonderful."

Jacob brought the buggy around while Matt said his good-byes to Mr. and Mrs. Muller. He smiled and nodded at Mary and Jonathan, who were sitting on the steps of the porch. He walked over to them and reached out his hand to Mary. She took it and started to say something but didn't.

Matt spoke to her softly, "You have a beautiful name, Mary. That was my mother's name." With that he turned away, and in a moment, he and Jacob were driving down the lane to the main road.

They were not far up the road when the question that had been on Jacob's mind came rushing out. "Matt, how did thee learn to fight like that? Thee took down three village toughs in just a few seconds."

Matt smiled at the question. "My Pa taught me, Jacob. When he was preparing to go to the army, he went into training for fighting with the Yankees. He ran several miles each morning after chores, and he did muscle exercises. I did that with him most of the time. My Ma wasn't very happy that he was teaching me fighting skills, but Pa said a boy needed to know how to take care of himself, and being fit and ready was the best way to stay out of a fight."

Matt smiled to himself as he told the story. "I was much smaller then, but I could run with him, and we did push-ups on the straw in one of the stalls and pull-ups on a frame he built onto the side of our barn. The thing with the pitchfork handle was something he taught me when he was training for hand-to-hand combat. We would take two old broom handles and work on defensive movements and attack. He did it in slow motion for me until I got the hang of it, and then we speeded it up. He would attack me, and I would fend him off, and then I would attack him, and he would catch my blows with his broom handle. It was fun to learn it, but I never used any of the skills until last night.

"A big part of the success with those three hoodlums was the fact that they did not expect me to fight. Surprise is a very effective weapon. My Pa always said, 'If you move quickly when the enemy doesn't expect it, the battle can be over almost before it starts.' That is what happened last night."

The horses had been moving down the road at a fast trot ever since the boys turned onto the main road. Shortly, they crested a ridge and could see Culpepper in the distance.

"Matt, where does thee think thee would want to go once we get into town?" Jacob asked.

Matt thought for a few minutes and said, "It would be good if we could find where they were camped before they moved north. I'm sure there is a road out of Culpepper to the north. Your father said that they had gone toward Front Royal. I need to find out how far that is and to find a connecting road."

When they entered the town of Culpepper, Matt had Jacob pull over in front of the first general store he saw. Inside, he learned from the clerk that the camp was just north of town. There was a second camp not too far up the road in Brandy Station. That camp was for JEB Stuart's cavalry and was much smaller than the first one.

As the clerk talked, Matt's mind was flooded by the memory of the renegades who had stolen Ol' Mose, leading to the injury to his face and eye. They had said the Yankees had surprised them one morning before they were awake and attacked their camp. The two men claimed that the Yankees had run off their horses and taken most of their supplies and materials. The reason they were down the road in southern Virginia where they met up with Matt was to get new horses. Or so they said.

Matt thought of his experiences with Ol' Mose the three or four times he got out of the corral. Even if he and Pa couldn't find him, the mule always came home on his own in a day or two. Pa told him that wild horses and mules would roam a territory several miles wide where they could get food and water. Horses and mules that had been raised on a farm with people would come back to wherever they were used to getting food and water. Generally, they wouldn't wander far.

"Jacob," Matt said suddenly, "can you take me just a bit farther up the road? I want to try out a possibility that I just thought of. Let's go up to the camp where the cavalry was at Brandy Station."

Matt was hesitant to tell Jacob his idea for fear it was just too far-fetched to come true. He was hoping that one or two horses might still be in the area after the cavalry had moved on. If they were, it was possible that he might be able to catch a hungry horse and set himself up to ride north instead of walk.

When they found the cavalry camp, it was just as the renegades had described it. The camp lay on the flat land between two ridges with a stream running down between. The renegades had said that the Yankees had attacked them from one ridge and ran them back into the woods on the other side of the valley. Matt looked around, hoping to see a shadow at the edge of the woods on the other side, but saw nothing in the distance that resembled a horse.

"Jacob, I am going to get off here. If you head back to the farm, you can make it by dusk. I am going to stay here through the afternoon. Perhaps in the early evening, any strays still in the area might wander back to this campsite to drink from the stream or graze on the meadow grass," Matt said. "If they do, I may have a chance to capture one."

Jacob objected, "Matt, I will stay with thee. It will be easier to catch a horse if there are two of us."

"I appreciate the offer, but I have imposed long enough. I want you to head back home now so your folks won't worry about you," said Matt.

Jacob continued to argue the issue, but Matt was firm that Jacob should be home by dusk so his folks wouldn't worry. Jacob climbed back in the buggy and turned it around. Matt felt the tears beginning to rise in his eyes. He was standing a few feet away, ready to wave good-bye to his new friend, when Jacob looped the reins around the brake and stepped down from the driver's seat again. He walked back behind the rear wheels and reached under the backseat. There was a black painted box there. He lifted the lid and reached inside. When he turned back to Matt, he had a rope in his hand.

Jacob smiled at Matt and said, "If thee does find a horse, thee will need some way to secure him."

The gesture from his young friend brought the tears to Matt's eyes again. What a fine family, and what good fortune they had happened by when they did! Matt thanked him as he took the rope and stood watching as Jacob moved back into the driver's seat, shook the reins gently on the backside of the horses, and the little buggy headed off down the road. Matt waved, but Jacob didn't look back.

Matt walked across the meadow where just days before the cavalry camp had been set up. He could see where they had tied the horses downstream along the bank where watering them would not have been a time-consuming task. He could also see trash here and there that had been left behind when the soldiers moved out. He hoped that trash wasn't the only thing they had left behind.

He waded across the shallow stream and felt the water cold on his bare feet. He found himself standing at the edge of the woods, looking out at the clearing. It would have been difficult for anyone to see him, but he could see the entire meadow clearly. Matt sat down and waited. It was a good three maybe four hours until dusk. He unrolled his blanket and put it against a tree. Before he knew it, he was asleep.

From time to time, Matt heard sounds of movement back in the woods. The brush was thick, and when he listened intently, the sounds seemed to disappear, so he heard only the rustle of the leaves in the slight wind that came through the trees. He drifted back and forth into sleep.

At about dusk, he heard another noise, and he came awake quietly. He looked around, getting his one good eye used to the dark. He could still see across the meadow, but the light was fading rapidly. He looked well down to the left as far as he could see along the stream bed. Nothing. His eye scanned down the stream to where the horses had been tied. Nothing. He leaned up to get a better vantage point and saw something in the corner of his eye. A movement. He stood up slowly and quietly stepped out from behind the tree that was blocking his view. There in the distance was a large dark horse. It was standing in the water drinking. Then a second horse, a gray one, came out of the woods and joined the dark one at the edge of the stream. They were about fifty yards from him and stood together motionless, drinking the cool water from the edge of the stream.

Matt's mind raced forward. How was the best way to catch one of the horses? He had been thinking of several possibilities of what he might do if a horse did, in fact, appear. Should he just walk up to them? Should he lure the horses with some grass? Could he keep from spooking them back into the woods?

He knew that the horses were used to being around people, but they had been away from humans for a couple of weeks. While they were used to hearing men's voices and seeing people around, their last experience with man was with guns firing and lots of noise and confusion. Matt began to talk softly. He was some distance away, but he knew the horses would hear him. With the first couple of words, he saw the horses' heads come up and turn in his direction. They pricked up their ears almost simultaneously.

Matt began to move along the edge of the woods. He wanted them to hear his voice, but he wanted to be careful that he did not scare them with any sudden movements that would spook them back into the woods. The dark horse puts his head back down to take more water. The gray one continued to watch Matt. As he moved closer, the dark horse lifted his head out of the water and took a few steps backward. It was obvious that this one, which stood closest to Matt, was walking with a slight limp. There was something the matter with his right front leg. He might walk back into the woods, but it was not likely that he would run.

Cautiously, Matt moved closer to the horses, continuing to speak softly to them. He wasn't sure how they would respond to the sight of the rope, so he held it behind his back. He had a loop ready in case he got close enough to one of the horses to get it over his head.

The gray horse moved away from him downstream a few steps. He stopped and looked back at Matt. The dark horse, the one with the bad leg, stood motionless at the edge of the water. He was watching

Matt intently. His ears were thrust forward toward Matt, as if to pick up any sound. Matt continued to talk quietly to the two horses, moving ever closer.

The gray horse took a few steps toward the edge of the woods. Matt stopped moving forward and held his breath for a few seconds. Then he began to talk again. The gray horse moved quickly into the woods. Matt then turned his full attention to the dark horse. He was still standing at the edge of the water, watching Matt's every move.

Finally, Matt was almost behind the dark horse, standing between him and the woods. He continued to talk to the horse. The words he used didn't mean anything, but his tone was soft and soothing. He did not want the horse to feel in jeopardy or to follow the gray one into the woods. As Matt carefully began to approach the horse, it turned to face him. Matt was now just a few feet away and thought, *It's now or never.* The horse backed a step into the water. Matt stopped moving but kept talking. He held out his hand so the horse could smell him. The horse quieted, and Matt began to approach again. Finally, he was close enough to lift the rope and gently place it over the horse's head. The horse was definitely a cavalry horse. It still wore a halter on its head.

Matt moved back, gently pulling on the rope. The horse followed. Matt was relieved. He had a horse!

The next order of business was to find out what was wrong with the horse's right leg. He wouldn't be much good if he was lame and couldn't carry Matt's weight. Matt tied the horse on a low-hanging tree limb and began to rub his hands over the horse's coat. He wanted the horse to get used to his hands so he could examine his leg. There were a few scratches on him, but nothing serious. Matt figured he probably got them running through the brush when the attack occurred or perhaps after he was free.

Finally, Matt leaned down and rubbed his hand along the horse's lower leg. He was feeling for the tendons along the lower part of the leg. Pa showed him once when Ol' Mose was having trouble. He said that if the two main tendons in his lower leg were bowed, he was a goner. Matt could feel the tendons, but neither seemed out of line. He squeezed them, and the horse didn't react. If they were sore, he would have shied. Matt continued to feel down the leg. He heard his Pa's voice in his ear: "The bump on the back of a horse's front leg would have the feel of a knot inside if everything was right." Matt felt a small bone there about the size of a small rock. So far, so good.

Matt turned the horse's hoof up and looked at it. The shoe was loose, and the nail on the side was hanging out. There was a rock under the shoe. It was hard to tell if the rock had gotten under the shoe and pushed the nail out or if the nail had gotten loose and allowed the rock to get in there. Either way, it wasn't a major problem. He reached in his pants pocket and pulled out his pocketknife. He took the back of the knife and put it under the head of the nail. With just a little effort, the nail came out too. The horse's hoof was clean, but it still had a loose shoe. He would need to find a blacksmith shop before he could ride him.

He led the horse back to the tree where he had left his pack and blanket, tying the horse where he could graze. There was nothing to be gained by heading out in the dark. The morning would be soon enough. He lay down on his blanket, but sleep was difficult because he felt such excitement in the pit of his stomach. His journey north had taken on a decided turn for the better. He had a horse!

GLORY HALLELUJAH IN THE LAND OF COTTON

The early morning light found Matt already up and getting ready to go. He was delighted with his newfound traveling companion, despite the fact that he was not going to be able to ride him until he could get a new nail in the horse's shoe. It was also likely that the horse's hoof would be sore from the rock under his shoe. You couldn't tell how long it had been under there. It was stuck pretty tight. It could have been days.

    Matt walked the horse out into the sun then stepped back and looked him over. What he had been identifying in his mind as a dark brown horse turned out to be bay-colored. He had a reddish-brown coat with black points. All four feet were black as well as his mane and ears. Bay horses were unusual, Matt thought, but when you saw one, you didn't forget them. They tended to be larger than most horses, and they were distinctive with their reddish-brown coat and black markings. Whoever owned this horse wouldn't be forgetting him soon.

    He wondered if the former owner had been killed in the Brandy Station fight or if the horse had just been run off by the Yankees, like the renegades had reported. He put his blanket in his pack, hung it over his shoulder, and picked up the end of the rope. He walked the horse back across the meadow to the road, and they started back toward Brandy Station.

    To Matt's relief, there was a blacksmith shop just at the northern edge of Brandy Station. It wasn't a real blacksmith shop like he had seen in Mt. Airy or the one where Hop Hopkins's father worked in Hillsville, but a small makeshift shop located at the back of a barn. The blacksmith, a big man with a curly beard, did a variety of different things, and he said he could fix the horse's shoe, though Matt would have to wait for him to finish another job first.

The blacksmith's farm was only slightly bigger than the small farm Matt had left in North Carolina. He sat under a tree across from the shop and watched the chickens walk back and forth across the road. *Whoever asked the question about why the chicken crossed the road evidently knew there was no real answer*, Matt thought, smiling to himself. Watching the chickens going back and forth didn't reveal any purposeful thinking on the fowls' part.

At last the blacksmith called Matt over and showed him what he had done with the horse's hoof. "Son, you had best not ride this horse for a day or two. His hoof is going to be fine, but it will be sore for a while," he said. "That will be twenty-five cents if it is Union money and fifty cents if it is Confederate."

Matt was out of change, but he reached into his pack and pulled out a Union dollar.

The man was obviously pleased. "Son, you will have to take Confederate change for your dollar. I don't have any Union change," he said.

"That will be fine with me as long as the Union money gets me double in Confederate money when you make the change," Matt said.

It was obvious that the man did not like Matt's response. "Listen here, sonny, I set the prices in my own business, not some kid who comes in from heaven knows where."

Not to be intimidated, Matt said, "You set the exchange rate. I'm just following your lead." He handed him the money.

The man did not look happy with that response but reached into a bag he had on his table and pulled out a dollar fifty in Confederate money. Matt took the money, thanked the man, and started to leave. Then the man asked a question that sounded more like an accusation. "Son, where are you headed with that stolen Confederate cavalry horse?"

"I did not steal this horse. I found him wandering out where JEB Stuart's cavalry unit camp was located," Matt said simply. "I'm on the way north to find the Army of Virginia. When I find them, this horse will be back where he belongs. I hope to catch the army by the time they get to Winchester or maybe a little farther north." He paused and asked, "Sir, how did you know it was a cavalry horse?"

The man responded, "Everyone who knows anything about the military can identify that horse by the bridle. Even if he wasn't wearing that bridle, there isn't a fine horse like this in the entire state of Virginia that hasn't been picked up by the army. When you catch up with the army, you will not have a problem, but between here and there, you need to be careful if the authorities catch you with a horse that doesn't belong to you."

"I'll be careful," Matt responded. He thought about the blacksmith's words as he led the horse up the road. If he put on the Confederate jacket and cap, there would be no question about the horse, but that would be disastrous if he ran into a Union patrol. If he didn't wear the uniform, he might be better off to make a new bridle out of the rope he had around the horse's neck and get rid of the bridle the horse was wearing. For the time being, he left the jacket and cap in his pack.

As they walked along, Matt smiled to himself as an idea popped in his head. One good thing about having the horse was that he would not have to carry the heavy gun anymore. He got in his pack and unrolled the leather carrying harness his Pa had rigged up that he had used on Ol' Mose. He fit it around the horse's chest just behind his front legs and placed the gun in the harness. It hung along the horse's side from his hip to his shoulder. It was a real relief to get rid of the weight of the gun. He looked at the horse's front legs as they walked, noticing that the horse was giving to the leg a bit but not nearly as much as before. Matt decided he would not ride him today at all and would look at him again tomorrow.

That night, Matt rigged some hobbles out of the end of the rope so the horse could move and graze but not wander too far. He laid his blanket out under a tree and sat looking at his beef jerky and bread for a long time before he took his first bite. His mind was on the dinner table at the Muller's house. What a meal he had during his night there, and now this. Oh well, it would get him by. The first night or two on the road, the beef jerky had been just fine. Now, it just made Matt think of what he was missing.

The next morning he put his pack on the horse and led him up and down the road several steps. He didn't seem to be giving to the front leg anymore. Matt decided to give riding him a try. He resolved to ride him down the hills and on the level but to walk along side of him when they had a hill to climb, just like he had done with Ol' Mose. By tomorrow he should be recovered enough for Matt to ride him. Then they would make faster time.

Matt led the horse into Jacksonton about midafternoon. He was still two days' walk from Front Royal, but when the horse was in good shape, he figured they could make about twenty miles a day. The army probably couldn't make half of that, so he hoped he would be making up ground quickly.

He tied the horse up on the rail in front of the only store in Jacksonton and went inside. There was a young clerk behind the counter. Matt greeted him and asked, "Did the Confederate cavalry come through here last week?"

The boy responded with a flood of words, as if he hadn't talked to anyone in a week. "Yes, they came through all right, but it was more like ten days ago," he said eagerly. "They were headed toward Front Royal and then north. One of their scouts stopped in here before the troops came through. He said that they had some problems back at Brandy Station and were not able to leave the area when Lee's army left Culpepper. After the scout left, the cavalry came through here so fast it was obvious they were in a lather to catch up with Lee. The word here is that the Yankees have taken Winchester again. Our boys ran them out of there last year, but they came back. Lee has about fifty thousand men and intends to take Winchester back as soon as he can get his men up there."

Matt listened intently and then asked the helpful clerk for the best route for catching up with the army.

He replied, "It is a shorter distance to Winchester going straight north, but the Rappahannock and the Potomac Rivers are between us and Winchester, and both are pretty deep and wide. You can avoid the Rappahannock by going to Front Royal, and the best place to ford the Potomac is just north of the city. There is a ferry there. There is a ferry on the Rappahannock too, but it is too small to carry much across, and the army wouldn't use it. It would take too long to get everything across."

Matt smiled to himself at the boy's wealth of information, hoping he didn't glean all of that from a short conversation with the scout who stopped by for a few minutes. He reflected that if the boy shared this much information with everyone who came into the store, the whole world probably knew where Lee was headed, including the Yankees.

"Do you have a map of the area I could look at?" he asked. " I need to catch up with Lee's army, and going cross-country and even across two rivers is not a serious problem if I can make up some time."

The boy pointed to the back wall of the store. Sure enough, there was a map there, and Matt walked back to take a closer look. It showed Culpepper, Rappahannock, Clarke, and Warren counties, all the land between Culpepper and Winchester. Front Royal was to the west, Culpepper to the south, and Winchester was well to the north. The Rappahannock River was just a couple of miles north of Jacksonton.

"Friend, can you show me where the ferry is on the Rappahannock River?" Matt asked.

The boy joined him, studied the map carefully, and put his finger on a spot on the river just a few miles north of Jacksonton. "Right about here," he said. "If you follow the road north, you can't miss it. At the north edge of town there are two roads. One goes west to Front Royal. The other will take you to the ferry across the Rappahannock."

Matt thanked him and headed toward the door. The clerk said, "Say, after all of that good information, aren't you going to buy something?"

Matt stopped just short of the door and looked back at the clerk. Then he looked at the shelves behind the counter. He spied a display of honey. He still had the beef jerky and bread he had bought at the store in Lynchburg, but he had run out of the honey back down the road. He walked over to the counter. "How much for a small tin of honey?" he asked.

The clerk retrieved one of the smaller tins from the shelf. "It is twenty cents," he responded.

Matt asked, "Is that Confederate or Union money?"

The boy smiled and said, "Confederate, of course."

Matt paid him the two Confederate dimes the blacksmith had given him as change back in Brandy Station. As he headed out the door, he heard the boy wish him good luck.

It was late afternoon when he left Jacksonton and approaching dusk when he led his horse up the bank of the Rappahannock River above the ferry. He looked down the hill. There was a little building at the edge of the river, and he could see the ferryboat out in the middle of the river. It was attached to a big rope that was tied to a tree on both banks of the river. The proprietor was on board, pulling the rope hard from the near side, sliding the ferryboat slowly toward the side where Matt waited. He was working without a shirt, but he had a Confederate cap on. Matt was about to head down the hill to the little building at the edge of the river when he heard horses' hooves on the road behind him.

Matt pulled the horse back into the brush on the side of the road. He could still see the river and the ferryboat clearly, but he couldn't see the road, and more to the point, no one on the road could see him. He wasn't sure who he might meet on this road and was not anxious to meet soldiers from either side of the conflict. Matt put his hand over the horse's nose to steady him and to keep him from making a noise that might reveal their hiding place.

As the horses crested the hill behind him, he heard the sound of a woman's voice coming from the small building down by the river. She was singing "The Battle Hymn of the Republic," which had become the Yankee army's marching song:

> *Glory, glory, hallelujah,*
> *Glory, glory, hallelujah,*
> *Glory, glory, hallelujah,*
> *His truth is marching on.*

Matt looked down at the ferryboat that was still in the middle of the river. He saw the proprietor let loose of the rope and move quickly to a box at the edge of the boat. He took off his gray Confederate cap and put it in the box. Matt began to smile. In a moment, the man was wearing a blue Yankee cap.

The lady's singing stopped as the horses pulled up in front of the building. Matt looked back at the ferryboat again and saw that the man was again pulling on the rope and was approaching the dock on Matt's side of the river. In a few more minutes, he had the gate down and was welcoming a Yankee patrol of five men and their horses onto the ferryboat. Before long he was back at the rope, moving them across the Rappahannock.

Matt watched the Yankee patrol disembark and disappear into the distance and again focused his attention on the proprietor. He was resting on a chair at the edge of the dock on the far side of the river. Matt was just about to leave his hiding place when he again heard the unmistakable sound of hoofbeats on the road. This time the riders' uniforms were gray. There were twelve men and horses, and Matt thought it was likely they were trailing the Yankee patrol that had just come by.

Matt heard the woman's voice again. This time she was singing a song more familiar and welcome to Confederate ears:

Oh, I wish I was in the land of cotton,
Old times they are not forgotten,
Look away, look away, look away
Dixie land.

Matt smiled to himself as he watched the scene across the river. As soon as the lady's voice begin to carry, the man moved quickly back to the box on the boat and retrieved his gray cap. In a few minutes the man was pulling on the rope that moved the ferry back across the river. The boat was not large enough to accommodate all the men and horses, so this time it took two trips and about thirty minutes. It was fully dark when the last Confederate soldier had disappeared up the bank on the other side of the Rappahannock. The man was making his way slowly back across the river, pulling the rope hand over hand.

When the ferry proprietor had his boat tied up on the dock, Matt got his first really good look at the man. He was about his Pa's age, maybe thirty-six or thirty-seven years old. He was strongly built with big shoulders and thick leather gloves on his hands. Matt left his hiding place on the bank and approached him about getting a ride across. "We need to wait awhile," the man said. "I charge fifty cents for a man and another fifty cents for a horse. I don't make a trip unless I can make at least five dollars, Confederate."

"How many trips do you take across on an average day?" Matt asked.

"Oh, eight or ten trips usually. There have been more lately with the military activity," the man responded.

Matt walked back over to his horse, thinking about the negative possibilities of his situation. He didn't want to end up on a trip across with either the Yankee or Confederate cavalry. Either group might take it on themselves to shoot him, either as a deserter or as an enemy combatant. He returned to the proprietor and asked, "Do you think you will be making any more trips tonight?"

"No, son. My wife and are about ready to close up for the night," the man responded. "We can operate at night if we have to, but if something went wrong, the rope broke or we were hit by a floating limb, it is hard to salvage the boat in the dark. Tomorrow is soon enough. You get some sleep, and I'll see you first thing in the morning."

Matt didn't like the prospect of waiting overnight and taking potluck on who came in the morning. Still, he didn't see any alternatives unless he was willing to swim. It was about seventy-five yards across. Two days ago he wouldn't have given the idea a second thought; he wouldn't have even considered it. But today, he had a horse. He had a big, strong horse that ought to be able to swim that river with little difficulty.

Matt went back to the horse and climbed on his back. The horse was quickly responsive, and Matt guided him down the gentle slope of the riverbank and a few steps into the water. The horse was about knee deep in the water and seemed to have no fear of it at all.

Matt guided the big horse back to shore and climbed down. He took off his shirt and rolled it up in his pack. He then tied the pack up high on the back of the horse's neck. He looked at the gun hanging on the side of the horse. If it was a working gun, he would have had a serious problem with it. It was too heavy for him to carry, and being underwater would foul both the barrel and the firing pin. Of course, that old gun didn't even have a firing pin, so the water couldn't do it any more damage.

As Matt was deliberating, the lights went out in the little building. A few seconds later, he saw the proprietor blow out the lantern at the dock and walk up to the building. It was almost completely dark. There were still a few streaks of light in the sky coming from the sunset, but here on the riverbank and looking at the water, it was very dark. Matt was immediately in a quandary. He wasn't sure whether to swim it now or to wait for the morning and take his chances riding across with some early travelers.

Matt heard the proprietor and his wife drive off in the buckboard that had been tied out behind the little building. Alone in the dark, Matt led the horse back up to the dock where the big rope hooked onto the pulley and the stabilizer went through the base of the boat and skimmed along the surface of the water. He thought that he could guide the horse across the water, and if he got in trouble, he could catch hold of the big rope and pull himself across. It was a risky plan that depended both on the horse being able to swim the river and him being able to hang on for the ride. In an instant, his decision was made.

Before he could change his mind, Matt guided the big horse into the water. He didn't seem at all reluctant. In a few seconds, both the horse and Matt were swimming in the river. The horse was doing fine, but way too quickly Matt felt himself getting tired. He held on tight to the rope around the horse's neck and felt the power in the thrust of the big animal's legs.

To his dismay, Matt realized they were drifting away from the big anchor rope on the ferry, and that was not a part of his plan. He could let go and swim back to the rope, or he could go with the horse. He decided to go with the horse, which seemed to know where he was going. Matt hung on and kicked with his legs to help as much as he could. They were drifting downstream, but they seemed to be getting closer to the other shore. Then Matt felt it. The horse's hooves had found solid ground under the water, and he was walking instead of swimming. In a few seconds he walked up on the shore with Matt alongside of him. Matt was breathing heavily, but the big horse seemed unbothered, like he did this every morning before breakfast.

Matt took the rope off the horse's neck and led him back toward the roadway that was now to the left of where they had drifted. He stopped at the top of the ridge overlooking the river and the ferry operator's building on the other side, admiring the strength of his horse. He patted him on the shoulder, giving him a few words of praise, and felt the water in his coat. Matt retrieved the curry brush from his pack and spent the next fifteen minutes rubbing the water out of the big fellow's coat.

Several things were on Matt's mind as he rubbed the shiny coat of the horse, not the least of which was that they had just saved a dollar, which he would have hated to give up to the ferryboat man. Another was that they needed a place to spend the night. The sun had completely set, but there was a bright moon. Before long he saw a stand of trees well off the road to the right, and he guided the big horse in that direction. In a few minutes he had hobbles on the horse and had laid his blanket out under a tree just at the edge of the woods.

Matt looked up at the sky and saw no clouds in any direction, just the big moon and several stars beginning to show up here and there. He took his change of clothes out of the pack, removed his wet pants, and laid them across a bush to dry. The dry clothes felt good, and the night was just about perfect for sleeping out under the stars.

ON THE ROAD TO WINCHESTER

Matt was on the road before first light. It felt comfortable to be astride his big horse and moving up the road. He thought there was little to compare between this horse and Ol' Mose. The old mule was aging and well past his prime. His Ma had talked about Ol' Mose following along behind the wagon when she and Matt's father had left Pennsylvania for North Carolina after they were married. That would mean that the old mule was at least sixteen years old when he died, maybe seventeen, older than Matt himself.

The horse was a big one by any standards, at least a foot taller at the shoulder than Ol' Mose, and powerfully built. If Matt didn't know that before the swim across the Rappahannock, he certainly knew it now. He could feel the strength of the big horse with every movement of his legs while they were in the water. When they were across the river, it was Matt who was breathing heavy. The big horse seemed to take it all in stride.

Matt thought such a fine animal needed a name. If an old mule had a name, surely a great bay horse in the prime of life needed a name. Matt thought of several names that came from books that his mother had him read when he was younger. Bucephalus came to mind. That was Alexander the Great's horse. How about Pegasus, the mythical horse who had wings? Robert E. Lee's horse was named Traveller. Everyone knew that. How about Rebel, because he certainly was a part of what the Yankees called the Rebel Army? None of those names seemed to fit.

Suddenly, Matt's mind went to the toy horse his Pa had made for him when he was small. It was just a cut-off broom handle with a homemade horse's head attached at the top. He rode that little stick horse all over the yard for months until its head fell off. He called his play horse Billy. Billy wouldn't quite do for this very big animal that Matt found himself riding here in the northern part of Virginia. How about…Big Billy? He thought for a minute. He liked it. Big Billy it would be.

Matt gave Big Billy a nudge with his knees, and the horse began an easy gallop. Matt hadn't planned to have the horse running this soon after his foot healed, but the gallop seemed to be what he wanted to do. It was probably a pace he was used to in traveling with the cavalry. Now that he thought about it, he hadn't seen cavalry units on the road but a few times. Each time they were in a gallop as if they had someplace important to go. Matt resolved to just let Big Billy have his head, and he held on tighter to the big horse's flowing mane. Having a saddle would certainly make the ride more comfortable, but just having a horse was sheer luxury.

The trees along the road were flying past. Matt wondered about the battle going on in Winchester. Perhaps it was already over. In that case, he would be seeing the movement of troops on the road headed back south if the north won, or east toward Washington, DC, if Lee had won. The south had taken Winchester before, and it was just not possible in his mind that Robert E. Lee with fifty thousand men would not take it again. Matt needed to be alert to the movement of troops. It was not likely that the Union Army would treat him very well if they came face-to-face with him on the road. He might lose his horse—or worse—if they caught him.

In the early afternoon he passed through Piedmont Station. It was little more than a crossroads with a store. He stopped at the store more to get off his horse for a few minutes and to see if there was any news about the battle for Winchester than that he needed to buy anything. The slender elderly lady behind the counter was pleased to see a potential customer come through the door.

"What can I do for you, young man?" she asked.

Matt responded, "I'm looking for some shoes. Do you have any fourteens in stock?"

She laughed. "Son, I'm not sure we have ever had any fourteens." She came out from behind the counter and looked down at his feet. "You do have some big feet," she said.

"Well, ma'am, do you have any canvas material?" Matt asked. "It is a very strong material you can wrap around your feet that protects almost like a pair of shoes."

She shook her head. "I'm not sure I ever heard of such a thing as canvas. We have several bolts of material, but it is mostly used to make dresses and shirts. I don't think any of it would work for wrapping feet."

Matt walked toward the back of the store, looking at the shelves. Most of the light in the store came from the windows at the front. The farther he went to the back, the more he was in the dark. He looked deep into the shadows and had a flashback of his Ma telling one of her stories. It was in a store like this near her home in Pennsylvania that his Ma described as the meeting place when she met his Pa. She loved to tell the story of their whirlwind romance, which lasted just from the Saturday afternoon they met at the store to Monday morning.

He was on a trip to Pennsylvania to buy some livestock. She was the seventeen-year-old daughter of a Quaker elder who lived on a farm near Lancaster with her parents and her two younger sisters. It was on a Saturday when they met by accident in a store just like this one, Matt imagined. Her father had gone to the bank, and she was shopping with her mother and sisters. His Ma said she turned around to the door when she heard heavy footsteps entering the store.

Matt could almost hear her voice now. "He was so big he filled up the doorway," she would say. He had heard the story so many times that he almost had it memorized, how she was immediately fascinated by the big county boy from North Carolina and how his father couldn't take his eyes off her. She said she could feel his eyes following her around the store and was flattered by the attention. She was in the back of the store when he approached her.

"My name is Isaac Mason. I'm just visiting here from North Carolina. What is your name?" he asked.

His Ma said she didn't know how to respond to this stranger. So she told him that they had not been properly introduced, and she didn't feel comfortable talking with him. He took a step toward her and asked her name again.

She remembered taking a step back and saying in a low voice so her mother and sisters couldn't hear, "Mary. My name is Mary."

"Then," his Ma would always add, "he smiled that big irresistible smile of his."

He said, "Well, now we have been properly introduced, and we both have Bible names. That must mean something important."

Matt heard the female voice from the front of the store. "Is there anything else I can help you with, young man?" she asked.

Matt was standing in front of the section for leatherwork. One of the things he saw hanging from a hook was a feedbag. Eventually he would need one for Big Billy.

"How much is your feedbag, ma'am?" he asked.

"That one is three dollars, son," she responded.

Matt regretfully hung it back on the hook and started back toward the front of the store. He stopped close to the front door and looked back at the lady. "Have you heard how the battle has gone over in Winchester, ma'am?"

The lady responded. "That battle was over day before yesterday. It only lasted the better part of a day. Lee and his troops ran the Yankees out of town to the north. You could hear the sounds of the cannons all the way over here."

"Is the Army of Virginia still in Winchester?" Matt asked eagerly.

"No, son, they may have left some troops behind, but the bulk of the army has moved on north up the pike toward Martinsburg," she said. "Are you headed that way?"

"Yes, ma'am. I'm hoping to catch up with the Army of Virginia. My Pa is with them, and I need to find him."

The lady moved closer and began talking in quiet tones, as if someone might overhear her. "Son, let me suggest that you go up the road a piece and then turn north toward Bluemont instead of going on into Winchester. That road between here and Winchester may be full of Yankee stragglers. You don't want to meet up with them. They are a bloodthirsty bunch of dastardly characters. When you reach Bluemont, you can turn back to the west toward Berryville. At Berryville you can turn north again and head for Charlestown, West Virginia. North of Charlestown you can catch the main road north that will take you to Martinsville. Lee's army will only move about six miles a day, so you should be able to catch them before they reach the Pennsylvania border.

"One other thing," she said. "Remember that Charlestown is in West Virginia, not Virginia. West Virginia is Yankee territory. Most of the people there have sons and husbands who are in the Union Army. They will not be as friendly to a Southerner like you. You may want to avoid any reference to where you are from or anything to do with the war."

The lady paused for a minute and looked at him with almost like a grandmother would. Her tone of voice told him that she was concerned for him. "Son, you need to be very careful," she said. "The Yankees are still in the area, and you are headed into the teeth of the conflict. And one other thing. The Army of Virginia is now called the Army of Northern Virginia. I'm not sure why they changed its name, but it could be so that the Yankees would think we have more men and armies traveling around Virginia than we really do. I know we have Lee's army north of Winchester now. Another part of that army is over in Richmond, and several other smaller units are moving independently here and there around the state. One of those may still be called the Army of Virginia. I just thought it might be of help for you to know that they have changed their name."

Matt nodded and smiled. "Thank you," he said gratefully.

"You be careful," she said.

When he was back on Big Billy heading toward Winchester, Matt thought about the lady's advice. He had intended to go on into Winchester if the South had taken the city. But what she said made sense, and he thought he might be better off to head north at his earliest opportunity. Heading to Bluemont sounded like good advice.

Matt urged Big Billy back into a light gallop, and before long, he was at a road that split with one fork going west and the other going north to Bluemont. There was a wooden sign that said Bluemont was eight miles distant. He took the north road.

If he had been walking, it would have taken him most of a day to reach Bluemont, but on Big Billy he was there in the late afternoon. He found a sign at the edge of town that said Berryville was another nine miles. He knew he probably wouldn't make Berryville by dark, but he turned and headed that way, resolved to make it as far as he could before holding up for the night.

Matt wasn't more than a couple of miles along the road when he saw a big cloud of dust ahead. He guided his big bay horse off the road and into the trees alongside a small stream. He continued to move alongside the road, wading in and out of the water, watching as a column of men appeared. They were indeed Yankees, and they looked very much the part of a defeated army. Matt knew this couldn't be all of them. He counted about 375 men on horseback, another four or five hundred walking, and several wagons that appeared to be carrying the wounded. They did not look like a unit that would be fit to fight again for several weeks, if then.

The caravan moved toward Washington, DC, while he moved slowly down the stream bed in the opposite direction. The soldiers seemed oblivious to his presence, but he stopped moving from time to time when their outriders came by. They were the only ones in the column who seemed to be concerned with knowing who might be close by, watching their movements. Finally, the column of Yankee soldiers was past. There were a few stragglers walking behind, and he let them pass as well before he returned to the road and continued his trek toward Berryville.

By this time it was nearing dark, and a light rain had started to fall. Matt rode on, looking for a dry place to hold up for the night. Nothing appeared along the road. At one point the big horse stumbled, and Matt got off him to check his front leg. When he did, he noticed that periodically, there were some very deep ruts in the road. Obviously, there had been rain over the past several days, and the wagons that had just come through were loaded down with lots of weight. He didn't feel he could take a chance on Big Billy stepping in a hole in the dark and breaking a leg or bowing a tendon, so he started walking and leading the big horse.

Matt had been walking for a couple of hours in the dark when the rain really started pouring down. He led Big Billy off the road and found a big oak tree to stand under. He could see lightning in the distance coming closer, and the thunder was almost constant. Standing under a tree with lightning in the area wasn't a good idea, so Matt returned to the road with Big Billy and kept walking. The rain seemed to come down harder and harder the farther they walked.

After what seemed like another couple of hours, they came to a lane that led down a hill. In a flash of lightning, he saw it led to a farmhouse with a big white barn just behind it. He decided to walk up the lane and see if he could find shelter there. He carefully negotiated the lane between the mud puddles while leading the horse. It was way too late for anyone to be up in the house, and there were no lights to be seen anywhere. He hoped he could find a place to get in out of the rain.

The closer he got to the house and barn, the more he realized that this was no ordinary farm. The lightning continued to light up the sky, and when it did, he could see the major buildings of the farm. The house and barn were both two stories tall. The barn was a huge building with several loft windows, each with pulley fixtures outside like the one at the Mullers' farm. To his left was a vineyard, and to his right was a wheat field. There was a big eight-point star painted in red on the side of the barn. Matt's heart leapt in his chest when he realized it was like the star that his mother had drawn on the cross that he had placed at the head of her grave. This must be a Quaker farm!

Matt made his way past the house toward the barn. The door was latched, but he was able to open it and get the two of them inside. As if to emphasize that this was what he needed to do, there was a big flash of lightning and a crash of thunder just as he ushered Big Billy through the door. When they were inside, he sensed immediately the presence of animals that had been brought in for the night.

In one stall, a cow began to moo, and shortly, he heard the familiar bray of a mule from another stall. He stood there in the dark with his dripping wet clothes. His big horse was waiting for him to do something. Matt decided that the first thing to do was to get out of his wet clothes and into something dry. He took down the pack that was tied to the horse's bridle and retrieved his change of clothing. Within a minute or two, he had on dry clothes, and his wet clothes were laid over a stall rail. The mule and the cow were both quiet now. He took out his curry brush and began to rub Big Billy's coat. Covering the big horse's body took about fifteen minutes, and while he worked on getting the water out of his horse's coat, he thought about what his Ma had told him about Quakers and the Amish. She said there were many Quakers and Amish in Pennsylvania. And evidently, in northern Virginia too. A statesman named William Penn who was instrumental in organizing the state of Pennsylvania was a Quaker. His Ma said that the Quakers and Amish tended to dress alike, and both groups farm for a living, so people get the two groups mixed up. She said that the Quakers were much more relaxed from a religious perspective.

"We owned businesses and traded with the 'English,' as we called them," she said.

When Matt finished with the horse, he looked around for someplace to lay his blanket. He settled on a couple of bales of hay up above the floor of the barn. The straw would make a good bed for the night. He intended to be up and out of the barn before anyone was awake in the house. That way no one would be the wiser about his clandestine visit to their barn. Exhausted, he settled down in his bed of hay.

Matt awoke the next morning to full sunlight and a voice saying, "Who are thee, young man?" He opened his eyes to see a middle-aged man standing over him, dressed in a black coat and a white shirt. He had on the traditional hat of the Quakers.

He had been found out! Matt attempted to respond. "Sir, I'm sorry for invading your barn. I didn't know what else to do last night. We were traveling up the road toward Berryville when the rain caught us. It was coming down in sheets, and lightning was everywhere. I would have knocked on your door and asked permission, but the house was dark, and I didn't want to wake anyone. I thought we would be gone by this time and would not be an imposition."

The man held up his hand for Matt to stop talking and said, "It is all right. There is no harm done. We are pleased that thee happened by our way. The scriptures say that we will meet many way strangers on the road and that we are to do them good as we have the means. Let's get thee inside. My wife is putting breakfast on the table, and thou can join us."

Matt couldn't think of anything to say but "Thank you."

The middle-aged man who had awakened him carried a lantern, and he had a small basket full of eggs. Obviously, he had been out of the house some time before he discovered Matt in the barn.

"What is thy name, son?" he asked.

"I am Matt Mason from Mt. Airy, North Carolina," Matt responded.

"What brings thee way up here all the way from North Carolina, young man?" he asked.

Matt explained to him about his mother dying and that he was looking for his Pa, who was with the Army of Northern Virginia. He used the new name the woman had shared with him at the general store in Piedmont Station. The farmer simply listened and nodded.

All the way to the house, all he could think of was how blessed he had been while making this odyssey from Mr. Airy all the way to the northern edge of Virginia. Except for the renegades who cost him Ol' Mose, everyone had been especially nice to him as he moved from place to place. Now, here he was at yet another home, this time with a family of the Society of Friends who were treating him like a visiting member of the family.

When they arrived in the kitchen, he was introduced to a cheery lady with blond hair tucked under a cap, who was holding a tin of biscuits that were hot from the stove. She appeared to be somewhat younger than her husband and was obviously pleased to have a guest for breakfast.

Matt learned that he was the guest of the Schendler family. A daughter about Matt's age joined them shortly after they arrived in the kitchen. Her name was Ami Ruth. They also had a son whose name was David. He was away, and it was his seat that Matt occupied at the kitchen table.

"Well, Ami Ruth, David, and Matthew. Three Bible names. If we had a second son, we would have named him Matthew," Mrs. Schendler said once all the introductions had been made.

Mr. Schendler smiled and nodded at his blond-haired daughter. "Ami was one of the officials in King Solomon's court, and Ruth was the loyal daughter-in-law of Naomi. She has a book in the Old Testament named after her. Most of the Friends in this area have named their children Bible names. Ami Ruth's best friend is named Mary Ann."

On the way into the house, Matt had looked around the place and decided it was the most complete farm he had ever seen. There were crops that included wheat and corn, a vineyard, and a vegetable patch that he could see. He made note of the cows, horses, and at least one mule.

"I lived on a small farm close to Mt. Airy, North Carolina," he told them. "We had two cows, a mule, and some chickens. Before my Pa left, we were preparing the fields around us for crops. I couldn't do it by myself, so we never had the beautiful fields he envisioned, like you have here. You have certainly made this into a model farm. I can't help noticing the eight-pointed star painted on the barn. So you are a Quaker family?" he asked.

Mr. Schendler responded, "Yes, we are members of the Society of Friends. Does thee know about our group?"

"Yes, sir, my mother was raised in a Quaker family," said Matt. "Her father was an elder in the Society. When Ma died, she had me erect a cross on her grave that had the eight-pointed star on it like the one painted on your barn. She said she wanted anyone who happened by to know that she was a Christian lady and was a member of the Society of Friends."

Matt noted that the four of his host family were all sitting with hands folded in front of them. He folded his hands as well and bowed his head. He heard the words of the prayer coming from Mr. Schendler at the head of the table. When it was over, he heard himself join the rest of the group with a murmured "Amen."

Mrs. Schendler voice came from the other end of the table. "How is it that thy father is off fighting with the Army of Northern Virginia?"

"My father is an English and does not have Quaker leanings," Matt said. "My parents met while he was on a trip to Lancaster, Pennsylvania. Ma raised me with Quaker teachings, but she was the only Quaker we knew of in our region of North Carolina. We didn't even have a church to go to except about once a month in Mt. Airy, and it was Methodist." Matt took a few more bites of food and then asked, "You said David is away. How old is he, and if I can ask, where has he gone?"

Matt noticed that Ami Ruth looked down at her plate. Mr. and Mrs. Schendler looked at each other before Mr. Schendler answered. "David is off in the army," the father said. "He is twenty now and was in Philadelphia at the Quaker Seminary. He knew we would not be happy with his decision to join the army, so he didn't tell us until he had already enlisted. Our son is in the Union Army."

Mrs. Schendler picked up the story. "David has some strong feelings that are in line with our faith. He does not believe in slavery. He believes that the Bible teaches that all are sons of God and made in his holy image. No man should be able to subjugate another. He says that he is fighting for his principles and that if he was not willing to fight for them and even die for them, then what good are principles anyway."

Matt responded, "We didn't believe in slavery either. Pa was very much upset by the dilemma the war created. All of his friends were signing up. Ma was completely opposed to his going, but he said that there were times when a man had to fight. He wasn't for slavery, but he was not for anyone else coming south and telling us how to live our lives." Matt paused and then added, "It was a difficult situation." The Schendlers nodded in sympathy.

While they talked, Matt looked around the room. He was amazed at the amenities in the kitchen. There was a sink with a pump for water. There was a big black iron stove with several burners for cooking. There were several kettles hanging against the wall within easy reach of the stove and the sink. Over in the corner, there was a box of kindling for the stove. When they came in through the back porch, he had noticed a second sink and a counter for preparing food.

With his stomach full, Matt thought of Big Billy out in the barn. "Sir, would you mind if I gave my horse some oats? I saw a supply out in the barn last night and wondered if I would have the chance to provide some for my horse. I'm pleased to pay for them with Union money, or I could do some work for you today."

"Mr. Schendler responded, "There are plenty of oats for your horse. You will find a bag already opened hanging on the wall by the front door of the barn. Take what you need. There is a spare feedbag hanging on a hook in the first stall. You may want to turn your horse out in the paddock for a while. I'm assuming that you can stay with us for a few days to rest from your journey."

Matt had not thought about staying, but he was enjoying the conversation and seeing the big farm. He also thought he would like to get to know Ami Ruth a bit, and he studied her as casually as he could as she sat across from him at the table. Matt had never known a girl his age and felt uneasy with his sudden preoccupation with an attractive young lady.

His mind moved immediately to his Ma's description of her upbringing in a Quaker home in Pennsylvania. He remembered her telling him, "My mother taught me all of the things I would need to know to keep a house. I could cook and sew. I could wring a chicken's neck, pluck its feathers, and cook it for supper, and I could do a hundred other things around a farm." She used to say this with pride. He imagined that Ami Ruth was raised the same way.

Matt forced his mind back to the conversation.

"I would appreciate staying another night if it doesn't put you out," he said. "I slept well in the barn and would be pleased to be there again tonight, if that is all right."

Matt was in the barn later when he heard a buckboard pull up in front of the house. He looked out through the door and saw a man dressed just like Mr. Schendler holding the reins. There was a young girl next to him on the driver's seat. She looked to be about Ami Ruth's age, which Matt judged to be fifteen or sixteen. Mrs. Schendler and Ami Ruth met them on the porch. The young girl climbed down from the driver's seat and ran up the steps to where they were standing. In a few seconds, the two girls went into the house, and the man lifted the reins against the backsides of the horses, and they turned to go down the lane. Mrs. Schendler stayed on the porch watching the buckboard drive away before she followed the girls inside.

Matt went to find Mr. Schendler. He was out behind the last paddock working on a part of the fence that needed repair. Matt offered to help, and his offer was immediately accepted. "There are some jobs that are two-man jobs," Mr. Schendler said. "This is one of them. I need thee to hold the corner post up while I set the cross pieces in place. Then we can anchor both to the posts at the gate. I can put the nails in them if thou can hold them up for me."

Matt had the easy job and stepped in to do his part. It took about twenty minutes to get the fence back up and in good repair. Just as they finished, Ami Ruth and her friend appeared with a water bucket and a ladle. She introduced Mary Ann to Matt while her father had a drink from the bucket. Mary Ann was also a blond-haired girl, more slightly built than Ami Ruth. Now that he could see her up close, Matt decided she was perhaps a year younger than Ami Ruth.

When the girls left, Matt saw that Mr. Schendler was smiling, and his eyes were twinkling. Matt asked why.

"That is the first time anyone other than my wife has ever brought me water when I was working out in the paddock. I think the real goal was for Ami Ruth to show off our guest to her friend," he said with a grin.

Matt was a bit embarrassed, but he smiled along with Mr. Schendler. He talked with his host about the farm, how long the family had been there, how much land was here, and where they took their goods to market.

Mr. Schendler said, "I could tell when we came upon it that it was good land, good for growing almost anything we wanted. Most of the farms in this area grow a lot of tobacco, which has a ready market in Winchester and can be easily shipped to Washington, DC, Baltimore, or Philadelphia from here.

"I'm not a tobacco grower. I am sure I could make more money if I focused on that crop. However, the fact that I grow a variety of other things and also have the animals makes what we produce each year even more in demand. Besides that, I tried a little tobacco in the beginning. I can't stand the smell of it when it begins to dry. It makes me sneeze and makes my eyes red and puffy." Then he added, "My best crop for the marketplace is wine."

"I noticed the vineyard as I came in last night," Matt said. "It looks like you started planting on the flat land close to your wheat field and then took it up the ridge to the top. Do you make your own wine?"

"What thee can't see, Matt, is that the vineyard goes across the ridge and down the other side and up the next ridge as well," Mr. Schendler said. "In between we have a barn where we make the wine."

"Sir, is making and selling wine a problem with the Friends?" Matt asked curiously.

"We thought it might be when we began," Mr. Schendler said. "No one else was doing it in this area. I thought a vineyard was a natural for the hillsides, and we began to plant the vines about a decade ago. There were some questions and some concerns at the Meeting House. I suggested that they read the scriptures. As his first miracle, Jesus turned water into wine at the wedding party in Cana. I told them that Jesus couldn't be against either making or drinking wine if he did that. After that, I didn't hear anything else on the subject."

Matt was curious about the farm's operation and said, "I would like to see your entire operation before I leave. It would be good to know how a successful farm operates."

"Well, that may take a couple of days, but let's start with a short tour around," Mr. Schendler said. "I need to go over to the winery anyway. It won't take but a minute to harness a horse to the buggy. Get thy shirt on, and we'll go."

Until Mr. Schendler mentioned it, Matt had not realized that he didn't have his shirt on. He had taken it off when he began to help with the fence. Going shirtless was Matt's natural state; many days back on the little farm in North Carolina, he did not put his shirt on all day. Then he thought about his being without his shirt when the two girls came with the water. That must have caused quite a sensation here on a Quaker farm. He would have to be more careful in the future.

Mr. Schendler and Matt spent the rest of the morning looking over the farm. It was a large tract of land, mostly bottom land but with some ridge land as well. From the road out front, he could see the house and barn, though both were shaded and the trees hid the size of those two major structures somewhat. The paddocks were on the back side of the barn and were hidden from the sight of those passing on the road.

Then the first ridge gave him a look at a part of the vineyard, though most of it was hidden by the ridge. It ran all across the valley behind and up the side of the next ridge. Obviously, this was a huge vineyard that provided the major cash crop of the farm. From the roadway, a casual observer's impression was that it was a fine little farm, well kept, and modestly prosperous. Its true proportions would impress anyone.

They stopped at the wine barn and went inside where several men were working. Matt didn't know anything about making wine, but obviously, Mr. Schendler and his men did. The smell of grapes permeated the place, and there were several big vats that were bigger around than Matt was tall.

Mr. Schendler took him down into a lower floor, which wasn't visible from the outside. There, in the cool of the basement, were dozens of barrels of wine. Mr. Schendler explained to Matt that each of the barrels was made from oak, and the wood played a role in creating the taste of the wine. He could change the taste of the wine by using different kinds of oak for the storage barrels and by storing the wine for longer periods. Matt found it all just amazing.

When they returned to the house, it was time for lunch. Matt could hear the handheld dinner bell ringing as they drove up the back lane from the winery barn. He stopped on the back porch where there was a pump and a basin, washed up, and hurried inside.

They called it lunch, but Matt thought for the middle of the day, it was worthy of being called a major dinner. The table was spread with about everything Matt could imagine. There were now five at the table with Matt, the Schendlers, and the two girls Ami Ruth and Mary Ann.

Mrs. Schendler took charge when all were seated at the table and asked Matt if he wanted to say the blessing. Matt felt himself gulp twice and then accepted what he judged to be a personal honor to say grace over such a feast.

Saying grace was not a new thing for Matt. He had heard his Ma say the blessing at their table three times a day for his entire life. She had begun teaching him to say the prayer before meals when he was about five years old.

Matt began as his Ma always did, "Lord, thank you for all of your many blessings. Thank you for your son, Jesus, who came to earth to show us how you want us to live. Thank you for new friends who take seriously your direction to feed those who want and to take in those who need. Bless now this food. Bless this family and keep their son David in the protective palm of your hand. These things we ask in Jesus's name, amen."

Almost in unison, the Schendler family and their young guest said, "Amen."

When Matt looked up, he saw the tears at the edge of Mrs. Schendler's eyes.

"That was a very nice prayer, Matt," said Mrs. Schendler. "It is a pleasure to have thee at our table."

The conversation around the table at lunch left Matt struggling over how to answer the many questions raised by his hosts and the two girls. He didn't want to tell them about burning the farm or losing Ol' Mose. He had already told them about his Ma dying. That was all he said on that subject, and they did not push him beyond that revelation. He liked the conversation around the table, listening to the give and take between the family members. He liked the feeling of being with a family. However, he wasn't sure he liked being the center of the give and take. He wasn't sure why; he would have to think about it.

Meanwhile, he dug his fork into the delicious baked beans on his plate and savored every bite.

A HOME AWAY FROM HOME

Matt went back to the barn after lunch. He filled the feedbag he found in the first stall with oats and put it on Big Billy's head. Before he could even get the cinch tightened on the back, he could hear the sound of the big horse's tongue reaching for the oats. He turned Big Billy out into the closest paddock, reminding himself that he needed to come back in a short time to take the feedbag off so the horse could graze if he wanted to. There was a water trough at the edge of the paddock, and the sun covered about half of the area so Big Billy could choose to stand in the warmth of the sun or stay covered in the shade with drinking water right there. The setting for his horse was just about perfect.

Matt stowed his pack up on the hay bales in the barn. The animals were moving through the barn at will now, and he didn't want to lose any of his beef jerky or the new tin of honey he had bought the day before. Ami Ruth and Mary Ann came to the barn as Matt was finishing putting his gear out of reach of the animals.

It was a surprise to see the girls in the barn. For Matt, being with girls anywhere was a strange situation. He had not known any girls his age in North Carolina. His vision of girls was always mixed up with his Ma, and he saw them at home in the kitchen or at least in the house. Seeing them in the barn seemed out of character. Still, here they were, and they had obviously come to see him. Mary Ann seemed shy at first, keeping her eyes on the ground, but Ami Ruth was not at all shy.

"Matt, where are thee from exactly?" she asked. "I told Mary Ann thee were from North Carolina, but I haven't ever been there, and Mary Ann says it is a big state, maybe larger than Virginia."

"It is a pretty big state, but we lived at Mt. Airy, which is just across the border from Virginia," he said. "We had a farm, but it was not at all like this one. You have a wonderful place here. Ours was just a small farm that my mother and father operated."

"Matt, how did thy mother die?" Ami Ruth asked gently. "Was she sick?"

"Yes," he responded. "She was sick for several months. Sometimes she was better and sometimes worse, but near the end she was in a lot of pain. She got very weak and couldn't get out of bed."

"It must be terrible to lose thy mother when thou are so young. Just how old are thee, Matt?" she asked.

"I will be sixteen in August," Matt responded. His voice was very low, and he spoke slowly. It was an uncomfortable topic for him, but he wanted to respond to Ami Ruth's questions. "It is terrible to lose your mother. I think it is terrible at any age. I don't know if it would have been different if Pa had been home with us. She seemed to lose hope without him. In the end she had lost a lot of weight and didn't have the strength to even get out of bed and walk to the front door. She stopped eating. She said it hurt too much. She lived mostly on hot tea, and sometimes she would eat some bread."

Mary Ann joined the conversation, asking, "So how long have thee been traveling, Matt?"

"I left home about three weeks ago. I have been across Fancy Gap in the mountains, to Big Lick, up to Lynchburg, to Scottsville, through Charlottesville, Culpepper, and Brandy Station before ending up here last night walking in a driving rain storm. Finding your barn was a real godsend."

"I don't think we have been to any of those places. How did thee make it all this way with a war going on all around thee?" Mary Ann asked.

"Actually, I didn't see any of the war until I got north of Culpepper," Matt said. "Down where I come from, there is a lot of talk of the war, but we really don't see any soldiers or any fighting. The war seems to be located farther north and in bigger cities like Winchester and Culpepper."

The two girls and Matt talked on into the afternoon. Matt learned that Mary Ann's folks were going to be gone for a couple of days, and she was staying with the Schendlers until they returned. Ami Ruth asked him about his eye and the scar on the right side of his face up close to his hairline. He had finally discarded the bandage during the heavy rain last night. He could now see out of his bad eye, and the swelling had gone down. It looked like he had a bad bruise, just a black eye. Matt told them the rabbit story, figuring they didn't need to know about the renegades and Ol' Mose.

The girls wanted to know about his school, and they told him about theirs. They wanted to know about the little church in Mt. Airy, the Methodist church. They were curious as to how it was different from the Meeting House they went to and what happened during services. The subjects seemed endless. Matt was enjoying the conversation. Then Ami Ruth opened up a totally different subject.

"Matt, does thee have a sweetheart?" she asked.

Matt wasn't sure how he wanted to answer that question. He did not have a sweetheart. In fact, there weren't any girls his age in the little country school he had attended; there weren't but twelve students, and nine of them were boys. He hemmed and hawed a bit then responded, "No, I don't have a sweetheart…right now. Maybe someday soon. Who knows?"

Both girls giggled, jumped up from the hay bale where they had been sitting, and headed for the door. Ami Ruth stopped at the barn door and looked back at him, hesitated, and then came back close to him. She spoke in a soft voice. "Matt, I heard my folks talking, and I want thee to be forewarned. Pa is going to invite thou to stay and live with us until this war is over. Without a Ma and your Pa off in the army, thou needs a place. We have a big farm and can always use an extra hand. We would make a good family for thee. When they ask, if thee wonders, I want thee to stay with us too."

With that last comment, she turned and ran out the door. Matt sat in stunned silence. What a great place! What a great family! What a great opportunity! Those thoughts dominated his mind for most of the afternoon. Sure, he needed to find his Pa, but this would be a wonderful place to live! He wasn't sure what would happen when he found his Pa, but there was nothing to go home to in North Carolina. Could he, perhaps, do both? Could he find his Pa and come back to take the Schendlers up on their offer? It was a serious question to think about.

That night after supper, Mr. Schendler suggested that he and Matt go to the porch and talk a bit. The question Matt had been thinking about most of the afternoon was not long in coming. Mr. Schendler said, "Matt, I have had a long conversation with Mrs. Schendler, and we were wondering what plans thee might have for the near future. We could use some help on the farm, and we think thee would fit in well here with us. Would thee like to stay on and become a part of our family?"

Matt appreciated that Ami Ruth had given him warning of what was coming. He let a few seconds pass before he began to respond. "I really like it here, sir. You have a wonderful place to live, and there is much that I could do to be of help. I like you and Mrs. Schendler and Ami Ruth really well. I would love to take you up on your offer if you can keep it open for me for a few weeks. You see, I really need to find my Pa. I think I can catch up with the army in a week or so. I need to let him know what happened back in North Carolina. That was my Ma's last request. She said I should find my Pa and tell him what has happened. I intend to do what she asked." Matt smiled before he said his next words. "After that, I'd be glad to come live with your family. Even my horse likes it here!"

Mr. Schendler smiled too, blue eyes twinkling, and he said, "All right, then it is settled, Matt Mason. Thou will go find the army and thy Pa, and then thee will come back before too long and become a part of our family. We will be very glad to have thee. Let's go in the house and tell Mrs. Schendler and Ami Ruth your answer."

When Mr. Schendler shared the conversation with his wife, daughter, and Mary Ann, it was as if a celebration had been kicked off. Mrs. Schendler went to the kitchen and brought in some muffins she had been baking. She put sugar and butter on top of them to make them all the more scrumptious. Mr. Schendler came in with a bottle of wine and a tray of cups. He put five of them on the table and said, "We would not ordinarily do such a thing with young people like thee, but this is a really special occasion. It is not every day when a person is added to a family. We need to celebrate with a taste of our own wine."

Matt watched Mr. Schendler pour half cups for himself and his spouse. He then poured just a thimble full of the red liquid into each of the other three cups. He said, "Just a splash for our young people. More is not good for thee, but a taste on this special occasion will be just right."

Matt hadn't ever tasted wine of any kind, red or white. He picked up the cup closest to him and tilted it up to his lips. He put his tongue into the liquid and took a few drops back into his mouth. It tasted heavenly. He quickly drank down the rest of his "taste." He could hear his mother's voice in his ear objecting. Then he closed his eyes for just a moment, and he could see her face. It was his mother as he remembered her when she was well, as she had always been. She was smiling. With that sign, if Matt had any second thoughts, they were gone.

The night passed all too quickly. He slept in the barn again and this time was up with first light. He picked up his blanket, took his pack down from the top of the hay bales, and prepared Big Billy for the next—and he hoped last—leg of his journey.

Ami Ruth stuck her head past the barn door and asked, "Matt, are thee dressed?"

Matt smiled at her. "Good morning, Ami Ruth. Yes, I'm almost ready to leave."

"Breakfast is ready," she said. "Thee should come as soon as thee can."

Matt stopped by the water pump and the basin on the back porch to wash his face and arrived at the kitchen just as Ami Ruth and Mary Ann were sitting down at the table. He joined them just in time to have a full plate of food placed in front of him. There was crispy bacon and fried eggs with toasted bread. Pots of honey, butter, and preserves sat before him on the table. In short, it was another wonderful breakfast. The ritual grace was said again, this time by Mrs. Schendler. Matt thought to himself that he would really have to watch it if he was to eat at this table every day. He might never be taller than his Pa, but he could certainly weigh more, and in a hurry.

When breakfast was over, Mr. Schendler went with Matt to the barn. He said, "Matt, I have a spare saddle that I want thee to have for thy trip. I think it will make thy trip more comfortable and will bring thee back to us more quickly."

Matt was shocked. "Thank you, sir!" he said. "I've never even ridden with a saddle before."

Mr. Schendler continued, "Matt, I am very impressed with thy horse. He is a wonderful stallion, very strong and well pointed. I have to ask, where did thee get him?"

Matt told him about capturing the horse at Brandy Station and about the problem with his shoe. He said, "I know it is a Confederate cavalry horse. But when I caught it, the cavalry had moved on and left him behind. He was anyone's for the taking."

"Matt, I wouldn't be surprised if he was the mount of some high-ranking officer. He is a most unusual cavalry horse. If I had him standing at stud here at the farm, he would be the most popular stallion in the area. I think he might become a whole new business of his own. He may be worth several hundred dollars, maybe thousands."

Matt knew he had a fine horse but had not thought of the possibility that he might belong to JEB Stuart or someone like him, that he might be recognized by soldiers or, worse, by an officer who had lost him in the confusion at Brandy Station. He had looked at Big Billy as a major asset to him in his quest to find his Pa. Now he had to consider that the big horse might be a potential liability as well.

Mr. Schendler brought out the saddle and helped Matt fit it onto Big Billy. It was obvious it had been on a much smaller horse, and the cinch had to be let out to fit around the big horse's chest just behind his front legs.

Matt heard himself saying "Thank you" over and over again was silently thanking providence for sending him to such fine people. He and Mr. Schendler led the big horse out to the front of the house. Mrs. Schendler was in the front yard waiting for them. She handed him a cloth bag that she called "just something for the road."

Mary Ann came out the front door and motioned to him. Matt went up the steps toward her and followed her into the house. Just inside the door, he came face-to-face with both Mary Ann and Ami Ruth.

Ami Ruth looked at him and smiled. She said, "Kiss me bye, Matt."

Matt was dumbfounded. He had never kissed a girl. His kisses from his mother had been of the simple peck-on-the-cheek variety. He didn't know what to do. Fortunately, Ami Ruth did.

She moved toward him, and he backed up to the wall. She pushed against him and pressed her lips to his. Then before he could react, it was over. She had kissed him! Both girls giggled and disappeared around the corner into the parlor. Matt was left standing alone, dazed. After a moment, he went back out the door toward the Schendlers, who were still standing in the yard holding Big Billy. He had a hard time looking them in the eye.

When Matt was up on Big Billy, the two girls came out the door onto the porch. He waved to them, and he heard Ami Ruth say, "Hurry back, Matt."

Halfway down the lane, he touched his fingers to his lips. "Hurry back," she had said. Oh yes, he would hurry back.

THE ARMY OF NORTHERN VIRGINIA

With Big Billy traveling at a light gallop, Matt soon passed through the small town of Berryville and headed for Charlestown, West Virginia. A sign on the edge of town said it was just twelve miles distant; he was confident that they could reach Charlestown well before dark.

As he traveled into West Virginia, Matt recalled the advice the lady in the store in Piedmont Station had given him a day or two back. She said West Virginia was Yankee country and that he should act accordingly. He should not expect any help from those who had husbands and sons fighting for the Union. The memory made Matt pause and rein in Big Billy. Here he was moving up the road at a gallop, seemingly without any regard for what might be just over the next rise or around the next corner. How careless!

Admittedly, Matt was enjoying the luxurious feel of his first ride on a saddle and the ease of staying on the horse's back without clenching his knees, but he needed to be careful lest he run into trouble. He resolved to slow to a trot as he approached each blind spot in the road, then let the big horse have his head on level ground where he could see far into the distance.

It was nearing late afternoon when Matt crested a hill and spied Charlestown, which he judged to be about two miles away. From the top of the ridge, he could see much of the road going into the city, and he didn't see any other riders. His intention was to go straight through the town without stopping. He didn't have need to stop for food, directions, news of the war, or the location of the Army of Northern Virginia. In fact, asking any questions at all in Charlestown might be the beginning of trouble.

The only thing Matt knew about Charlestown was that it was where the famous abolitionist John Brown met his fate at the end of a rope. His mother had taught him about how Brown tried to create a rebellion of slaves in Harper's Ferry, a few miles to the east of Charlestown. The abolitionist thought he could instigate a popular uprising among the slaves that would begin the process of freeing those unfortunate souls. The rebellion did not materialize, leaving John Brown and a handful of men, including three of his sons, hiding in an armory in the middle of the town. The army made short work of his failed rebellion, killing two of Brown's sons and hanging John Brown there in the county seat of Charlestown. Why Matt remembered just that about Charlestown, West Virginia, was a mystery to him. He knew his folks were opposed to slavery, and so it would have been a topic taught in his homeschooling. He seemed to have a never-ending list of little-known facts and stories that appeared in his mind at strange and inopportune times. Such was his Ma's homeschooling. He was sure he never heard of John Brown at the little schoolhouse he had attended, where many of the students came from farms that had slaves.

Matt guided Big Billy through the residential streets of the town, avoiding the main street. Even so, he didn't take a deep breath until he was back on the northbound road headed toward the small town of Bunker Hill, West Virginia. Beyond Bunker Hill were Martinsburg and Williamsport. Matt was sure he would catch the army by the time it reached Williamsport. He expected that Confederate troops would still be there getting their army across the Potomac River.

It was dark when Matt reached the outskirts of Bunker Hill. Hoping to avoid discovery, he found a clearing in a wooded area well off a side road. There was a small stream coming down from the ridge above the road and to provide water for himself and Big Billy. Matt thought about putting the hobbles on his horse but rejected the idea, deciding instead to tie him to a small tree. That gave him enough room to move a bit to reach grass to eat, but not to wander off. As he got out the rope that Jacob had given him, his mind moved to his stay with the

Mullers. Had that been three or four days ago, or was it a week? Time had all run together. He felt like he had been on the road for months instead of just over three weeks.

Matt laid his blanket down on the ground next to the stream and sat down, listening to the water trickle through the rocks. He did not dare build a fire, and he was grateful for the bag of food Mrs. Schendler had given him that morning. Even with a full stomach, sleep did not come quickly; he was sensitive to every sound. From time to time Big Billy would move over to the stream for a short drink. Twice Matt heard what he thought were footsteps, and both times he instinctively reached under his blanket for the big gun that he had stored there on previous nights. Tonight he had left it hanging in the halter on his horse. Now why did he do that? Why indeed? The gun was useless. After lying there for what seemed like hours, Matt got up from his blanket, walked over to Big Billy, and retrieved the gun. It might not be worth anything as a working gun, but no one knew that but Matt. He finally drifted off into an uneasy sleep.

He was relieved when the first rays of light found his little campsite. All during the long night, his mind had been filled with thoughts that tomorrow he might finally catch up with the Army of Northern Virginia. Tomorrow he might see his Pa. Tomorrow, tomorrow… well, tomorrow was now today! He could feel a growing excitement and stepped lively as he cleared his campsite, despite the lack of sleep.

In a few short minutes, Matt was up on Big Billy. He guided him through the woods and back to the road. It was going to be a day to be very careful. He did not want to get so close and not reach his goal of finding his Pa. He reviewed in his mind the unit his Pa was in. He was in the artillery assigned to General Henry Heth's army. That artillery unit was headed up by Colonel Edward Porter Alexander. Matt remembered exactly, as if that name was tattooed on his chest. According to his Pa, Colonel Alexander had ranked third in his class at West Point and was an instructor in engineering there at the start of the war. He left the Union Army and joined the Army of Georgia, and later he was tapped by General Lee himself to head up his artillery unit in the Army of Northern Virginia.

An early letter from his Pa told him all he needed to know about Colonel Alexander. Pa said he was "the best damn artillery officer in either army." Colonel Edward Porter Alexander. He would not forget that name.

Matt and Big Billy were through Bunker Hill and headed up the road north before there was a light on in any of the half dozen buildings in the little town. No one was stirring on the streets at all. He nudged his big horse into a light gallop, and they headed up the road toward Martinsburg. A sign at the edge of Bunker Hill said that Martinsburg was nine miles to the north. He could make that by noon if nothing slowed him down.

Matt wasn't more than a mile or two up the road when he ran up on a slow-moving wagon train. It was the supply wagons of Lee's army! Lee had more than fifty thousand men, and hundreds of wagons were needed to carry supplies. It seemed to Matt that the hundreds of wagons were all on the road between him and Martinsburg, blocking his way and slowing his progress toward his Pa.

Who said, "The best-laid plans of mice and men often go astray"? Matt's mind wandered backward to his Ma's "classroom," the little table next to the front-room window. She had been an admirer of the Scottish poet Robert Burns and made Matt memorize several of his poems, mostly the ones that had morals for future consideration. One of those poems was about a mouse. What were those words? Matt struggled to remember. Then the poem began to come to him, just as Burns wrote it in his Scottish dialect. And of course, his Ma taught the poem to him exactly as Burns wrote it.

> *But Mousie, Thou are no thy-lane,*
> *In proving foresight may be in vain.*
> *The best laid schemes o' mice an' men*
> *Gang aft a-gley.*

He pondered the words "gang aft a-gley." Plans often go astray, Burns was saying. And so they do. Here Matt was needing to get on up the road, and fate put an army of wagons in his way to slow him down. It wouldn't do any good to lose patience and get upset. The army couldn't move any faster. Matt's plans had certainly gone astray more than once on this trek. On the bright side, even at this slow pace, he knew he could catch up with the army before the day was over.

Matt took a little spur road off to the left and stopped under a tree out of sight from the wagon train. There he took his gray jacket and Confederate cap from the pack and put them both on. From a distance, he would look like a soldier on official business. It wasn't likely that any Yankees would be on the road ahead of him, considering Lee's fifty thousand men and hundreds of wagons occupying it, and he felt safe in his Confederate garb.

In a few minutes, Matt was maneuvering Big Billy up the road around wagon after wagon. Occasionally, he would find a man on horseback on the road next to the wagons. He tried to recognize arm patches and insignia to see if the rider was an officer, someone who could question his presence there or his destination. Mostly he was able to maneuver to the other side of the wagon and was past the potential problem before the other rider knew he was there. A couple of times he and Big Billy crested hills that allowed Matt to see well off into the distance. Each time the road was crowded with wagons and horses as far as he could see.

The wagon train came into the city limits of Martinsburg and made its way right down the main street through the town. As soon as Matt arrived at the edge of town, he turned off the main road and spurred Big Billy into a trot down a residential street parallel to the route of the wagons. He passed several dozen wagons with his alternate route and came out on the road still in the wagon train just north of town. A sign there said Williamsport was seven miles ahead. It was late afternoon, and he had already lost hope of finding his Pa among fifty thousand soldiers before nightfall.

Matt kept weaving around the wagons, and finally, he saw what proved to be the first of the military camps. It was spread out on the flat land on both sides of the road. In the distance he saw what appeared to be a wall of trees, a tell-tale sign that there was a river nearby He had caught up with the army, arrayed along the Potomac River, and he was finally at his destination! Matt continued to wind his way around the wagons, making his way up the last gentle ridge toward the river.

It was dark by the time Matt and Big Billy climbed the last hill just south of Williamsport. He was on top of the ridge overlooking the flood plain and observing the tops of tents that seemed to cover the land as far as he could see in both directions. The landscape was dotted with campfires, and he could smell the burning wood smoke. It was like the whole Confederate army was spread out before him. He thought he had seen many soldiers during his travels on the road that day, but that had been like seeing a little town of people compared to this metropolis. What he was looking at was as many people as were in Raleigh, Durham, and Mt. Airy altogether, more than Matt had ever seen in one place in his life.

Matt heard the sounds of horses in the distance, and he felt Big Billy's excitement as he sensed other horses close by. Similarly, Matt felt a rush of excitement, as if he sensed his Pa down there somewhere among all those thousands of men. Still, he was worried about riding up on sentries or other unsuspecting soldiers in the dark. As anxious as he was to find his Pa, Matt decided not to venture into the camp after dark. It would be better if he could walk in leading his horse in full daylight, when everyone could see that he was not a soldier and meant no harm. Then he could ask where Heth's artillery unit was located. He could look for Pa somewhere in that throng of men below. If Pa was all right, he would find him by midmorning.

Matt guided Big Billy off the road into the brush and trees just below the top of the ridge. He took the rope from the loop on the back of the saddle and tied Big Billy up to a low-hanging tree limb. He did not want the big horse to wander off during the night. The urge to go find the horses he could sense at the camp would be strong; horses were herd animals who craved each other's company, just as people did. At this time especially, Matt needed him to stay close.

Raking up a pile of dead leaves as a mattress, Matt laid his blanket down for the night. Again, he did not build a fire, and he was sensitive to the gray jacket and cap he had been wearing all day. He took them off and stowed them in his pack. As Mrs. Schendler's "something for the road" was gone, he got out his beef jerky and bread and opened the tin of honey. This would do for tonight. Perhaps he could find something more filling to eat when he entered the camp in the morning.

Sleep did not come easily that night. He was just south of the Potomac River. His Ma had said that she and Pa were married in a little house behind a Quaker church about an hour south of the Potomac River. He wondered if he had passed it along the way. He had a vision of his Ma and Pa riding on a wagon headed south down the route he had just traveled, leading a cow and a younger Ol' Mose behind the wagon. He couldn't help but smile.

It wasn't even daybreak when Matt heard noises on the road close by. There were two men on horseback. He heard one of them say, "The man I saw last night was about here when I lost sight of him." Immediately, Matt realized they were looking for him. He thought about hiding but decided against it.

"If you are looking for me, I'm over here," Matt called out.

In no time a horse's head poked through the bushes, followed by a burly man with a heavy beard wearing a Confederate uniform. He yelled for his partner, and soon both of them were standing in the small clearing with Matt.

"What are you doing here, boy?" the burly man demanded belligerently.

"I'm here looking for my Pa. He is with General Heth's artillery unit," he responded.

"Tell us who you are and where you are from, boy," the man spoke forcefully.

"I am Matt Mason from Mt. Airy, North Carolina," Matt said. "My Pa is Isaac Mason, but people call him Zeke."

It was not lost on Matt that the burly man was asking him questions while the second man, a tall thin man with a moustache, had his rifle pointed at his chest. They were being careful until they were sure he was who he said he was.

"You don't talk like a Southern boy," the burly man said.

"No, sir, I was raised Quaker, and I just talk the way I was taught," Matt said.

The man with the gun trained on him spoke up. "Boy, you ought to know better than to ride up on a military camp in time of war. You could get yourself shot," he said.

"I'm sorry if I caused a problem for you. I rode along with the wagon train of supplies for as long as I could. I stayed up here because I didn't want to risk riding into camp in the dark," Matt said.

The second man seemed to accept the explanation but turned his eyes on Big Billy. "That is a good-looking horse you got there," he said. "Where did you get him?"

"I've had him for a while," Matt said defensively. He didn't want to tell a blatant lie, but he didn't think the truth would help much with these two soldiers. Matt knew he had better be careful talking about the horse. If they knew he captured Big Billy back at Brandy Station, he could count on losing him. The big horse had just been his for a week, but Matt had developed a real pride of ownership, and he certainly appreciated being able to ride rather than walk.

"Well, get your gear together, and we will take you into camp," the burly man said. "We can ask at the officers' tent where Heth's unit is. I think they are on up the river a piece. That is where the shallowest water is and where they are taking the cannons across."

In a few minutes, they were all three riding down the ridge road into the camp.

About halfway through the camp, they stopped in front of a large tent. The burly man dismounted and spoke to a soldier who was standing by the door flap. Matt stayed on Big Billy while the talking was going on. The soldier went inside and shortly came back out. He spoke again to Matt's guide, who relayed the message to Matt.

"I was right," he said. "Heth's artillery unit is up the river. They are working at getting the cannons across. If you go over to the edge of the river and head upstream, you just need to follow the river through the stand of trees and listen for the sounds of men and horses working hard."

"Thank you, sir," Matt said sincerely. "I appreciate your help." It had been so easy! He might see his Pa that morning.

Matt followed the man's directions. He was sensitive to the fact that everyone seemed to be watching him as he and Big Billy passed. Here and there, other horses were standing near the tents, but there weren't many of them, maybe ten or twelve in all. None of them were nearly as big as Big Billy. When a man rode past him, Matt noticed that he was almost half a body higher than the other rider. Matt dismounted when he reached the river and began to lead the horse, thinking maybe his horse wouldn't look so big and noticeable without a tall rider in the saddle.

Walking along with Big Billy, Matt passed by rows and rows of tents. The men were in varying stages of dress, some in their underwear, some half-dressed, and some fully uniformed in the familiar gray jackets. Most of them had their Confederate uniform hats on, and almost all of the men had beards. Some of them looked up as he passed, but no one said anything to him.

From time to time Matt saw someone who looked to be his age or even younger. He wondered if they were like him, in the camp with their fathers, or if in fact they were full-fledged infantrymen carrying a rifle into battle. Matt tried to imagine himself lined up with other men marching into battle with a rifle over his shoulder. He tried to imagine it, but the image just would not materialize.

There were cooking fires next to almost every tent where the men were preparing breakfast. As he passed one campfire, Matt smelled hog jowls and grits, and he felt hunger pangs flare up in his stomach. He paused for a moment, breathing in the aroma. One of the men at the campfire nodded and smiled at Matt, so he stopped to ask him if he knew where Heth's artillery group was. The man yelled into the tent for someone, and a second man came out. They conferred and agreed that the unit Matt was looking for was farther up the river. One of the men saw Matt eyeing the kettle on the fire and asked if he was hungry. Matt smiled and told the man he could eat a horse.

The man smiled back at Matt and said, "If you stay around long enough, you may just get that opportunity. I don't have any horse right now, but you are welcome to a helping of some of the stew I have on the fire—if you are brave enough to eat it."

"I'd be much obliged," Matt said. The man handed him a small tin bowl and spoon. Soon he was sitting on a duffel bag and eating hot stew. It could have been made of almost anything—horse, mule, or squirrel—and Matt would have eaten it and thought it tasted good.

When the stew was gone, Matt thanked the man, excused himself, and headed up the river again. Within minutes he was outside the main camp and looking at several smaller camps in the woods ahead and up the hillside to his left. Through the trees, he heard the sounds of horses neighing and men yelling. With a few more steps, the trees parted, and Matt saw several horses hitched to small cannons.

He looked down to the Potomac. Out on the river, several large flat rocks were sticking up above the water level. It was obvious that the Potomac was at low ebb. The men could roll the cannon wheels from rock to rock, and there seemed to be only one place in the river where the horses and cannons were having a hard time. Each of the cannons had a wooden base built around it, and these were used as floats to help hold the cannons up when the water was too deep for them to touch bottom.

Four men were assigned to each cannon. Two held ropes, one climbed up on the wooden framework with the cannon, and the fourth rode on the back of the horse that was pulling the load from rock to rock and through the water. It was obvious that it took all their strength to steady the cannons as they moved into the deeper water.

Matt tied Big Billy to a small tree and walked up to a man who was calling out orders and seemed to be in charge. The man glanced up at Matt but went on with what he was doing. Finally the man regarded him and asked, "What can we do for you, young man?"

"Sir, I hope I have found General Henry Heth's artillery unit," he said. "I'm Matt Mason from North Carolina. I'm looking for my Pa, Zeke Mason. Can you tell me where I can find him?"

The man casually pointed out toward the middle of the river. "There," he said.

Following his finger, Matt saw a cluster of men about a hundred yards away. One of them, bigger than the rest, was certainly Zeke Mason. Matt could feel his excitement rising in his chest. He had not seen his Pa now in two years.

Matt walked up the river bank to get a better perspective of the group and his Pa. He hoped that Pa would look over this way, but he and the other men were too busy with the cannon and horse.

Matt sat down on a big rock about twenty yards above the edge of the river where he was out of the way, yet able to see everything that was going on. He felt weak-kneed with the anticipation of again being with his father. He smiled to himself as he watched his Pa working with the other men out on the river. It reminded him of the good times back on the little farm in North Carolina when he went with his Pa early in the morning to haul rocks for a fence or to fix the gate of the paddock after Ol' Mose or one of the cows had disappeared in the night.

He savored that good feeling while he waited for the minutes to pass when he would be face-to-face with his Pa.

SHARING THE STORY

⁓⁓✦⁓⁓

After watching for almost an hour, Matt decided to wade out on the rocks to where the cluster of men were. He checked Big Billy to be sure he was tightly secured and then walked down to the river. What looked to be a simple pathway rock to rock from his perspective on the bank turned out to be not so easy to follow. There was some deep water between the rocks, and Matt found himself wading up to his waist in a place or two.

He had almost reached the cluster of men when he heard his Pa's familiar deep voice. He was instructing two of the men to help an injured man get back to shore. Pa's eyes met Matt's from across the last deep water between them. At first there was no recognition in Pa's eyes, and then his face broke into a broad grin.

"Matt, I almost didn't recognize you!" he said. "You must have grown a foot, and your hair isn't blond anymore, but you still have your Ma's face. It is sure good to see you! Hold off for a minute, and we will talk on shore when we get this cannon the rest of the way."

They both heard the voice of the boss man from the shore yelling again.

Pa looked at Matt and then at the horse that was hitched to the cannon. He said, "Matt, we need a rider. Get up on the horse. Hold on tight and ride him just like Ol' Mose at home. Kick him in the ribs and yell at him to get him to move, or he will just stand there."

Matt put one foot on the side shaft that attached the horse to the wooden framework, stepped up, and swung his leg over the sweating animal. He kicked, and the horse moved forward, pulling the framework and the cannon along with him. The two men in the water were holding the ropes taut to steady the framework so the cannon would not slip off into the water.

In a few minutes, they were through the last of the water, and the cannon rolled up on the opposite bank of the river. Pa was following the cannon just a few feet back, ready to pitch in wherever he might be needed. When they were safely on the bank, the other two men started taking the ropes off the wooden framework. Pa grabbed Matt in a bear hug and said, "Son, what in the world are you doing here?"

Matt just sputtered. All the words he had saved up to tell his Pa were stuck in his throat. He didn't know if this was the time to tell him about Ma and the farm, but before he could get a word out, one of the other men was yelling at them.

Pa said, "Hold on, son, we have to get these last four cannons across the river. Then we can take a breather and talk a bit. Go sit up under that tree and wait for me." Pa walked back into the river and stepped rock by rock to the other side. As Matt watched, they inched the rest of the cannons across the river until they had them lined up side by side on the bank. Only then did Isaac Mason take his red handkerchief out, wipe his face, and come over to where Matt was waiting. He grabbed Matt again in a bear hug, and both of them began to wipe tears.

While Matt had watched the men moving the cannons, he had formed the words he needed to tell Pa about losing Ma. The tears came freely from both of them. Matt knew he was crying partly from the feeling of loss and partly from the relief of being able to share his grief with his Pa. He had barely gotten the words out when Pa raised his hand again to quiet him and pointed back across the river. Several more cannons had been rolled down to the river's edge and were awaiting his attention. "Come on, son," he said. "We've got more work to do."

The two of them made their way back across the river. The men seemed to be waiting for Pa to arrive before they all stood up, ready to go back to work. When Matt and Pa got close to the south bank, Pa yelled at the group over the noise of the river splashing over the rocks. He said, "Boys, this is my son, Matt. He is going to be with us for a while and will be a rider. Let's get the rest of these cannons across before sundown."

Matt pulled his shirt off and laid it over a bush near the bank. The job he was given was not difficult. He was to climb onto the horse and keep him headed across the river. He was to try to keep the horse moving forward so the men following could maintain enough tension on the ropes to keep the cannons upright in the wooden frames. There were ten more cannons to move when Matt stepped in to help, and it took the group the rest of the afternoon to complete the job. It was almost dark when they stopped to return to camp.

Matt told his Pa that he had a surprise for him when they got back to the south bank of the river. Instead, it was Matt who got the surprise. When he reached the tree where he had tied up Big Billy, the horse was not there. Matt's pack was lying on the ground, but the gun and his horse were gone. The gun wasn't a problem as it didn't work anyway, but someone had taken Big Billy! He quickly told his Pa about the big horse he had captured at Brandy Station.

Zeke Mason walked over to the man running his crew and asked him if knew anything about the missing horse. He said, "Yes sir, I do. That is a civilian horse, and he has been confiscated for the military. The lieutenant in charge of the horses came by and took him about two hours ago."

"That man had no right to take the boy's horse," Isaac said in a voice that could be heard quite a distance away. At six-feet-five and 250 pounds, Isaac Mason could be an intimidating man, and it was obvious from his response that the other man was intimidated.

"Don't yell at me," he said. "I'm in charge of moving the cannons, not looking after horses. You need to talk to someone else."

Matt was nearing panic. "Where can we go to find him, Pa?" he asked.

"Son, we can find him. That is the easy part. The problem is that the army is very short of horses for the wagons and the cannons. The cavalry gets their pick of horses, and they lost a bunch of them in a face-off with the Yankees back at Brandy Station. We have been struggling ever since. We have been picking up a horse or two at every farm we have passed since we left Culpepper. They are paying about ten dollars a horse, Confederate money. We may get you some money for the horse, but getting him back may be about impossible. We will see when we find him."

The army's horses were staked out in three groups, and it was well into the night when Pa and Matt found Big Billy. He was tied up with the horses that were closest to the ridge away from the riverbank. When they approached Big Billy, he began to react to Matt immediately. It was obvious that he was glad to see his young master. The sounds coming from his throat indicated instant recognition.

Pa spoke to Matt in a low voice, "You stay by the horses, and I will be back before long." He then headed off to talk to the officer in charge.

Matt leaned against the big horse and fought the tears. He had developed a real affection for the big bay and was already grieving his loss. He wondered if he should have left him with the Schendlers back on the Berryville farm. He wondered what role Big Billy would play in the war effort. He had seen horses pulling the wagons and helping to hoist the cannons across the river and knew how hard it was on them. Pa said the cavalry got their pick of the horses. Surely, Big Billy would be picked up by someone in the cavalry. That would be better than pulling a cannon. He wondered if he would ever get the big horse back.

When Pa came back, Matt could tell from his face that the news was not good. "Son, they tell me they are about thirty horses short of what they need," Pa said. "They have been buying what they could and confiscating the rest to make up the difference. Here is ten dollars they are giving you for compensation."

Matt held the money in his hand for the longest time. He didn't want it. He wanted his horse.

Pa's camp was up by the ridge with three other men Matt had seen helping to move the cannons. Matt felt lucky to have his pack. It could have disappeared along with Big Billy back on the riverfront. He took the blanket and laid it out close to Pa's.

That night it was all he could do to put aside his thoughts of Big Billy and focus on telling his Pa about Ma and the loss of their little farm. He recounted the details of Ma's illness and how bad it was, that she was in pain all the time, and every time she did manage to get to sleep how she would moan and groan and sometimes wake up crying in the middle of the night.

"When she was close to the end, she gave me instructions about what to do with the animals," he said. "She sent me to town to get supplies I would need for the trip to find you, and we paid for them with the last four chickens and Bossy. And Ma wanted some special tea that I made for her from some plants from down close to the stream."

Tears began to roll as Matt told Pa about the grave up on the hill and about burning the buildings after Ma died. He thought his father might be upset about the house and barn, but Pa smiled when Matt told him about burning them down. Pa said, "I always said that if the thieving bankers ever came for my land, they would find nothing there but a pile of ashes. Your Ma knew how I felt about that, and she saw to it. Son, tell me again about taking the cow to the Martins and your trip down to the store in Mt. Airy."

Matt went through the story again in detail. He talked about taking the cow to their neighbors and their reluctance to accept it. "I told them it was just a loan until their baby was older, or they probably wouldn't have taken it. They both came out on the porch to meet me when I arrived. Mrs. Martin was holding the baby, and it was making kind of a quiet crying noise. They turned Bess down at first, but then she whispered something in Mr. Martin's ear, and they both went inside for a moment. When they came back out, she said they would take the cow. I don't think he was happy about it, but I think she gave him her thoughts inside, and in the end, her judgment prevailed. Anyway, they have Bess, and the baby has milk.

"The trip to the store was pretty well just as Ma predicted. They traded some beef jerky for the chickens and seemed pleased to buy the cow. The man balked a bit at paying for it in Union money, but it was just as Ma said, he had the money under the drawer in his cash box, and he dug it out when I insisted," Matt said. "I think that is about it, Pa."

"How about cutting the sprouts for Ma's tea on the way home?" Pa asked quietly.

Matt responded, "Oh, Ma told me just where to look to get what she wanted. She said the plants looked like Queen Anne's lace on the tops, but instead of being knee-high, they were as tall as me or taller. She said I wouldn't find them anyplace but down around the stream. She was right. They were right where she said they were." He thought a minute. "Pa, Ma called it old people's tea. What did she mean?"

Pa didn't answer right away, and when he spoke, he didn't exactly address Matt's question. He said, "You were right about your Ma being close to the end of her limit in handling the pain. She knew she was not going to last much longer, and she was resolved to go out at her own time and in her own way. That was just like your Ma. She was never one to just let loose and let things go. She believed in planning ahead and having an influence on life. That was your Ma. Those are traits to admire, Matt. You need to remember that about your Ma."

As Pa talked, Matt looked closely at how his Pa was dressed and had a flashback to his Ma talking about Pa and his clothes. Pa had his gray army hat on his head, but only the pants he wore were issued by the Confederate army. And they were in tatters. His Ma had said that the hardest part of her married life was keeping his Pa in clothes. She said that he was such a big man that none of the stores carried clothes large enough to fit him, and she had to make everything he wore. She said his clothes took a beating every day, and looking at his Pa as he sat there in the dim light of the campfire, Matt was very much aware of the truth of his Ma's words. He looked much more the part of a hard-working farmer than he did a soldier fighting for the Southern Army.

Both Matt and Pa were wiping their eyes after this serious exchange about Ma's last days. Then Pa's voice dropped softer, and he sounded even more serious that Matt had to lean in close to hear him.

"Matt, I have been in this war now for two solid years," Pa said. "I have known many good men who I have come to appreciate, many good friends I have had to watch die in battle. I think a man gets hardened to it. I am sorry to lose your Ma. She was a wonderful wife and mother. You are a good representative of what she created for both of us. We were both lucky to have her in our lives this long. I guess you have grown up a lot since I have been gone. Watching your Ma fade away must have been really hard. I am so sorry. I am sorry for both of us. I am sorry that I was not there to go through the illness with her.

This war has cost everyone dearly. I have lost the last two years of my time with your mother, and that is what I hate more than anything."

Pa raised his voice a bit as he went on. "Matt, this army is going to move on up into Pennsylvania. I have heard that General Lee intends to loop up through southern Pennsylvania, take Harrisburg, and swing down north of Washington, DC, to catch the Yankees between us and the rest of his army that is down in Richmond. General Richard Ewell was in charge there until he came with Lee to replace Stonewall Jackson. I'm not sure who is in charge there now, but they are in Richmond waiting on us to become the north part of a two-part pincer action on Washington, DC. If we can get them in a vise, they just might quit and leave us alone. This war could be over in weeks.

"I can't be concerned about what the army is going to do or not do. I will be with them until this war is over, however it comes out. My primary concern is to keep you out of it and safe until it is all over. Your mother wanted that, and I want it too. You can travel with us for a time, and it will get you some meals and a place to sleep. When we get ready to fight, I want you out of here and well away before the first musket ball comes our way. In the meantime, you can help us move the cannons. We don't have enough men to do this job, and you are becoming quite a man."

Matt and Pa talked on into the night. Matt told about the long walk north and how he lost Ol' Mose. He wasn't sure he wanted to tell his Pa about his confrontation with the renegades, but Pa asked him about the scar on his face and the traces of the black eye. He told Pa about the hospital, the Muller and Schendler families, and even about the three village toughs at the Mullers' house. Pa got a real laugh out of that story. He told Matt he was really proud of him, that he had done a good turn for his new friends. Pa showed some obvious pride about teaching his son how to fight with a broom handle.

"You never know when things you learn along the way will become important," Pa said. "You should remember that learning is a lifelong process, and everything you know today is built on top of things you learned yesterday. Your Ma would love the moral of that. She would say that learning is a value in itself. You should try to learn something important every day."

That night, Matt bedded down next to his Pa for the first time in more than two years. Right before he dropped off to sleep, he reflected that arriving at the army camp had been a mixed blessing. He was very happy to have found his Pa; it made him feel safe again for the first time since he had left home. At the same time, he hated that he had lost Big Billy. He would blame that on the war. Ma always said, "No one wins in a war." Matt was sure, like in so many other things, that she was right.

Matt woke up to the sound of movement in the camp. His Pa was already up and ready for the day. There was a cooking fire going, and the stew he ate was even better than the dish he had shared with the soldiers the morning before. The cannons were all across the river, and that seemed to be what the army was waiting for before moving on north into Pennsylvania.

Within an hour, the entire camp of Heth's artillery unit had waded across the river. From the north bank of the Potomac, Matt looked back to the bank where he had spent the night and saw hundreds of wagons lined up, preparing to cross. They were following the path of the cannon movers, taking advantage of the flat rocks and the low ebb of the river. It was a natural crossing point, though there was the one really deep spot in the middle of the river. That one spot required ropes to be attached to the back of each wagon to steady it when it was floating in the current, and it took several men to handle each wagon just as it had with the cannons the day before.

Heth's infantry unit had crossed the river and was long gone when the wagon train was finally across the river. It must have taken a full two days to get them all across because that was how long the cannons sat on the side of the road, waiting for the wagons to catch up with them. Finally, the wagon train and the cannons were all together, and they began to move north.

From that point on, each day was pretty well like the last. The wagon train moved north for three days to a point just south of Chambersburg in southern Pennsylvania. Then they turned due east. When they made that turn, they were looking directly into the mountains on the east side of the Shenandoah Valley. Those mountains stretched as far as they could see both north and south. The road north was on level ground, but the generals directed them into the mountains.

The scuttlebutt among the men was that someone must have lost their mind to take them into the mountains when they could have stayed on the road north and traveled on level ground toward Harrisburg if, in fact, that was their destination.

"What could the generals be thinking?" a man seated by Matt at the campfire grumbled one night. "They seem to talk only to each other and to God."

The others around the fire agreed that the generals certainly were not talking to the men who had to move all of this equipment up the road every day.

The mountains seemed to grow taller each day as the men coaxed the horses forward with their heavy loads. Then as they passed the little town of Blackgap, the mountains seemed to part in front of them. They could make out a way through, and the road they were on that seemed to run right into the mountains actually turned slightly right and then left and found a passageway between the bluffs on both sides. The rumor passed from wagon to wagon was that it came out on the other side of the range at a little place called Cashtown on the piedmont in southern Pennsylvania.

The caravan traveled about a half day between the mountains that rose several hundred feet above them on both sides. Then they could begin to see the last of the ridges to the right and left of them. Finally, the winding road began to go downhill in a slight grade. From what seemed to be the last ridge in the mountain pass, Matt could see the flat lands stretching endlessly in the distance. The army was well ahead of the wagons and cannons, and they had already started to set up camp all around the little village of Cashtown. The always-present rumors continued to pass between the wagons. The latest one said that they were not far from a larger Pennsylvania town called Gettysburg.

SHOPPING FOR SHOES IN GETTYSBURG

In a short while, the artillery unit made camp outside Cashtown. The men quickly pitched tents and built cooking fires. That night, Matt and Pa sat down around the fire with several other men and ate hot porridge that was bubbling in a kettle. There was no butter or salt, but Matt was so hungry he ate his bowl quickly and wished there was more.

Most of the men were used to sleeping outside as it was late June in southern Pennsylvania with mild weather. A blanket between Matt and the ground and a flap over his legs was enough to provide comfort unless it rained. When it did, Pa told him the men would have to double up in the tents. It had been threatening to rain and seemed to be raining every day or two to the west in the mountains of eastern Pennsylvania up toward Pittsburgh. The rain hadn't found them yet on the east side of the mountain range next to Cashtown, and so Matt and Pa bedded down each night under the trees close to the cannons.

Pa did not come with Matt to the place they had staked out to sleep that first night near Cashtown, so Matt fell asleep alone. He woke suddenly when he felt his Pa's hand on his shoulder and heard his voice whispering in his ear. "Matt, get up quietly and follow me," he said.

Matt obeyed his father. In a few minutes they were at the edge of the camp, and Pa walked up to two horses that were tied to a small bush. Pa didn't speak but signaled for Matt to mount one of the horses, and in a short minute they had ridden off into the darkness. They skirted the artillery camp as well as the larger army camp that was farther to the east. They were back on the road before Matt said a word. He pulled his horse up alongside of his Pa and asked, "Where are we going?"

"Son, it is time you had some shoes," Pa said. "Gettysburg is about six miles down this road, and the word is that they have a shoe factory that has been supplying shoes to the Yankees. It may be time that we liberated at least one pair of shoes for you. About a fourth of our men don't have shoes, and I think the reason for the detour from the road to Harrisburg may have more to do with that shoe factory than anything else. If the military goes there in the morning, they will clean that place out, and there won't be any shoes left for a civilian like you.

"The word from the scouts is that the Yankees are up protecting Philadelphia and Harrisburg. We aren't likely to run into any Yankees here in this area."

Matt kept his voice low as the horses carried them down the road toward Gettysburg. He told his Pa about stopping at several stores looking for shoes as he traveled north but that none had sizes above twelves. He told his Pa that he would need at least thirteens and maybe fourteens. Pa looked at Matt's face and then at the foot that was draped around the side of the horse. Matt heard a low whistle.

"Son, that is a big foot," he said. "How tall are you now?"

Matt responded, "I think I am just over six feet tall right now. Ma thought I would be as tall as you, but I don't think so. I weigh about 160 pounds."

Pa shook his head. "Matt, I've lost track. Are you sixteen yet?" he asked.

"No, sir. I will be sixteen in August," Matt replied.

Matt and Pa rode for a while in silence. They crested a rise, and there spread out in front of them were the lights of the little country town of Gettysburg. Pa put up his hand, and they stopped there on the rise overlooking the town.

"I'm looking for a place where we can tie our horses," Pa said. "A couple of Confederates just can't go riding down the main street in a Yankee town without expecting to get shot at. We need to be quiet, and we need to stay out of sight. It is around midnight right now, and there probably won't be anyone on the street, but we can't be too careful."

Pa pointed to a clump of trees over to the right in a big field. He nudged his horse, and they headed in that direction. Matt was thankful that there was no moon tonight. It would be better if they could stay in the dark as long as possible. Pa and Matt tied the horses in the clump of trees. Pa took off the uniform jacket and cap he had been wearing and draped them over the saddle.

"Matt, if something bad happens and we get separated, you find your way back to this clump of trees and the horses," Pa said quietly. "Don't wait on me. Ride up on that rise that we stopped on earlier where you can see over this whole area. If you see people coming after you, hightail it back to our unit with the army. I don't think anyone will chase you there. Just assume I will be along shortly. I will catch up with you either on the way back or at the tent."

Pa's voice was low, but his tone of voice said this was serious, and Matt knew he was to do exactly what he said. Matt responded with the words that seemed most natural when he was dealing with his Pa. "Yes, sir."

Matt and Pa walked into the little town from a side street. They looked both ways down that street and moved on to the next street. Matt wasn't sure what a shoe factory would look like, and finding the right place was obviously going to be harder than either of them had imagined.

Without warning, a shot rang out. Both Pa and Matt dived behind a watering trough. Pa looked around the edge. "Did you see where that shot came from?" he asked Matt.

"I think I saw a flash from a rifle down that street. I'm not sure who shot, and I don't know if they were shooting at us," Matt responded.

"I think, for sure, they were shooting at us. I felt that musket ball miss my head by about an inch," Pa said.

Matt peered up over the watering trough. Down the street he could see several figures moving in the dark. One of them passed a lighted window, and the blue uniform of a Yankee soldier was obvious. They could hear men shouting. "It's Yankees for sure, Pa," Matt said. "They are coming this way!"

"Well," Pa said, "let's don't be here when they get here." Pa stuck his rifle up over the watering trough. He said, "As soon as I shoot the gun, you run back the way we came, and remember what I told you about getting your horse and riding up to that rise."

"I'm staying with you, Pa," Matt argued.

Pa looked at Matt with that look that he always got when there was to be no argument. He said, "Matt, move."

He shot, and Matt ran. Matt could hear several other shots in the darkness and knew they had to be coming from the Yankees. Pa had a single-shot rifle, and he wouldn't have time to reload. Matt had reached the field on the edge of town when the shots stopped. He looked back toward the town; his eyes were used to the dark now, and he could see the terrain pretty well. Soon he found the clump of bushes and the two horses.

Pa had said to get on the horse and ride up the rise to the top and to look back for trouble. Matt did just that. When he topped the rise, he reined in the horse, turned around, and looked back. To his relief, he saw his Pa following the same path Matt had just taken, and he felt himself inhale deeply for the first time in at least twenty minutes.

They did not speak when Pa joined Matt at the top of the rise, and the two of them urged their horses up the road into the darkness. Before long they were skirting the army's encampment on the east side of the little village of Cashtown, and within minutes they were back by the trees near the cannons. Now Pa had a real dilemma. There were not supposed to be any Yankees in Gettysburg, but the pair of shoe shoppers had sure ran into a bunch of them. Should Pa go to the officers' tent, tell what they had seen, and run the risk of being disciplined for leaving camp, or should he just keep quiet?

A few minutes later, Matt stood outside of the officers' tent, listening to rising voices he did not recognize. He could hear them calling Pa on the carpet for leaving camp without permission. Pa didn't tell them he wasn't alone or what he was doing in Gettysburg. That wasn't pertinent to the issue that he had run into Yankees where there weren't supposed to be any Yankees.

One of the voices asked him how many Yankees he saw and whether they were local militia or army regulars. Matt couldn't hear Pa's response, but there was an immediate flurry of activity, and before Pa left the tent, a man came out and got on his horse and road off.

He had a leather pouch hanging around his neck. It appeared he was a courier being sent with a message to General Lee about what Pa had seen in Gettysburg.

Pa came out of the tent. "Let's go, Matt," he said grimly, and they walked back to the trees by the cannons.

MEETING THE YANKEES

July 1, 1863

Even before dawn, Matt and the men of Alexander's artillery unit could hear the unmistakable sounds of horses on the move in the distance. They scrambled to strike camp, following the small cavalry unit and infantry column that took the road toward Gettysburg. Alexander's artillery was the last of the fighting units bringing up the rear while the wagons with supplies stayed behind them and off the road. As they moved forward, Matt could hear the sounds of rifle fire coming from just down the road and could see the infantry column breaking down and spreading out across the open terrain.

A single horseman galloped up, stopping for just a few seconds beside their unit. The man yelled, "There is Yankee cavalry on the road! They have dismounted and are behind a fence down the hill. We need the cannons up front to bombard the Yankee positions!"

A serious look came over Pa's face as he listened, and when the rider galloped off, he turned to his son. "Matt, you stay in the rear until everyone has moved up," he ordered. "And then you head for that stand of trees on the hill over yonder." He pointed about half a mile north.

Matt knew not to argue. Within a few minutes, the infantry group was out of sight over the hill, and the cannons were on the move, traveling down the same road that he and Pa had taken the night before in their futile search for shoes. From their moonlight ride, Matt knew the little town of Gettysburg was just over that next rise.

Matt moved into the field on the side of the road to watch the men maneuver the horses and cannons into a broad line, set just behind the crest of the rise. He then broke into a dogtrot toward the trees Pa had pointed at. From the grove of trees, he looked back and saw that the horses had been unhitched and the cannons were lined up side by side. He counted 160 of them, stretching way off in the distance to the right. A man stood at the far end of the line with a signal flag. As Matt watched, he swooped the flag to the ground and then lifted it up and waved it over his head. In response, the men moved the cannons almost in perfect unison forward to the crest of the hill.

With the cannons in place, Matt began to see the infantry take up positions just behind the cannons. It was obvious that the men were waiting for the cannons to do their damage before they entered the fray.

During the lull, Matt climbed up in an oak tree with low-hanging branches so he could better see the battle unfold. He continued to climb until he was almost to the top of the tree. From that vantage point, he could clearly see the Yankees' positions on the rise. They were lined up behind a fence that bordered the opposite bank of a little stream. Farther up the side of the hill, he could see clusters of horses with soldiers in blue holding them. It was obvious that they had ridden their horses to that point, dismounted, and taken up positions behind the only cover they could find. Matt didn't see any cannons on the other side of the little valley where the Yankees were.

He heard himself say, "Those Yankees are really in for it when our cannons begin to fire."

Almost as soon as the words were out of his mouth, one cannon fired. Just one. Matt knew his Pa and the other artillery soldiers were watching where the cannonball landed so they would know how to set the rest of the cannons. Evidently, the ball fell either long or short because in a minute, they fired just one cannon again. They spent a few moments adjusting the cannons, and when they were ready, all of the cannons fired at once. The sound was deafening, and the smoke made it impossible for Matt to see the action down in the valley and across to the other ridge.

JOURNEY TO GETTYSBURG

As the smoke cleared, Matt could see the Confederate infantry troops begin to move across the top of the hill and disappear down the other side. He could hear so much rapid rifle fire, cannon concussion, and men yelling that the sounds all ran together. Officers on horseback were riding up and down behind the battle line, yelling encouragement to the men. From time to time, one of the officers would fall off his horse, and it didn't take much imagination to know that he had been shot. It took a few minutes for the thought to sink into Matt's mind that he had never seen anyone die. He had been asleep when Ma died.

The battle went on for several hours between the two ridges as Matt watched in the tree. The Confederate men would move forward, and then the Yankees would counterattack. It was hard to tell who was winning. Matt was fascinated by the action, the confusion, and the noise, but he was horrified by the death and destruction. As more and more men fell the medical wagons rolled over the hill picking up the wounded, dying, and dead soldiers.

Then as quickly as it started, the battle ended. The Yankees began to pull back. The sounds of gunfire slowed and then stopped. The Yankees remounted their horses and disappeared across the top of the ridge, riding toward Gettysburg, with the Confederate troops in hot pursuit.

Matt climbed down from the tree and began to walk slowly toward the line of cannons. The horses that had pulled the cannons were being taken back up to where the cannons were poised on the crest of the hill. They were ready to be reattached to the cannons to move them forward toward their next point of enemy contact. He looked down the line and, with a great feeling of relief, sighted his Pa beside a cannon about halfway down the line. He walked until he was just behind that cannon and stood for the longest time without saying a word while they hitched up their pull horse and packed up their powder and cannonballs. When they were ready to move out, Matt joined his Pa.

The morale of the men was running sky-high. They were laughing and talking about the Yankees turning tail and running for the cover of the little town with their army in hot pursuit. When a medical wagon rolled up next to them on the road, one of the drivers yelled, "News! News!" The men gathered around him, and he announced, "General

Ewell's Second Corps just arrived at the north edge of Gettysburg! That was probably what made the Yankees turn tail and run. They were way up close to Harrisburg. They must have got word that the Yankees were in Gettysburg while they were camped out last night. They broke camp and marched all night to get here in time to run up on the Yankees' backside."

Matt thought back to last night, standing outside of the officers' tent and listening to his Pa tell them that there were Yankees in Gettysburg. The messenger sent out to General Lee must have started a chain reaction. Alexander sent word to Lee, and in turn, Lee sent word to Ewell and probably the other generals who were spread all over the geography in southern Pennsylvania. The end result was that Heth's unit met the Yankees here on a hillside northwest of Gettysburg. They ended up hightailing it back into the town to escape getting caught between Heth's men facing off with them from the front and Ewell's Second Corps coming up from behind.

It may have been just happenstance that put the Yankees in that vise, Matt thought, but in the newspapers, it will look like another brilliant move on the part of General Robert E. Lee. To think, it really started with his Pa finding out that the Yankees were in Gettysburg and telling Colonel Alexander! Pa always said it was a smart general who listens to his men.

Heth's army camped northwest of Gettysburg that night. There were no fires—cook fires were never lit when the enemy was close by as no army wanted to run the risk of a surprise attack in the night—so Matt and the men ate hardtack, the little biscuit made from flour, water, and salt. It was the one staple fighting men could always count on when they were on the road and away from their cook fires.

The talk around the camp was all about the victory of the day and reports of the ongoing battle over in Gettysburg. The word they heard from messengers coming from General Ewell's army was that the Yankees had been chased clear through Gettysburg and been whipped good. They were regrouping just to the south of the little town. They also heard that Ewell's army had captured about four thousand Yankees at the north edge of the town. Four thousand!

Later that night, Matt watched as a column of captured Yankees marched by on the way to some back line destination. They would probably end up in some prisoner of war camp back in Virginia. They were a thoroughly defeated–looking bunch who were not likely to fight again in this war.

There was lots of talk among the men that night. Even if the excitement of the day had not kept everyone awake that night, the sounds of battle in Gettysburg a couple of miles down the road would have. Whether it's a contest, a game, or a battle, everyone loves to win, and spirits were soaring among the men that night. With every exploding cannonball and every musket shot in the distance, it was easy to imagine their boys carrying the fight and the Yankees on the run.

Matt had many questions for his Pa, but with all of the give and take between the men, he didn't get to ask them. Listening to the men talk was always a learning experience for Matt, and sometimes he had to be careful not to smile or even laugh out loud. Hearing about the cannons that night was a case in point. Matt wasn't sure who was talking as the voices came to him out of the dark.

"Every cannon fired, every one. Can you believe it?" one voice said.

A second voice responded, "That was amazing. There is always something wrong with one of them. Either the powder is wet or the firing mechanism doesn't work, something."

"At least we can always count on the cannonballs going off," the first voice said.

"Yeah, they do explode, we just can't always be sure if it will be at the right time. It could be sometime next month," said another voice.

Matt was smiling despite himself, but no one could see him in the dark.

When exhaustion did overtake them, the men laid their blankets out on the ground and tried to get some sleep. They knew this battle was not over, and tomorrow they would have a new assignment that would most likely test their skills and their bravery.

Matt had been amazed from the beginning of his time traveling with the army at how good their information sources were. They didn't get much information at all from the officers, but everyone seemed to keep their eyes and ears open for any rumor that might float through. When a soldier picked up some new scrap of intelligence, it moved through the camp like wildfire. The rumors said they were going to move north from the Potomac. They moved north. The rumors said they were going to turn due east at Champersburg and go through the mountains. They turned due east. The rumors said there were Yankees in Gettysburg. There were Yankees in Gettysburg. Of course, that last rumor was started by his Pa, and it wasn't a rumor.

The most prevalent rumor that night said that the Yankee army had moved all the way through Gettysburg and were clustered just south of the town near a small cemetery. Another rumor said that General Lee ordered General Ewell to continue attacking the Yankees through the night, but General Ewell decided to wait until morning. His men had been on a forced march the night before and had been fighting ever since they arrived. They needed rest and food. Matt's Pa said that General Ewell probably thought that with the superior numbers the Confederates had in the field here at Gettysburg, he could win the fight more easily in the morning with a rested army than he could at night as tired as his men were.

The last rumor before Matt, his Pa, and the other men lay down for the night was that the cannons were going to be moved south of town in the morning and set up along a ridge to the southeast near a seminary. Matt fell asleep with the words "seminary on a ridge south of Gettysburg" on his mind. Setting up a battle line next to a seminary—a bastion of peace, harmony, and Christian love—had to be one of the major ironies of war.

July 2, 1863

Matt awoke to the roar of cannons and gunfire. His blanket was wet from a light rain that had started about midnight. At the time there was nothing to do but pull the blanket up and try to stay as dry as possible. Heth's unit was camped just northwest of Gettysburg, and the sounds of battle were coming from both the east side and south of Gettysburg. Everyone in the camp was scurrying about as cannons were being hitched to horses and army troops were forming for a march into the thick of the battle.

There was no time for breakfast, so the men grabbed more hardtack, filled their canteens with water, and made do. There would be time enough for eating a real meal when the fighting was done. Until then, the hunger pains would sit in their stomachs alongside of the butterflies that always accompanied moving forward toward battle.

Matt quickly found his Pa in the confusion. He said, "Matt, our orders are to move the cannons straight south down close to a seminary located somewhere below the town, so the rumors we heard last night were right. Evidently, we are not going into battle right away, so you can stay with us a little longer."

There was no mistaking the relief the men felt that they were not going to be moving closer to the ominous sounds they were hearing in the distance. When the unit was ready to move, Pa told Matt to get on the lead horse on a four-horse hitch pulling a two-cannon caisson. Within minutes, the big cannon caisson was in line with the other cannons, and the entire line was moving down the dirt road that had turned to mud overnight.

They passed Gettysburg, and Matt could see smoke and flashes of fire from just to the other side of the little town. Much of it seemed to be coming from a hillside that was just visible to the southeast. Word passed among the men on the road that most of the fighting was at a place called Culp's Hill, and it was Ewell's Second Corps in the fray.

"There must have been more than thirty-five thousand of our soldiers fighting in that battle yesterday," Pa said as he shared the news with Matt. "I heard Ewell had twenty thousand soldiers with him when he arrived yesterday, then General Jubal Early and General Trimble's men joined in. I doubt there have been that many men on a battlefield in this country's history."

It took about an hour to get the cannons down the road to the little seminary that sat on top of the ridge south of town. The ridge was covered with trees beside a heavy wood that provided further cover. The men moved the cannons into a holding location south of the two-story seminary building.

Pa motioned to the upstairs of the building. "General Lee has his headquarters in this building," he told Matt. "From the top of the building, he and his officers can see all the way across to the Union lines south of Gettysburg by the cemetery."

The artillery soldiers were not sure exactly why they had been deployed to this site when the fighting was going on over on the other side of the little town. Pa said, "It is likely we are going to serve as the first strike in some big battle, but we don't know yet. We will get our orders, or at least we will begin to hear rumors about our next battle before long." The men began to speak of their location as Seminary Ridge.

The Union lines were about a mile due east of the Seminary Ridge location, and Matt could hear gunfire farther from the south. He asked Pa about it.

Pa responded, "The rumor is that our troops under General Longstreet are moving to take a small hill called Little Round Top that is just at the south edge of the battlefield." Matt thought about this and mapped the situation in his mind. He reasoned that with Ewell's troops at Culp Hill and Longstreet's to the south, General Lee was planning to attack the Yankees at both ends of their lines.

They waited for orders all morning and through the early afternoon. Tensions remained high with the sounds of battle continuing both east and south of Seminary Ridge. Still, there were no orders for the artillery unit. The men passed the day checking and rechecking the cannons and making sure that the powder was dry and cannonballs were close by for easy access. Late in the day, a mounted officer arrived and ordered the men to move the cannons down the hill through the woods. Moving cannons downhill was easier than uphill, but there was lots of brush and clutter to clear to make way for the cannons. Moving them down the hill took most of the rest of the afternoon and into the evening.

Eventually, the entire line of cannons came to rest at the bottom of the hill, camouflaged by the brush and trees. Pa ordered Matt to stay out of the way, so he climbed into a tree. "And I don't want you to become the target of a sharpshooter," Pa added. "You stay on the back side of the trunk."

Matt didn't have to be told twice. There was a constant sound of musket balls flying through the tree leaves and bushes that shielded their position from Yankee eyes. From his vantage point, Matt could see horses coming and going from the seminary building back up the hill. Pa had said they were couriers from the battlefront. Matt looked in vain for Big Billy, thinking he would make a fine mount for a courier.

Late in the afternoon, a large troop of men in gray marched in and took up positions just to the south of the cannon unit in the woods. Matt couldn't begin to tell how many there were but figured there were thousands. He heard someone say that they were under the command of a General George Pickett. It was a name he had not heard before.

About dusk, Matt began to hear the sounds of approaching horses, and down the road came a huge contingent of cavalry. Pa walked over to his tree and said, "It's General JEB Stuart and his men, coming back from a scouting trip." The horses and men stopped just north of the seminary building, and the men began to tend to their horses. There were not as many men as there had been in the marching troop that had come through earlier, but with the horses, they filled the open field just north of the building.

Matt looked out on a sea of gray uniforms and sweaty horses in the field. Again he found himself looking for Big Billy. Pa had said the cavalry got their pick of the horses. Big Billy could serve the Confederacy much better as the mount of a cavalry officer than pulling a wagon or cannon, Matt knew, but no matter how hard he strained his eyes, he did not see his big horse.

Cook fires were out of the question again that night so Matt climbed down from his tree and broke out the beef jerky he had been carrying in his pack. Since losing Big Billy, the pack had become a fixture on his back. He caught his Pa's attention and gave him some beef jerky and shared the last of the bread he had been carrying for more than a week. It was stale and dry, but it was something to fill the stomach. Most of the men had eaten nothing at all; most did not even have canteens. Pa called it "a very lean night" and had little to say. He went off to sleep under the cannon caisson with the other men in his crew.

When darkness fell, Matt could occasionally hear rifle shots in the distance, but they eventually died out, and all he heard were the summer night sounds of crickets and tree frogs. He watched the martins and bats hunting up their evening meal of insects and finally drifted off into an uneasy sleep at the base of the tree.

July 3, 1863

Morning came early. The sounds of horses moving and men talking in the distance brought everyone to their feet before daylight. Again there were no cooking fires, and men made do with hardtack, beef jerky, and a long pull on their canteens. Again, Matt shared beef jerky with Pa, and Pa gave him some of the hardtack issued by the army.

The camp vibrated with anticipation of the action to come. Everyone seemed to feel that today would be the day when the battle at Gettysburg would be settled.

Over their meager breakfast, Pa spoke quietly. "Son, I'm afraid I have let you stay with us too long," he said. "We are going into a major battle today. It is time you left here, and you should head west as fast as you can move. You can stay with us until we move the cannons out into position for firing. Then you have to leave."

Matt started to protest, saying he could climb the tree again, that he was sure the Confederates would chase the Yankees away just as they had the first day, but Pa raised his hand and continued talking. "It makes no difference how the battle goes. Hundreds of cannons will be fired, and many men will be killed. Cannon balls, riprap, and bullets will fill the air. You are to be no place close to any of the battle action."

His voice grew quieter and even more serious. "When the battle is over, it is likely that both our boys and the Yankees will withdraw to take care of the wounded and dead. When things quiet down, you can come back to the seminary building, and most likely, you will find our artillery unit somewhere close by. It I have survived the battle, that is where you will find me."

Matt searched Pa's face for signs of fear but saw only concern for his son and a steely determination to make the best of what was to come. Wordlessly, Matt reached out for Pa, and he soon had him in another of his big bear hugs. Pa then held Matt at arm's length, his big hands clamped on his shoulders. "Son, never worry that your Ma and

I loved each other and loved you more than life," he said. "You became the center of our world, and whatever happens today, we will always be there in the back of your mind, supporting you in everything you do. I hope I see you again when this is all over. But if I don't, you remember that you are a Mason, and Masons do what is necessary and what is right. God gave you some wonderful abilities, some wonderful gifts. Use them well."

Matt was overcome with emotion. All he could do was nod at his father. Then Pa was gone—to do what was necessary and what was right. He climbed back into his tree to watch the cannons being moved into position. Suddenly, Matt realized that Pa did not say what he was to do if he did not find him at the seminary building after the battle. The idea of his Pa not making it through the battle was too impossible to contemplate, too painful. Pa was one of those strong personalities whose presence would always prevail. He would, wouldn't he? He would be there when Matt came back to find him, wouldn't he?

About midmorning, the cannons began moving out. This time they moved directly to the east and through the trees. In less than an hour, all of the cannons were lined up along the edge of the woods. In his tree, Matt counted the cannons as they left, losing count at 140. He could only imagine what it was like to hear all of them firing at once. He wondered about the devastation they would rain on the opposition over on the ridge by the cemetery.

When all the cannons were in position, Matt came down from the tree and began retracing his steps to the campsite from the night before last to wait out the battle there. Another column of Confederate infantry was marching on the road, so he waited for the group to get past. He felt conspicuous watching the troops marching down the road toward the battle lines and decided to move farther off the road into the woods above the little stream that ran down the back side of the ridge. He could easily hear the men on the road, and he resolved to stay there until the newly arriving troops had passed.

EVERYONE GOES TO BATTLE

From his hiding place, Matt could hear the troops marching down the road, but his attention was diverted by a sudden rustling in the bushes followed by the barrel of a rifle poking through the underbrush. He was reminded immediately of the two renegades invading his makeshift camp below Bent Mountain. The memory was even stronger when two men in Confederate uniforms joined him in the clearing.

One of the men had a bad scar on his face, and he held a rifle aimed squarely at Matt's chest. The other man seemed to be in charge. He had a full beard and sergeant's stripes on his sleeve. In a rough voice, he said, "Who are you, boy?"

"I'm Matt Mason from Mr. Airy, North Carolina, sir," he responded.

"What are you doing hiding in here?" he asked.

Matt protested, "I'm not hiding, sir. I'm just waiting for the troops to get past."

The two men looked at each other, and the man with the scar demanded, "What is your unit?"

"I don't have a unit, sir. I came to see my Pa. He is with Heth's artillery," Matt said.

The scar-faced man looked over at the sergeant and declared, "No one comes to visit at a battlefront. This one is a deserter, and he doesn't even have a decent story."

"I assure you, sir. I am not a deserter," Matt said desperately. "My Ma died, and I had to come and find my Pa. I found him at the river crossing in Virginia. He is with Heth's unit, and I have been traveling with them for a few days. He told me to get away from the battlefield, and I was headed back to where we made camp."

The scar-faced man grabbed Matt's pack. "Let's see what you have in here," he said.

Matt's heart leaped into his throat. The Confederate cap and jacket were still in his pack! The man opened the pack and dumped the contents on the ground.

"Well, looky here," he said. He lifted the jacket up with his gun barrel. "It says here you are in the Twenty-First Division. You would have to be a deserter or a thief to have either this uniform jacket or that cap, boy."

Right at that instant, with fear filling every pore of his skin, Matt heard his mother's voice in his ear saying, "Matthew, 'Be sure that your sins will find you out.' That's in Numbers 32: 23." He had heard her say that enough times that it was imprinted on his brain.

He had been wearing that jacket and cap on and off ever since Big Lick. He used it to get transportation to Lynchburg, to Scottsville, to Charlottesville, to get into the Ladies' Relief Hospital, and even as a disguise while he was riding Big Billy, a Confederate cavalry horse. He had not felt good about any of that, but it had been easier to do it each time. He had been taught that sin, deceptions, or transgressions of any kind get easier every time you do them. Now, he was about to pay for his deception.

The sergeant motioned Matt to his feet with rifle barrel. He said, "My inclination is to just shoot you right now and save the time and effort of hanging you later. But we need every man we can get. You will probably be dead by suppertime anyway. We will give you a choice. We can shoot you right now as a deserter, or you can rejoin this fight. Take your pick."

"I don't know what to say or how to explain my situation," Matt said, his voice cracking. "I'm not in a unit. My Pa said I was to get away from the fighting and to come back here after the battle. I was just waiting for the troops to pass. Why can't you believe me?"

The two men looked at each other, and the scar-faced man said, "Well, you are either in a unit now or you are dead. What's your choice?"

Matt picked up his pack and started to say something else, but before he could speak, the sergeant snarled, "Keep your mouth shut, boy. You are just making your situation worse. And we'll take that pack, if you don't mind." He handed it to the scar-faced man and said, "Keep this as evidence if we need it."

Matt started to object but held his tongue. He hated to lose his money, blanket, and other possessions he had been carrying since he left home, but the two men were not listening to him.

The scar-faced man motioned with his gun for Matt to walk through the underbrush, where the troops were still marching past. When one of the officers in charge of a unit marched by, the sergeant said something to him. The officer stepped out of the formation and looked closely at Matt, and then he grabbed his arm. The column was marching by in twos. A few seconds later, a soldier came by marching alone, and the officer pushed Matt into the line and walked along beside them. "Son, do you have a gun?" he asked.

"No, sir. I had one, but the firing pin blew up and burned my face," Matt said. He pulled the hair back on the side of his face so the officer could see his scar.

"Well, I can't have you going into battle without a gun," the officer said. He left the line, and in a moment, he was back with a flag in his hand. "Do you know anything about using a signal flag?"

"No, sir. I've seen them used, but I don't know what the signals are," Matt responded.

The officer said, "Well, you stay close to me when we get into action, and I will tell you what to do with the flag. I swear, if you run, I will shoot you in the back. Do you hear?"

Matt said miserably, "I understand, sir. I won't run." The officer left, and Matt continued marching down the road, his mind spinning. He looked over at the man to his left. "What outfit is this, sir?" he asked.

The man responded, "This is General Isaac Trimble's Brigade, but it don't make no difference because we are all going to be dead in a little while anyway." Matt started to respond to the man, but he was looking away, and Matt could see tears in his eyes. He didn't know what to say anyway, so he kept quiet and marched along.

The marching column came to a halt, and all of the men turned to the east and walked off the road into the woods. Matt soon became aware that there were many other men already in the woods. His unit kept moving through the woods until bright sunlight began filtering in between the trees. As the woods opened up, he could see cannons lined up toward the south of his position. He strained his eyes to spot his Pa, but it was hard to make out any individual while looking out into the bright sunlight.

In the distance, there was an endless sea of men dressed in blue stretched along that ridge. Matt could also see their cannons lined up along the ridge facing the ones of the Confederate forces, and he began to feel a tightness in his throat that seemed to slide all the way down to his stomach. He even began feeling sick, but fought the nausea by taking very deep and slow breaths. His thoughts were interrupted by the bleat of a bugle, followed by a voice yelling something he couldn't distinguish in the distance. Suddenly, there was a deafening roar as all of the cannons fired at once. The air was so full of smoke that he could no longer see the ridge where the Yankees were.

Matt wondered what had happened to the practice of testing the distance with one cannon at a time until the setting for the range was right. Did the artillery men know where those cannonballs would fall before they fired them off? Or were they just hoping? He couldn't tell with all the smoke.

In a matter of minutes, the Yankee big guns answered shot for shot. Matt had learned his lesson last night about hiding behind the trunk of a tree. He heard the Yankee cannonballs landing in the woods all around. When one hit, he heard the yells and cries of injured men, quickly followed by the sounds of medics rushing to help them.

All of the men Matt had marched with were leaning against trees, awaiting direction from the officers. Twice an officer came by, and Matt tried to tell him he wasn't in the army, that he had just come to find his Pa. Neither listened to him. They had bigger problems than an out-of-place boy and just left him sitting behind the tree.

After two hours of the big guns firing off over and over, silence fell. Matt heard the bugle call again, and the men around him stood up and moved forward to the edge of the trees, like sleepwalkers. Almost as a single man, they left the shelter of the trees and lined up side by side. They stood there for what seemed to be the longest time, their coats forming a long gray line. The officer who had given Matt the flag arrived just as the order came to move out.

Matt was at the far right of the second line of Trimble's unit, a line stretching a quarter mile up the line of trees along the edge of the ridge. To Matt's right was a long double line of men that the man he had talked to earlier had identified as General Pickett's brigade. They stretched out of sight to the south. All were moving forward purposefully, walking rather than running in one great double line. Way down the line, Matt saw what appeared to be a general out in front of his troops. He was walking ahead with his hat perched on top of his sword, stopping every few steps to yell back at the men who were following.

Incredulous, Matt asked the man to his right, "Who is that man out in front with his hat on top of his sword?"

The man squinted in the direction Matt pointed. "It's hard to tell from here, but I think that's General Armstead," he said. "He's the only one in Pickett's command who would pull such a crazy stunt. Some Yankee sharpshooter is going to pick him off before he gets halfway across, you wait and see."

As they moved forward, the Yankee cannons started up again, but the sound they were making was different, and they were not lobbing cannonballs up into the woods. He heard the man beside him curse and say the dreaded words: "Grape shot." He knew from conversations with Pa and the others in camp that grape shot was composed of riprap, metal, chains, rocks—anything hard and destructive that could be fitted into the muzzle of a cannon. When it blasted out, the grape shot scattered and cut down the marching men in a swath several feet wide. As quick as the gap opened in the line, men moved up to fill it, and the wave of soldiers continued walking to the ridge where the Yankees were waiting, leaving the wounded and dead men behind them.

All around Matt, men were falling, and blood was everywhere. To his horror, he saw that his bare feet were covered with blood, and he wondered if he had been shot, but he felt no pain and assumed he had not. Not far ahead, he saw a stone fence, and dead and dying men were lying behind it. When he was a few feet from the fence, Matt felt something hit him hard from behind, knocking the breath out of him, and for a terrible moment, he thought he had been shot. He fell to the ground, gasping, and when he opened his eyes, he was staring into his Pa's face.

Matt heard the familiar deep voice shout, "What the hell are you doing here, Matt? I told you to get away!"

"They caught me along the road!" Matt said. "They thought I was a deserter. They made me come with them and put me in the second line with this flag. What are you doing here, Pa? I thought you would be back with the cannons!"

"I was there until we ran out of ammunition!" his father said, shouting over the battle noise. "Then they gave us rifles and told us to fill in the gaps and move forward toward the Yankee lines with Trimble's troops. I caught sight of you back a ways and prayed you would still be okay when I reached you. You have blood all over you! Were you hit?"

"I'm okay, Pa. The blood on my feet is not mine. The ground is soaked with it," Matt said.

Pa leaned in close and whispered in Matt's ear. "Son, I have to move on with the other men in my unit. You are to stay here and lay really still until I come back for you. It won't be too long, not more than an hour or so." He pushed his face away and looked deep into Matt's eyes. "Do you understand, son?"

"I understand," Matt responded.

Suddenly, the weight of Pa's body lifted, and he was gone. Matt turned over and watched him until he disappeared in the confusion of the battle, and then he closed his eyes and lay still. Eventually, the sounds of battle quieted. He could hear the moans of men on the ground close around him and the sounds of men walking and helping each other move back across the open field toward the trees where they had spent the morning. No one stopped to see about Matt or any of the men who were lying on the ground close to the fence. Every once in a while, he opened his eyes to a slit to look around, but he didn't move a muscle.

The heat of the July afternoon and the smell of the dead dominated his senses, and he could also hear the soft moans of the injured and, occasionally, a gunshot far off to the south. Evidently, the battle was over on this site, at least for the time being. Finally, completely exhausted, Matt drifted off to sleep.

He was startled awake by something poking him in the back. He opened his eyes, lifted his head, and looked up into the face of a very large man wearing a white coat. The big man pulled him up to a sitting position. Even though it was dark, Matt could see bodies all around him, and a lantern sitting on the ground at the big man's feet cast a yellow light on a fearsome scene. Matt briefly wondered if he was dead, but the sound of the man's voice and the shock of coming awake to such a scene let him know that he wasn't. He knew heaven would not look like this, and he did not believe he deserved to be in hell.

The white-coated man shouted to another man close by. "I've got a live one here!" he said. "He has lost lots of blood, but he is alive. I'm going to take him back to the medical wagon."

Matt found himself being hoisted up on the shoulder of the big man, who carried him easily. Matt almost told him that he had not been wounded but thought better of it and just let the man carry him. From his position over the man's shoulder, he saw bodies everywhere. Worse, he saw parts of bodies—arms, legs, even a man with no head. Here and there, men in white coats were walking among the bodies, looking for men who were wounded but not dead. His mind moved to Pa and the heavy fighting. He wondered if Pa had been wounded—or worse.

In a few minutes, the man in white carried Matt into the trees that bordered the bottom of Seminary Ridge. How long ago had it been when thousands of men were standing there, poised to fight? Hours? It felt like days. Now, there was nothing but devastation. Entire trees were knocked down. There were holes in the ground. Men were sitting and lying against tree trunks, and the acrid smell of burnt gunpowder filled Matt's nostrils. As he continued up the road slung over the man's shoulder, he could see the seminary building ahead where only a few hours ago, General Lee had been standing on the roof, looking over the battlefield with his field glasses.

Now the seminary building had become a field hospital. The ground was covered with men, some lying on blankets and some just lying on the grass and dirt. Many were moaning, and some were calling out for help. Some had bloodstained bandages on their arms and legs. Others were still bleeding, waiting for attention from the doctors and nurses. Matt saw several dogs moving among the injured men. Hands were moving almost constantly, trying to keep the mosquitoes at bay.

The big man set Matt down on the back of a wagon and looked into his face. He said, "Son, can you understand what I am saying?"

Matt nodded his head.

The man smiled slightly. "You stay right here, son. The doctors will get to you when they can. I've got to go back to the battlefield."

Matt felt his lips mouth the words "Thank you," and then the big man nodded and turned away. Matt watched as he retraced his steps back across the road and into the woods.

For several minutes, Matt lay on the back of the wagon, checking and rechecking his arms and legs for wounds. He didn't feel anything wrong, though he could see why the big man thought he was wounded. His legs were covered with blood from his bare feet up to his thighs. It was someone else's blood, maybe several other peoples' blood.

Behind him, Matt heard the pitiful sounds of the wounded men in the wagon, and he could hear and see the doctors ministering to the wounded just through the open door of the seminary building. No one had yet come to evaluate his condition, and all the people around him seemed preoccupied with their own wounds or someone else's. Making a quick decision, Matt rolled over and dropped down onto the ground behind the wagon. Crouching, he began to make his way through the lines of wounded soldiers to the woods across the open ground where he remembered he would find a small stream.

Away from the lantern light and activity of the field hospital, Matt could still hear the sounds of the wounded men, and from time to time, he heard someone scream. He imagined that surgery was going on like he had witnessed back at the military hospital in Lynchburg, that someone was losing a leg or an arm. Finding the creek, he waded in up to his knees and began to wash the dried blood off his legs and feet with the cold water. He continued to scrub his legs long after the blood was gone.

RETREAT

Much later, Matt climbed out of the streambed and staggered up the rise through the woods, entering the wheat field on the other side. There was no moon, and everything was dark. He walked quickly through the field with wheat up to his waist. It was winter wheat that would be ready for harvest before long, and it swished as his legs passed through the stalks.

He could hear the sounds of men talking low in the distance. He thought the voices were Southern, but he felt he couldn't take a chance with either Union or Confederate soldiers. He didn't want to be shot or captured again as a deserter. Twice he crouched down into the wheat to hide from others moving in the same direction he was going.

There was a stand of trees in the distance, and he made his way toward it. When he entered the wood, he knew immediately there were others there as well. Again, he chose not to make his presence known and stopped beside a big oak tree at the edge of the woods where he could look back across the wheat field. From his vantage point, he could see flickering lights of campfires, which he imagined were necessitated by the doctors and nurses working with the dead and dying. There would be no cooking fires on this night.

Matt's mind went over and over the last time he had seen Pa. After their meeting behind the fence in the middle of the battle, he had been able to watch his father for a few seconds as he ran toward the Yankee lines. Very quickly he disappeared in the tangle of bodies and the smoke of burnt gunpowder. He wondered if that was the last time he would see his Pa alive.

His mind was racing now. He wondered if Pa was among the wounded, or if he was still lying out in that field with the dead. There was no way to find out other than by going back to the medical encampment and walking among the litters to look for him. Matt resolved to wait until daylight to do just that. He knew there were thousands of wounded and many more thousands of dead.

There was another possibility too, one that had not occurred to him before. Pa might have been captured by the Yankees. If Pa was captured or dead, there was no way for Matt to find him. If he had been wounded, there was a slight chance he could find him. However slim the chance, he would take it.

Sleep came fitfully that night. Matt had seen too many horrible things on the battlefield. He couldn't get comfortable. He didn't have his blanket or his pack. His pack had disappeared when he had been pressed into service by the two men who claimed he was a deserter, and his small supply of food and his cash had disappeared with his pack. This night, he was in the same boat as so many others. He was tired, hungry, and cold. Worse, he had no idea what had happened to his Pa.

When daylight came, Matt made his way back across the wheat field to the field hospital around the seminary. Already, the medical wagons were lined up down the road, and the wounded were being loaded into them. The army was making preparations to retreat along the Cashtown road, the same way they had come in four days before. It was a sobering sight.

Matt had no idea how many medical wagons were already lined up, but it seemed like hundreds; the line stretched south as far as he could see. Many wounded men still lay on litters on the ground, some moaning, others asleep or unconscious. Doctors moved among them. He watched one doctor pull a cover up over a patient's face. Matt knew what that meant. If he had thought of the worst human situation he could have imagined, he could not have thought of this. He half hoped he did not find his Pa in such a condition.

Matt took a quick look into one of the wagons to see how many men were inside. He counted twelve in this first one. Most were leaning against the sides while others were lying flat in the bed of the wagon. One man asked for water. The sight was overwhelming. Feeling dizzy,

Matt went to lean against the outside wall of the seminary building until his head cleared. There he overheard one of the doctors talking to an officer who obviously had the responsibility to move the wounded. The officer told the doctor that he had about six hundred wagons, more or less, for transporting the wounded. His orders were to move out as quickly as he could get the wagons loaded and not to stop until he had them at Williamsport. They were to cross the Potomac there. He said his orders were to move the wounded men who had the best chance for recovery. The rest would stay behind.

Quickly, Matt calculated what this operation would involve. If there were six hundred wagons with twelve wounded in each one, that would be more than seven thousand men on the wagons! Williamsport was four to five days' travel in a wagon if everything went right. He wondered about food and water, about medical attention along the way. It was all too much. This had the makings of a human disaster.

He decided his best chance of finding his Pa was to get up to the first wagon and then go back wagon to wagon, calling out Pa's name. He started up the row of wagons in a dogtrot, and the farther he jogged, the longer the wagon train seemed to be. He was more than a mile up the road when he neared the first couple of wagons. A man on horseback came by and said something to the driver in the first wagon, about fifty yards ahead. In a few seconds, he heard the pop of the skinner's whip, and the first wagon began to move.

Matt missed the first few wagons but began his search as the eighth one came by. His mind was again churning with numbers. He had missed eight wagons, and thus, he had not checked the first one hundred men who were on the wagons. Could his Pa have been in one of them? He couldn't worry about it.

He climbed up on the back of each of the wagons in turn and called out his Pa's name. A few times someone would answer back that there was no one there by that name, but in most cases there was no answer. Matt tried to scan the faces he saw in the wagons, but he saw no one who was familiar. Each new wagonload of men he looked into was a repetition of the last. Men were crammed in side by side with all manner of wounds and injuries. As close as Matt could tell, there was no food or water, no nurse to minister to their needs, no way to deal with body processes. It was just as he had characterized it earlier, a human disaster waiting to happen. In what must have been the eighteenth or twentieth wagon, a man responded to his voice.

He said, "I know Zeke Mason. Who are you?"

Matt made his way into the wagon until he was next to the man. "I'm his son, Matt Mason," he said eagerly. "Do you know where I can find him?"

The man responded, "I remember you. You helped us get the last of the cannons across the river back in Virginia. I was with your Pa until about halfway across the field yesterday, and then I lost sight of him. Son, as painful as it is to say, I'm sure your Pa was killed up close to the rock fence like most of the other men from the artillery unit. As close as I can tell, me and one other man were the only ones who made it out alive."

Then the man looked down at his leg and spoke softly. "I'm going to be very lucky if I don't lose my leg."

Wordlessly, Matt climbed down and went on to the other wagons. For sure, it would be very difficult to find his Pa in this mass of broken humanity. What if he was still lying dead near the stone fence? Matt thought of going back on the battlefield to look for him, but that was out of the question. There were too many Yankee sharpshooters with itchy trigger fingers on that ridge. He thought of returning to the hospital and going through the rooms, but he knew that was just one of many hospitals the army had hastily thrown together to handle the badly wounded. He didn't know where the others were, and Pa could be in any of them.

He kept up his effort to search each of the wagons as they came by. There were no more voice responses. By late afternoon, the wagons were still coming, and Matt was exhausted from climbing up and down, and his bare feet were bruised and sore. Yet it was the only chance he had to find his Pa, so he couldn't give up. Finally, around dusk, the last wagon passed him by. He had lost count at 622 wagons. He was sure there were at least another hundred after he stopped counting.

In the early evening, Matt made his way back over to the seminary building where the doctors and nurses were still working feverishly with the worst of the wounded. He had not had anything to eat now for two days, and he was feeling sick and light-headed. He circled the building and, following his nose, found a makeshift kitchen where food was being prepared. He waited by the door until one of the cooks came out for a breather. He asked if he could trouble her for a drink and perhaps something to eat. She disappeared back inside, and in a short minute, she reappeared with a canteen of water and a small bag of food. Inside the bag he found a half loaf of bread, a tomato, and a string of beef jerky. Matt thanked her and went off to the edge of the woods to eat his feast.

It was just the barest of rations, but it tasted so good. What had his mother always said? "Hunger is the best sauce." When his meal was about half gone, Matt fought the urge to eat the rest. Instead, he wrapped it up and hung the bag from his belt and the canteen around his neck. He walked slowly back to the little stand of trees where he had slept the night before.

The big charge that ended the Battle of Gettysburg was more than twenty-four hours ago now. Many of the wounded were still on the battlefield, and the air hung with the smell of decaying bodies. Flies were everywhere and sometimes in the distance Matt could see birds of prey were clustered around what he assumed was a dead body. There was no way to estimate the number of dead bodies that were still lying on the battlefield, but with well over a hundred thousand soldiers in a life-or-death struggle for three days, surely twenty thousand wouldn't be too high an estimate. Matt was sure he had seen half or more of that number in the field where he had laid on the ground for most of yesterday afternoon. He tried to wipe those visions out of his mind but couldn't. He suspected that if he lived to be one hundred years old, he would still carry a vision of that field littered with the dead and dying.

Matt spent another restless night on the ground under the trees at the edge of the wheat field. Before the sun was up the next morning, he had made a decision. He was going to make his way back to Williamsport. All of the medical wagons would stop there to transport the wounded across the Potomac River. If his Pa was alive, that is he would find him. If not, he could cross the river and make his way back to the Schendler Farm near Berryville.

In some ways, Matt didn't care much for his plan. He didn't want to leave the battlefield without knowing about his Pa, but he didn't feel he had a choice. The only word he had about his Pa came from the wounded man in the wagon, and he had told Matt Zeke Mason was dead. Yes, his Pa could be dead, but he might be wounded too. He also might have been captured by the Yankees. If he didn't find his Pa at Williamsport, Matt could still hold on to the hope that he had been captured. Yes, he would go to Williamsport. It wasn't a great plan, but it was better than no plan at all.

Matt had two choices for a route to Williamsport. He could follow the wagon train of wounded up by Cashtown and through the mountains, or he could follow the route of the army, which was already in full retreat. He had earlier heard talk of the two routes from Williamsport to Gettysburg. The one they chose for the wagon train came north on the west side of the mountains. The other route went through two little towns called Waynesboro and Fairfield. The army had obviously chosen to go back the other route, the southwest route, through those little towns.

He figured that the southwest route would get him to Williamsport fastest, and he could be there when the wagon train arrived. That would give him the best chance of rechecking the wagons for Pa. He also admitted to himself that there was way too much misery and depression traveling with the hospital wagons and a certain amount of danger. If the Union troops chose to follow and capture the wagons, they could do it easily. The army was already on the move, and there was no protection for the injured in the wagon train.

The Confederate Army, even in retreat, was still formidable. There were at least forty thousand fighting men under the leadership of some of the best generals in either army. Both sides had great losses at Gettysburg. It was not likely that either side would mount another major confrontation so quickly. Both needed time to regroup. It was likely that the Yankees would follow and harass them some, but most likely they would keep their distance.

Matt reasoned that the Confederate Army was headed south to friendly country. They would shake off this defeat, rack it up as one loss against a whole list of victories, and they would be ready for the next engagement. The South was winning this war and had been for all of the two years of the fighting. Sure, this was a withdrawal, but not necessarily a loss. But even as he ran those thoughts through his mind, Matt wondered if they were true. Was he just becoming a die-hard cheerleader for the army his Pa fought for?

As soon as it was daylight, Matt started his trek, walking south on the dirt road they had moved the cannons on less than a week ago. His feet hurt, and to add to the misery, a slow rain started and quickly turned the road into mud. Matt knew the army was out in front of him, and without the rain he would have been able to follow their dust. Instead, with the rain and thousands of feet wading in the mud in front of him, traveling south toward Fairfield was pure misery. He thought longingly about his little bag of food but decided he would need it more later on. Instead, he had a big drink of water from his canteen.

As he reached the top of a rise, Matt heard the sound of several horses coming up the road. He moved to the side as a Confederate cavalry group rode by. None of the men riding by seemed to notice him. That was just the first of several groups he saw that morning. The Army of Northern Virginia was on the march, and they had patrols out behind them where they had just left the enemy. They also probably had patrols out on both sides of the main body of soldiers and in front as well. The cavalry was the eyes and ears of an army.

It continued to rain all day and into the evening. As darkness fell, Matt looked for a place to get in out of the weather and grab a few hours of sleep, but he saw nothing that looked promising. By the time it was pitch-dark, he had given up hope of finding a place to stop. Instead, he just kept putting one foot in front of another, moving slowly along toward Williamsport. He knew the army was four or five miles in front of him and imagined that they were doing the same thing. He envisioned them putting more and more miles between themselves and that little town called Gettysburg that before last week, none of them had ever heard of and now wished they never had.

Many hours later, when the sky was getting lighter and dawn was close, Matt saw a farm off in the distance to the right of the main road. The barn had the familiar look of an Amish or Quaker barn, but Matt couldn't be sure. He knew that if he approached the wrong people for help, he could get himself shot. Hesitantly, he walked up the lane, stopping every twenty steps or so. There were lights on in the house, and he was sure the family was up. He wanted to give the farmer time to warn him off before shooting him, if he was so inclined.

When he was so close to the gate that he would have to open it to enter the front yard, he began to clearly see the barn out behind the house. When he identified the eight-point star on the side, he couldn't suppress a big smile. As a small boy, he had never realized how important his Ma's Quaker heritage might be someday. Having some knowledge and understanding of the Quaker ways had been of great help before he reached Gettysburg as he made his way north. Now, it might get him shelter from the rain and, perhaps, even something to eat.

Matt approached the steps to the back porch door but had not reached them when a voice behind him said, "Who are thee, young man?"

Matt turned around and found himself face-to-face with an older man dressed in the traditional white shirt and black hat of a Quaker. The man wasn't alone; there were two younger men approaching Matt from the sides, also in Quaker garb. The older man was not carrying anything in his hands, but the younger two each held a pitchfork. Matt reasoned that they might have been pitching hay, but more likely, a pitchfork was as close as they would get to carrying a weapon.

He responded directly to the older man. "Sir, I'm Matt Mason from Mt. Airy, North Carolina, sir. I got caught in the rain, and I have been walking all night looking for some place to get dry. I was hoping I could stop over in your barn for a while."

"The Confederate Army passed by this way in the middle of the night. Are thou in that army, young man?" the man asked.

"No, sir," Matt answered honestly. "I came up here looking for my Pa, who was in the army. We had not heard from him for several months, and my Ma sent me to find him. I think he might have been killed in the battle outside Gettysburg."

The man addressed one of the others. "Adam, tell thy Ma that we need some food for this wayfaring stranger. And see if thee has some clothes that he could wear."

Adam obediently ran up the steps and disappeared in the back door.

The older man looked back at Matt and said, "Let's take thee to the barn. It is warm and dry there. Thee can change clothes, have some breakfast, and rest a bit."

Matt was overcome with thankfulness. Once again, a Quaker family was living out the principles of their faith. He could clearly hear his Ma's voice in his ear: "Matthew, say it with me: 'For I was hungry and you fed me. I was thirsty and you gave me a drink. I was a stranger and you invited me in.' Matthew 25: 35."

Matt wondered just how much influence his Ma had over his life and who he had become. When he was growing up on the little farm near Mt. Airy, he had few conscious thoughts about his Ma's Quaker family or the training and influences those folks had on Ma. Now, he had to admit that by extension, they had influenced him as well. Because of the families he had come in contact with on this odyssey, he was more and more appreciative of these people who lived their faith and acted with benevolence without expecting anything in return. He had said to himself this morning that if he lived to be one hundred years of age, he would never forget what he had seen at Gettysburg. He knew that he would never forget these Quaker families and their kindnesses either.

He smiled to himself and thought, *May it always be so.*

Matt had barely finished changing into the clothes Adam brought when a small, sturdy lady with a gray apron over her cotton dress appeared at the door of the barn. She held a tray covered with a piece of cloth. Matt could smell the warm food before she set it down on the table in the corner, and his mouth watered in anticipation. The older man followed her. He lit a lantern and set it on the table next to the tray. It brightened the barn significantly and cast shadows against the wall. Matt felt his hunger pains more strongly than ever, but he tried to remember his manners.

"I introduced myself earlier," he said to the couple. "I am Matt Mason from Mt. Airy, North Carolina. Could you tell me your names so I would know to whom I am beholden?"

The man smiled and nodded at his wife and said, "Son, we are the Glicks. I am Killion, and this is my wife Elizabeth. The young men are our boys, Adam and John."

"I want you to know how much I appreciate your taking me in, considering the times and all. You are here in the middle of a war, and it is dangerous to trust a stranger," said Matt.

"It is our pleasure to be of help to those who need it," said Mr. Glick. "I can't help but notice that you don't speak like most we come in contact with from the Deep South. Are you, perhaps, a member of the Society of Friends?"

"Sir, my Ma was from Lancaster, Pennsylvania. Her father was a Quaker elder. She taught me Quaker ways, but we didn't have a meeting house in our county. If I talk differently from others you know, it probably is because of my Ma's training and influence," he said.

Unable to restrain himself further, Matt reached for the food on the tray in front of him. The dominant dish was a bowl of thick soup. It was obviously hot off the stove as steam was still coming up from it. Soon he was eating as fast as he could, with a spoon in one hand and a piece of bread in the other. It wasn't a feast like he had at the Schendler Farm, but in Matt's state of hunger, it tasted wonderful. Before he knew it, the tray was empty, and he was downing the glass of milk that provided the final capstone on the first meal Matt had eaten in…in…he couldn't remember when.

Mr. and Mrs. Glick gathered up the tray and left for the house. Adam laid out a horse blanket over a couple of bales of hay for him, and Matt fell asleep as soon as he hit the hay. He wasn't sure how long he slept, but he felt like a new person when he awoke.

Adam was still sitting there and greeted him with a smile and the words, "How did thee sleep, friend?"

When Matt ventured out of the barn, the rains had let up and the sun was out. It was midday and promised to be steamy but not overly hot. Matt had stood with Adam in the yard for just a few minutes when the Mr. and Mrs. Glick and John appeared. He thanked his host and hostess and said he would be taking his leave.

Mr. Glick whispered something to his son John, and the younger man disappeared out the door. As they were standing together in the yard saying their good-byes, John returned. He had a pullover shirt in his hands, which he offered to Matt. Matt started to refuse but thought better of it. He took the pullover and tried it on. It had an attached hood that could be pulled up over Matt's head.

"My wife made one for each of the boys," Mr. Glick said.

Matt said, "I've never seen anything quite like this." He addressed Mrs. Glick. "Where did you get the idea for it?"

She smiled, "I don't know. I was reading in my Bible one night, and a garment with a head piece was described. I had been working with some heavy material, making some winter clothes for the boys. Adding the head piece just seemed practical. Thee can let it hang down thy back, or if thee gets cold, thee can pull it up over thy head."

Next, Adam handed him a bag with a strap on it. He said, "Here, Matt, thee will need something to carry your clothes in. Mother put some food for the road in here too."

The bag was similar to the pack he had lost at the edge of the battlefield just a few days ago. "Thank you," he said, overcome with gratitude. "And thank you all again."

He walked off down the lane toward the main road with a full stomach, a new change of clothes, his next meal, and a pullover shirt with a hood. The Glick family stood in the yard and waved him off. *Amazing*, Matt thought. *Just amazing*.

As he walked on toward Williamsport, Matt felt much better about his prospects. It had stopped raining. He wasn't hungry anymore. The sun was shining, and he was about two days' walk from Williamsport. He wasn't sure what he would find when he reached that little city, but he was more and more certain that Williamsport was where his destiny would play out. He was anxious to get there.

WILLIAMSPORT

The next two days passed in a blur as Matt walked through the Pennsylvania countryside and the outskirts of the city of Hagerstown, Maryland. It rained on and off, which made the road a quagmire of mud and rocks. Matt had to be careful where he put his feet. The mud could suck him in down to his knees if he didn't hit firm ground, and the sharp rocks that had been used to repair the road could cut his feet. It occurred to Matt that the road was going to need major repair now, after forty thousand men, horses, and wagons had sloshed over it on the way to the river.

With a canteen full of water and the food from Mrs. Glick, Matt was not likely to go hungry, but with every step, he wondered if he would ever find shoes to fit his size 14 feet. Even if he found shoes though, he had lost his money when his pack was taken from him at the battle in Gettysburg three days ago. He had no money for shoes or anything else.

Finally, Matt was through Hagerstown. Williamsport was just a mile down the road, and he knew by the businesses bordering the road that he was approaching the Potomac River. On the left was a large lumberyard. He remembered the big timber rafts he had seen during his boat ride down the James River that brought new-cut trees to the saw mills that dotted the river's edge here and there. Such big cargoes had to move on a river. On the right was a boat shop. They advertised both new boats and repairs. The presence of a lumberyard and the boat shop were obvious clues that he was getting close to the river.

There was a lot of activity going on at the lumberyard. Matt paused for a few minutes to watch men carrying boards and loading them on wagons. He followed the wagons down toward the river and stopped on the ridge overlooking the riverbank below. His eyes widened in surprise. There below him was a very different Potomac River from the one he had seen two weeks before, when he and his Pa had helped move the cannons across. The river certainly wasn't at low ebb now. Since the Army of Northern Virginia had made its way across in late June, rains had come over and over, raising the river by several feet. He didn't see any of the big flat rocks that had made moving the cannons relatively easy.

Matt looked on with amazement. How could one river look so different in just a few weeks? And how would the army ever get the wagons and cannons across the river? It was obvious that the army engineers' solution to that problem was to build a bridge; that was what the wagon loads of lumber were for. Already, the bridge was taking shape on the close side of the river, with crews of men working furiously with saws and hammers.

Standing close to several soldiers, Matt listened in on their conversation. He soon gathered that the engineers had tried to span the river before with little luck. It seemed that each time they pushed the extension of the bridge out into the Potomac, the current, which was much stronger now, had taken the end of the bridge and dislocated it from its anchor on the shore.

Everyone watching in the little group of "sidewalk superintendents" had advice for the engineers. Some said there was no way to hold the bridge in the middle unless they could sink anchors into the floor of the river. Naysayers speculated that the depth of the river was too great after the recent rains to sink anything into the river bottom. Others suggested that they find some heavy rope and tie it across the river from trees on both sides and anchor the bridge to the rope. Someone pointed out that would be great if they had a rope long enough and strong enough to span the river, but if the army had such a rope, they would already have it in place. At least they would already have it stretched out down the bank, ready to use at the right time.

All the time Matt was standing there, he was hearing gunshots in the distance. He asked one of the soldiers what the shots were. The answer was chilling. "The Yankees have sent a division of men to harass us and to try to keep us from crossing the river," he said. "General Lee set up a defensive line to protect us, but the Yankees keep riding small boats downstream to where the engineers are working. They'll shoot at anything in a gray coat, but their favorite targets are the engineers."

Matt thought about the prospect of working out on the river with no cover while the Yankee sharpshooters tried to pick gray coats off one by one. He didn't envy that job at all and decided to stay away from the river. Asking around, he found out when and where the wagon train of wounded was expected to arrive.

It arrived later than afternoon, setting up on the flood plain just north of downtown Williamsport. Matt spent the afternoon walking among the wagons, saying his Pa's name over and over. There were only 120 wagons in the caravan when it arrived, hundreds less than the numbers that had retreated from Gettysburg. He wanted to ask one of the drivers about the other wagons but held his tongue.

When he had finished looking in all the wagons, he sat down on a rock wall that bordered the roadway where the wagons were parked. Several wounded men had already climbed down out of the wagons and were sitting in the sun. Some were ambulatory with injuries to their upper bodies, while others had bandages over parts of their faces. One man had blackened peeling skin on his face that looked like Matt's did a couple of weeks back. He knew exactly how that soldier had been injured and decided to ask him about the rest of the wagons.

"They are gone," the man said. "All of them are gone."

"What do you mean, they are gone?" Matt asked.

The man looked vacantly at Matt. It was obvious he didn't want to talk about it, but all of a sudden the words just came spilling out. "It was horrible," he said. "The wagons kept breaking down. We didn't have any tools to fix them, so they were just abandoned on the side of the road.

"At first we tried to take the wounded men into the other wagons, but there were just too many. The weight was too much, and it caused other wagons to break down. Sharpshooters were everywhere in the woods, everywhere. They were shooting at our drivers. One day dozens of civilians came at us out of the woods on both sides of the road with axes and chopped at the spokes on our wagons to make the wheels break down. We had a few guns and were able to shoot some of them, but there were too many. Most of our wagons are sitting on the side of the road from Cashtown through the pass to Black Gap and south. The men in those wagons are dead, or if they are lucky, they may be headed for prisoner-of-war camps. We won't see them again here."

Matt couldn't believe what he was hearing. He couldn't believe that the Confederate Army would leave six to eight thousand wounded men unprotected in enemy territory. Still, the evidence was in the six hundred wagons and more he had counted three days ago compared to the 120 he could count now.

That night, he slept at the edge of the soldiers' camp just north of Williamsport. He ate the last of his beef jerky and bread. He wasn't sure where his next meal would come from, but it seemed necessary that he eat all he had on hand in order to keep his strength up. Tomorrow, he was going to figure out how to get across the Potomac and south toward Winchester and Berryville. It was obvious that his Pa wasn't in any of the wagons, and if he had been in one of the others that didn't make it, he was probably dead now or headed to a Yankee prison camp. Staying around Williamsport with the army without his Pa to fend for him was not going to be a part of his plan.

Several times through the night, Matt heard activity down on the riverfront. The lumber wagons continued to roll back and forth between the lumberyard and the site of the unfinished bridge. He also heard some shots from time to time, though not as many as the previous afternoon.

At first light the next morning, Matt walked to the bridge and was amazed to find that it was very different from what had been taking shape the afternoon before. It was now a pontoon bridge. The soldiers must have gone up and down the river, confiscating every boat they could find. There had to be fifty of them in place connected to each other by boards from the lumberyard and forming a single-file walking path. It was probably three hundred yards long, stretching across the

Potomac. Men were already lining up on the bank to begin the walk across the river.

Matt asked one of the officers who seemed to be in charge where he should look for the cannons. He still hoped that someone in that artillery unit might have been with Pa when the battle started between the two ridges at Gettysburg. Someone might have seen what happened to Pa.

The officer directed him to the cannons that were just south of the downtown, lined up side by side on the ridge above the river. He remembered that when they left Williamsport three weeks earlier, there were more than 160 cannons. He counted seventy lined up for transport. He didn't see any familiar faces working with the cannons, and no one he asked knew about Zeke Mason and his artillery unit.

Matt was digesting the realization that there were probably no survivors from his father's unit when another thing struck him as odd: there were no horses with the cannons.

"Sir," he asked one of the men, "where are the horses?"

The man responded, "They came before dawn this morning and took the horses. They told us they could not take the cannons across the river. It seems the bridge they are building will only work for soldiers, people who can walk. The cannons and the wagons are too heavy for a pontoon bridge."

"So what about the horses?" Matt asked.

"We can't take the wagons or the cannons, and we can't leave them behind for the Yankees. Son, we are getting ready to destroy the wagons and the cannons and—"

As if on cue, Matt and the man he was talking to both jerked their heads toward the sound of gunfire and the hysterical sound of horses in panic. The man looked at Matt and shook his head. "They are shooting the horses," he said. "We can't leave them behind for the Yankees."

The words hit Matt like a lightning bolt.

"Shooting the horses?" he said. "Surely not! Why can't they swim them?" But Matt didn't wait for an answer. Before he knew what he was doing, Matt began to run toward the sounds of the rifle shots. Big Billy might be with the horses! The gunshots had begun slowly but were speeding up now. He didn't know how many horses were to be shot, and he might already be too late. He had to get there fast, and he was already running as fast as he could.

In the distance about a hundred yards away, he saw a line of men standing along the top of a ravine. There was smoke hanging over them, testifying to the firing of the rifles. Some of the men had stopped to reload their single-shot rifles; others were still shooting. Matt could hear the horses squealing and snorting, moving against each other, trying to get away from the imminent danger.

Matt ran through the line of shooters at full speed. He was yelling at the top of his lungs. "Stop, stop! That's my horse!"

Actually, he didn't know if Big Billy was down in the ravine with what appeared to be dozens of horses, but he needed them to stop shooting so he could look for the big bay.

The gunshots slowed and then stopped altogether. An officer moved toward him with a menacing look on his face. Matt was still yelling as loud as he could while frantically looking over the horses, trying to see if Big Billy was in the herd. Most of the horses were already lying on the ground, but a dozen or so were still standing. One of the horses still on his feet was, for sure, Big Billy.

Matt ran down into the ravine. The officer who had been moving toward him stopped at the edge of the slope and put his hands up in the air. His gesture was one of loss of control but served as well for the men to hold their fire. Most of the men had already put their guns down. No one liked this duty, but orders were orders.

Big Billy was standing in the middle of the mayhem. He watched Matt as he carefully stepped around the dead and dying horses and approached his big friend. When he was close enough, Matt reached out and took hold of the halter that was around Big Billy's head. A cheer went up from the men who, just a few minutes ago, had been shooting at the horses. No one wanted to shoot the horses; if they could save just one, it was worth a big cheer.

Matt quickly saw that Big Billy was bleeding from a wound in his chest. Blood was running down his front leg. He could not tell if a musket ball had lodged in his chest or if it was a through-and-through shot. He tugged on the harness. Big Billy stretched out his neck and shuffled his front hooves, but he didn't move forward. Matt walked around to the horse's side and looked at Big Billy's hindquarters. Blood ran from an open wound high on his flank. It was obvious to Matt that this was not a through-and-through. Most likely, there was a musket ball lodged in the flank. The pain must be severe.

He pulled the halter again, and Big Billy moved only slightly. Matt paused, weighing his options. The big bay horse was shot in the chest and in the left flank. Either wound might kill him. Matt might end up having to put Big Billy out of his misery himself later on in the day. But he wouldn't know that until he could get him out of this mess to examine him and see what could be done.

Matt moved his head closer to Big Billy's and talked to the big red stallion softly while pulling on the halter. This time Big Billy made a strange sound from deep in his throat and began to move forward. With that movement, the men around the edge of the ravine began to cheer again. It was obvious they were not happy to have been assigned this duty, and to see even one horse saved was a cause for celebration. There hadn't been many reasons to celebrate in recent days.

Matt led the big horse slowly up the side of the ravine and back into a stand of trees that bordered the river. He reached into the pack that Adam Glick had given him, pulled out his spare shirt, and used it to wipe the blood away from the wound on Big Billy's chest. To his relief, he saw this was a superficial wound. It was obvious that the musket ball had come across his chest and taken out a chunk of flesh.

The wound on his side, however, was a different situation altogether. It was high on his flank and might have penetrated all the way to the bone. If so, it would be very hard to get out, and it had to come out to keep the wound from festering. A lead musket ball was as good as poison for killing a man if it was left inside, and the same was true for a horse. Matt wondered what to do. With all of the horses that traveled with the army, there would be some veterinarians traveling with them. Surely there must be at least one at this camp.

Matt led Big Billy slowly over to the medical tents and tied him to a small tree just at the edge of the clearing around the tents. He wanted to ask someone if they knew of a veterinarian close by. He waited until he saw a doctor step outside for a breather. Matt walked up to him and asked if he knew where he could find someone to examine his horse.

The doctor said there were several, but he did not know where to tell him to look. "What's the problem, son?" he asked.

"It's my horse," Matt said. "He has a musket ball in his flank."

"Well, horses aren't my specialty," the doctor said with a weary grin. "Where is he?"

Matt motioned toward Big Billy, who was standing over next to the line of trees.

"When I have time, I'll take a look," he said.

Matt went back over to Big Billy and held the big horse's halter rope. He took his blood-covered shirt and dabbed at the wound on Big Billy's flank, which was still oozing blood. True to his word, in a short time the doctor came out and took a long look at both of Big Billy's wounds.

"That is a beautiful animal, son. I can see why he was worth saving. A flesh wound in a horse isn't any different from a flesh wound in a man. We won't have any problem with the one on his chest. We just need to keep it clean and to keep some medicine on it. The flank wound is something else again. That one is deep, and the ball may be lodged against a bone. It is in the wrong place and could be a major problem. Give me just a minute to get some of my instruments, and I will be back out to look again," he promised.

Matt couldn't believe his good fortune in finding a human doctor who had a love of horses. Surely he could fix Big Billy up as good as new!

When the doctor came back, he had a couple of big medical instruments. It was obvious that he was going to try to get the musket ball out of the big horse's flank.

"Son, hold this directly on the open wound," he said. He handed Matt a tin that was extremely cold to the touch. The doctor talked to Matt in a quiet voice as he worked. "Ice doesn't cure anything, but the cold will deaden the flesh around the wound so that the horse will feel less pain. It may help him hold still for me. You are very important in this process. You have to keep your horse very still. He can't move while I am probing for the ball. It is all a matter of how much trust this horse has in you. If he moves too much, I may not be able to get the musket ball out. In that case, you might as well put him out of his misery today because he will be dead of fever in about a week."

Matt held the cold tin up next to the wound. Big Billy made that rumbling noise down deep in his throat that Matt had heard from time to time in the past. He hoped it meant that he was feeling the trust the doctor was talking about. When the doctor was ready to probe for the musket ball, he moved back by the horse's flank and sent Matt to hold Big Billy's head. Matt prayed a silent prayer as he watched the doctor push the metal probe into the horse's flank about four inches deep. The horse made that sound again from deep in his throat, but he didn't move.

"There it is," the doctor said. "It is pretty deep, but I think I can get it. This is the crucial time, son. Hold him very still."

Matt began to talk softly to the horse. The words were not important, but the tone of voice certainly was. He was trying to let Big Billy feel the love and the security that he was sending to him. In a few seconds, he heard the doctor take a deep breath and withdraw the instrument. At the end of it, Matt could see the musket ball. He had gotten it out!

The doctor gave Matt instructions for taking care of the wound, and Matt listened intently. "Wait right here for a minute," he said. "I've got something for you to use." He went back into the tent and came back out in a few minutes with a tin of salve. Then he walked back to Big Billy's wound. He had a small container in his hand. He pressed a lever on the back of the container, and liquid shot into the air a couple of feet. He turned the front of the container to the wound and squeezed the lever again. Matt could see the liquid squirt into the wound and run out down the big horse's flank. The big horse started to rear and almost pulled Matt off his feet.

The doctor laughed. "I guess if we felt the sting he is feeling we would jump too! Don't worry though, I think he is going to be just fine. Take the salve from the tin and fill the wound with a finger full each morning and evening until it is all gone. It will keep the dirt out of the wound while it heals up."

Matt smiled as he stroked Big Billy's nose. "Doctor, how long will it be before I can ride him?" he asked.

"He should be all right in a week or so," the doctor said. "I suspect you can ride him before that, but don't ride him hard. He needs time for the muscle in his flank to heal, and it is going to be sore for several days."

Matt thanked the doctor over and over again. He didn't feel that words were sufficient, but he didn't have anything else he could use to show his appreciation.

The doctor smiled at Matt and said, "Son, that is a beautiful animal. I wish he was mine. You take good care of him, and I'm sure he will be a fine horse for you for many years after this lousy war is over." He turned and headed back into the tent.

Matt led the big horse back through the trees toward his little makeshift camp along the bank of the river west of Williamsport. He caught himself reaching up to rub Big Billy's neck several times as they walked along the river.

He thought back over the events of the day. Finding Big Billy again was just luck. If he had arrived more than a few seconds later, the big horse might have been dead. Then to find a doctor who would take the time to look at him and could fix him so quickly was just luck piled on top of luck. *Or*, Matt thought, *maybe it was the good Lord intervening in my life.* Matt's Ma always said there were no accidents in life. Everything happened for a purpose, and he could hear her voice in his ear as she quoted yet another of her favorite Bible verses: "'All things work together for good to them that love God, to them who are called according to his purpose,' Romans 8: 28."

That night, Matt and Big Billy slept at the north edge of the military camp just outside of the circle of tents. There were sentries posted about every thirty or forty yards, and one was very close to where Matt lay down to rest while Big Billy munched some grass and slept standing up as horses do.

Matt spent a restless night. He had felt some security when he arrived at Williamsport. Being close to the army provided a feeling of protection with forty thousand soldiers close by, but he wasn't feeling it now. Being there was necessary if he was to find his Pa. Now, he was resigned to the uneasy feeling that he wasn't going to find him. His Pa might be dead on the battlefield back at Gettysburg. He could be among the wounded abandoned by the army on the side of the road between Gettysburg and Williamsport. Either of those possibilities was almost unthinkable.

But Pa could be a prisoner of the Yankees and headed for a prisoner-of-war camp somewhere in the north. He could hang on to that thought. His Pa might be alive. He might be able to come home when this war is over. He wasn't sure where home was, but he was going to do his best to make a home for himself and his big horse back on that farm near Berryville, Virginia. By the time his Pa would be free to come home again, he would have done his best to create a new home for them.

The feeling that was growing strongest in Matt's mind was that he needed to get away from the army and the risk that any minute he might lose Big Billy again to the military, who seemed to be able to just whisk in at anytime and take whatever they wanted.

It was a good feeling to have such thoughts moving around in his mind. It was time he took charge of the future. After so much tragedy, maybe things were beginning to shape up. Whatever tomorrow might bring, Matt was convinced that he needed to stop following the army and begin to make his own tracks, to strike out in his own direction. He needed to stop being dependent on anyone else and begin to make his own future.

Tomorrow, he and Big Billy were going to find a way across that river and were going to head for the Schendler Farm. The Schendlers were going to look very good to him after what he had been through over the past several weeks.

HEADING TO A NEW HOME

Matt was on his feet with first light. He looked at the wound on Big Billy's flank and then at the surface wound on his chest. Neither looked festered. He took the medicine that the doctor had given him and rubbed it gently on the chest wound, and then did the same to the wound on his flank. Already, the hole in the horse's flank seemed more like an indentation and no longer looked like he could put his finger in it three or four inches deep like last night. Nevertheless, he took a liberal amount of the salve and pushed it into the wound as far as he could. He wanted to be sure that the wound stayed as clean as he could make it.

Their makeshift campsite was just outside of the army camp upriver from Williamsport. He had thought a long time last night about the best way to head for his new home at the Schendler Farm. He thought it might be a shorter journey if he went back down the river, and it would take him into more populated areas where he was more likely to meet Union and Confederate patrols. With the river swollen as it was, the farther downriver he went, the less likely fording the river would be an option. They would have to find a ferry. Matt wasn't sure riding a ferry was a good idea with all the army activity centered on ferries, moving men and horses and wagons back and forth.

Matt also didn't relish going back through the army camp where he ran the greatest risk of losing Big Billy again. He had pretty well decided on heading upstream until they found a place to cross. According to the word from the soldiers, he would be headed into a less populated area where there would be less army activity on either side of the river.

So the decision was made. Matt left the rope around Big Billy's neck and used it to lead the big horse. He was anxious for the time when he could ride him but knew that would be down the road at least two or three days, maybe even a week. They moved through the woods along the riverbank and stayed off the river road. He knew that the Yankees had been harassing the engineers while they built the pontoon bridge, and they were launching their small boats somewhere upstream. He wanted to skirt that trouble if he could. The Yankees might be using that road for approaching the river.

Matt and Big Billy were about two hours up the river when they came to the edge of a clearing. Big Billy was making a strange noise down in his throat, and he was very restless. Responding to his uneasiness, Matt carefully looked out through the trees. There, in the middle of the clearing, stood another horse.

The horse was a black one, smaller than Big Billy, and it was wearing a saddle with saddlebags and a harness. Judging from his tack, the horse looked like he belonged to the army—the Yankee army. Big Billy made a snorting noise, and Matt immediately turned to the big horse and put his hand over his nose.

Matt quickly looked back to see if there was any movement in the clearing. The Yankee horse was standing at alert and looking in their direction, nostrils flared at the sight and smell of another of his kind. Big Billy made another noise deep in his throat, and Matt began to look for an escape route. Much more of this horse-to-horse communication, and someone was bound to know of their presence.

The horse in the clearing began to move toward Matt and Big Billy. There was nothing for Matt to do. The black horse just kept coming in their direction. Shortly, he was poking his nose through the bushes where they were sheltered. Matt wondered if this horse was abandoned, if it had run away, or if its owner had been shot, or worse, in some conflict. Matt decided to investigate further. He thought if he left Big Billy behind for a few minutes while he checked things out, the Yankee horse would stay with him. Then Matt could see beyond the edges of the clearing without anyone seeing him.

He tied Big Billy to a tree limb and began creeping through the trees toward the river. He had almost reached the riverbank when he spotted a piece of blue material in the high grass. Matt crept closer and found a Union cavalry soldier lying in the grass.

Matt held his breath and listened, but there was no sign of life from the downed man. He came out of the brush and knelt beside him. There was no need for a close examination to know why he was on the ground. The soldier had a vicious whelp on his face. Something had hit him very hard.

Matt looked around. A pathway ran along the ridge above the riverbank. The soldier, obviously, had been riding along that pathway when something hit him hard enough to knock him off his horse. Matt looked up, and there, just above the pathway, he saw a low-hanging limb. Just to be sure, Matt bent close to the man to see if he was breathing. He wasn't. This man would not be fighting against the Confederates again.

For a moment, Matt considered what to do. Much of the time when Matt was in a quandary, he would hear his Ma or Pa's voice in his ear with some good advice. This time it was Pa's voice that he heard: "The Lord helps those who help themselves." His Pa quoted that "scripture" often, but sometimes his Ma would whisper to Matt that it was a nice saying but was not scriptural. She attributed that saying to Ben Franklin. Pa said he didn't care who said it; it was true.

Matt decided to check the man's uniform for sidearms, a pistol, or perhaps any money or food he might be carrying. Sure enough, he found the soldier's pistol in a holster around his waist and money in a leather pouch attached to his belt. It wasn't much, about ten dollars in Union money, of course, but it might come in handy down the road. There was also some food. The Union soldier certainly wouldn't need it anymore. He looked longingly at the man's boots, but the dead soldier had small feet. Matt would have to wait longer for his size fourteens.

Matt then looked at the black horse. He might have been ridden hard last night, but he had been grazing in the tall grass for at least several hours. He might even have gone down to the edge of the river for a drink. Matt checked the horse over for injuries. He seemed in good shape. Then he saw something peeking out of the back of the saddle.

It was the butt of a rifle. He reached up and pulled the rifle out of its scabbard.

Matt had seen many different types of rifles, but never anything like this. Most of the rifles that were carried by Confederate soldiers were Smith & Wesson single-shot rifles. They were state-of-the-art in the 1850s. This was something very different. Matt examined the rifle closely, looking at the brand name on the barrel. It said Henry. Matt had heard of a new repeating rifle that was carried by some of the Union soldiers. The army didn't have enough of them to issue to everyone, but some of their men had what they called a carbine rifle that could shoot maybe five or six times in a minute. He must be holding one of those new rifles in his hands! The next question in his mind was about ammunition. Was the Union soldier carrying ammunition for this new rifle? A quick search of the soldier's saddlebags revealed three boxes of shells. The label on the boxes said "Carbine shells for the Henry Model 60 Rifle."

He couldn't believe his luck; he had stumbled onto the mother lode. He now had a second horse that looked to be in good shape, along with a saddle and saddlebags. He had some food and some money. He also had a rifle that no Confederate soldier had, a Henry repeating rifle, the same rifle that he had heard Southern soldiers talk about with envy. They said the Yankees could load that rifle on Sunday and shoot it all week without reloading. Matt smiled. He didn't believe such a preposterous boast, but having the rifle was a major plus, one that might come in handy down the road.

Glowing with his good luck, Matt climbed on the Yankee horse and tied Big Billy's rope to the saddle horn. He had anticipated walking for the next two or three days, but now he was riding and was the proud owner of not one but two fine horses. Also, he had a rifle, and not just any rifle. It was a Henry 60 repeating rifle with three boxes of rim fire shells. And he had a pistol. Neither he nor his Pa had ever had a pistol.

Matt left the Yankee soldier on the ground where he lay. He thought about burying him but decided against it. Others would come that way looking for him. They would assume that he had been knocked off his horse by the tree limb, and the horse had wandered away. If Matt buried him, no one would ever know what happened to him. That, at least, was the extent of his reasoning on the matter, though time was a consideration in the back of Matt's mind. His major desire was to get far away from Williamsport as quickly as possible. He knew he was in Yankee territory, but it was sparsely settled country, and he was not likely to meet up with anyone if he didn't want to.

With his newfound food supply, a canteen full of water, and two horses, he had no reason to venture into one of the small towns up the river. He was looking for a place to ford the river, and he would ride upriver until he found what he was looking for.

At midday, Matt skirted the little town of Big Pool. He briefly wondered why they called it Big Pool, but he didn't stop to ask anyone. He could see that the river was still too wide and deep to ford at that point, so he resolved to keep following the winding river until he found the right crossing place. The sign on the road just north of Big Pool said that Hancock was the next town north, about twelve miles distant.

Matt arrived just down the river from Hancock at about dusk. He looked for the densest woods he could find and hid himself and both of his horses there within sight of the river. Because he did not want to chance being seen by anyone, he decided there would be no campfire. The Yankee's saddlebags provided one more treasure that was much appreciated as Matt made the trek toward his new home: a blanket. He pulled it out and laid it on the ground. Now, maybe he could get a good night's sleep.

Despite the comfort of the blanket, food, and weaponry, Matt did not sleep well. He had not felt comfortable riding north and west all day. It seemed like he was going in the wrong direction. He wondered if he had made the wrong decision about heading upriver rather than downriver from Williamsport. At the same time, he knew he couldn't second-guess a decision that had brought him both a horse and a Henry 60 rifle.

Either way though, it was too late for a different decision. He was a full day's ride west of Williamsport and just to the east of Hancock. He had confidence that his new mount could swim the river at almost any place he chose. Matt had watched Big Billy closely the last couple of miles before stopping and knew the big horse was still giving to the wound. That meant he needed a shallow or at least a narrow place to ford the river. Once they were across, he could follow the country roads southeast toward Winchester.

Matt was pretty sure he wouldn't begin to feel comfortable until he was at Winchester, back in Virginia, back in Confederate home country.

He was up before daylight, mounted on the black horse, and on the road toward Hancock, passing along the outskirts and heading on up the river road. The Potomac River was narrower now, and immediately north of Hancock, it seemed to change in personality. The channel of the river tightened up, and in some places its width was less than fifty yards. Unfortunately, the current seemed to be moving faster as well. Could he and his two horses swim across in the rapid current? Matt knew that at some point he would just have to give it a try, and he began seriously looking for a place to cross.

He came out of the woods near the river about midday to find a fisherman sitting on the bank with a line in the water. He was an older guy, dressed a bit more formally than Matt would have thought was appropriate for a serious fisherman. He looked like he had just been to church and then come down to the river to fish. Matt decided to chance a conversation with the man. "Hello!" he said. "Are you catching anything?"

The man looked at him, making a quick assessment of this young man with two horses. He responded, "No, son, not yet. I got here a little late this morning, and I think they stopped biting before I got a line in the water." He eyed him up and down. "Where are you headed?"

Matt thought it best just to tell the man the truth about wanting to get across the Potomac. "I'm looking for the best place to ford the river. Can you tell me where I might find it?"

"Where are you going when you get across?" the man asked.

"My destination is Winchester, sir," he responded.

"Well, if I was headed for Winchester, I think I would go on down to Paw Paw. That is just a little place on the West Virginia side, but the river slows down there, and it is narrower. You also have a pretty easy way to get across the Chesapeake and Ohio Canal. They have a bridge crossing there."

The canal was news to Matt. "Tell me about the canal," he said.

"It runs alongside of the Potomac all the way down to Washington, DC," the man said. "It is man-made and uses the water from the Potomac. It sets on the south side of the river all the way. You can't cross one without crossing the other. But at Paw Paw, you have a slow-running river and an overpass across the canal. If I was headed for Winchester, that is what I would do."

"How far is it to Paw Paw?" Matt asked.

"It is probably another sixteen or eighteen miles as the crow flies," said the man.

"Thank you, sir. I hope you begin to catch something pretty soon," Matt said.

"Well," replied the man, "if I catch something, I have to clean it. I just like to fish. Most of the time I just pitch them back in anyway."

Matt grinned and had another thought. "Sir, does this river road take me to Paw Paw?" he asked.

The man smiled, obviously pleased that the young man seemed to be taking his advice about going down to Paw Paw for his crossing. He said, "Yes, it does. For the most part, it is a pretty straight road to the last bend in the river before Paw Paw. You will see a sign there that points you to a little ferry that is just big enough for a couple of men and horses. You might find that to your liking rather than swimming your horses. That second one you are leading looks kind of gimpy."

Matt thanked the man, mounted his horse, and headed off down the road. He felt pretty confident about the man's directions. Surely the man would have had no reason to tell him about the canal if he wasn't trying to be of help.

It was early evening when Matt came upon the sign on the river road that said Paw Paw. As the sign directed, he turned and headed due south. When he crested the bank above the river, he saw the ferryboat the fisherman had described tied up at the edge. The lights were coming up in a few houses across the river. The river seemed pretty calm here, and if he decided to swim the horses, it probably wouldn't be much of a problem.

Matt rode up to the ferry, which appeared to be locked up for the night. He was looking around the riverbank for a place to walk the horses in when a man came out from under a tree at the edge of the river.

"Can I help you with something, young man?" he asked. He was an older man who walked with a limp. Matt got the immediate impression that he might have been in the military, probably the Union Army, and had been wounded.

"I'm not sure, sir," Matt responded. I need to get across, but it looks as if you have closed up for the night. Are you still open for business, or will it be tomorrow before you are taking passengers again?"

"The price is fifty cents for a man and fifty cents for a horse. For you, I'll throw in the second horse for free. I'm not above making another dollar before I close out the day," he said.

"Is that in Union or Confederate money?" Matt asked. As soon as he asked the question, he wished he hadn't. This was Union country, and one could assume that only Confederates would have other than Union money.

"Union money is all we take here, son. What are you carrying?" the man asked, narrowing his eyes.

"I have Union money, sir," Matt said quickly. "I'll be pleased to pay you a dollar for a trip across."

In truth, Matt hated to part with a dollar, but it seemed to be the best way for him to show his good will toward the man and to prove that he had Union money. He did not want to come across as being anti-Union here in Union country.

They were about halfway across the river when the man struck up a conversation with Matt again. "Those are some fine-looking horses you have there, son. Where did you get them?" he asked.

Matt was not sure how to answer to question, but before he could think, he heard himself blurt out, "Oh, the bay is mine and has been for a long time. Some Rebs decided to use us for target practice back up the road close to Williamsport, and he took a ball in his flank. I couldn't ride him on this trek, so I needed another horse until he got well. I still need to stay off my bay horse for a few days."

He wished he could have taken the words back as they were met with ominous silence from the ferryboat owner. As the silence lengthened, Matt moved between his two horses and slipped out the Henry rifle, holding it behind the Union horse next to the saddle scabbard. They were almost at the south bank when the man spoke again.

"Son, you and I both know that black is a Union cavalry horse," he said. "I'm not sure how you got him, but I doubt he was up for sale in Williamsport. I'm going to give you a couple of choices. You can leave that horse with me to turn back over to the Union army, or I will introduce you to the sheriff in Paw Paw. He is my brother and is on a first-name basis with the army in this neck of the woods."

Matt could not see the man's hands but decided it was likely that he had a pistol there already pointed at him. Shielded by the Union horse, Matt thought that if he could show some strength, the man might back down. He spoke to him in a low but firm voice. "Sir, I don't want any trouble with you or the sheriff. I did not steal this horse. The good Lord provided it to me right when I needed it so I could get back home. I didn't know why the good Lord also provided me with this Henry Model 60 repeating rifle at the time, but I understand better now."

With those words, Matt cocked the rifle. The ferry operator heard the tell-tale click of the cocking mechanism. Matt continued talking. "Now, sir, I intend to take my two horses and continue on my way. I suspect you are holding a gun on me as we speak. I think it would be the wisest course of action for you to just put your pistol back where you found it and let me pass. We could each just go our own way. What do you say?"

The man turned his back on Matt and appeared to put his gun back where it came from. He turned back around and said, "I don't have a gun on you, son. All right?" At that point, the ferryboat bumped against the wharf on the south side of the river, and the man moved to open the gate for Matt and the two horses. "How about my dollar?" he demanded.

Matt waited until he was off the ferryboat before he handed the man the Union dollar. "Here is your dollar, sir."

Still holding the rifle in plain view of the operator, Matt waited until he was across the ridge above the river before climbing aboard the horse and slipping the rifle back into its scabbard. He took a deep breath for the first time since confrontation with the ferryboat operator began in the middle of the river. He felt weak all over, the way he had back in the middle of the field in Gettysburg when his father had knocked him to the ground and told him to stay there.

He nudged the black horse and headed off toward the few lights he could see in the little village. From the crossroads in Paw Paw, he saw the bridge across the canal. It was not until he crossed over it that Matt began to feel safe again. He knew that telling the man about his Henry 60 rifle was probably the final weight that tipped the scale to his side.

Suddenly, Matt felt a chill run down his spine as he realized that he had never fired the rifle and wasn't even sure where the safety was or if it was on or off. He resolved to remedy that deficiency as soon as he was out by himself where he could take some target practice. He wasn't sure what he would have done if his bluff had not worked.

It was the darkest time of night when Matt decided to stop. He maneuvered his two horses over into a stand of trees that were at the edge of a farmer's wheat field. Like the wheat field in Gettysburg, this was winter wheat, about waist high and almost ready for harvest. It provided pretty good camouflage for Matt and the horses, who stayed back just at the edge of the woods.

The wheat field caused all the memories and emotions of the battle at Gettysburg to come rushing back. He wondered if it would always be this way, if innocent things like a wheat field would trigger memories in his mind forever, or if they would fade with time. He couldn't imagine the memories fading, but he prayed they would.

Matt thought that with a good day tomorrow, he could spend the night in Winchester, Virginia. He had about seven miles to travel in West Virginia before he crossed the border into Confederate country, then he had another ten miles or so to Winchester. If he was walking, it would have taken him two hard days to cover that ground. On horseback he could do it one day. If all went well, he would be at the Schendler Farm about noon on the day following.

THE RAVAGES OF WAR

Late the next day, as Matt and his horses approached Winchester, the traffic picked up significantly. He could tell the city's population was swelled by the presence of the Army of Northern Virginia. Cavalry patrols were out, and in the distance, he could see the dust from forty thousand sets of feet on the dirt road.

His plan required him to cross through the outskirts of Winchester and travel another ten miles east to just beyond Berryville. He wasn't in a hurry, figuring he could take his time and pick his way through. It was his hope to reach the other side of the city before anyone realized he had been there.

As he came closer to Winchester, Matt was shocked to pass several farms that were burned to the ground. Winchester sat in the middle of the north end of the Shenandoah Valley and was one of the best farming areas in Virginia. It was obvious that when the Union Army pulled out of the area to escape Lee's troops several weeks ago, they had used a "scorched earth" tactic. They had destroyed everything they could find in the valley both north and south of Winchester that might benefit the Confederate Army.

Obviously, no one was escaping this war, either soldier or civilian, and that included the farmers in this fertile valley. Matt saw a hastily painted sign left by the some Union soldier on the side of a burned-out barn that read as follows:

To the Rebs,

If you wonder what is ahead of you up the valley, just think of this. If a crow flies in either direction from Winchester, he had better carry his own rations. There is nothing left to eat for 70 miles.

The Army of the Potomac

The sign was painted on the only part of the barn that still stood. The rest had been burned to the ground. Matt noted that the sign was shot full of holes. Obviously, some of Lee's soldiers did not like the message and had used the side of the barn for target practice as they walked by.

It was dusk when he reached the edge of Winchester. The army had stopped marching and had begun to set up for the night. Tents were coming up, and cooking fires were being lit. Matt could smell stew cooking, but he wasn't concerned about his own meal. He still had some of the Yankee soldier's food, and he knew that as soon as he arrived at the Schendler Farm, he would never have to worry about food again.

Matt began to look for a place to camp for the night. He did not want to be in among the army tents, but he did see some advantage to being close to forty thousand soldiers. He had to admit that he felt pretty secure with them close by. At the same time, he couldn't wait to get some miles between himself and the lines of soldiers, the tents, and the cooking fires. Mostly, he couldn't wait to put as much distance as possible between himself and the thoughts and memories of his time in the heat of battle. That went double for his time climbing in and out of the wagons of the dead and dying men. He hoped that time and distance would ease the pain of those thoughts, though he had no hope that those memories would ever be totally erased from his mind.

He took the saddle off the union horse and tied both horses to a tree limb for the night. He did not see a stream close by but knew that he would need to find water for the horses before he traveled too far in the morning. There was plenty of grass for grazing at his little camp, and he would be able to feed the horses with oats when he arrived at the Schendler Farm.

Once again, Matt settled in for what turned out to be a restless night. He was anxious to get to the farm, and he knew it was just half a day's ride away. Although he had only spent two nights at the farm, thoughts of living there with the Schendler family had been constantly on his mind since he left them less than three weeks ago.

He was up before daylight. Already, Matt could hear the army camp beginning to come awake with the sounds of horses moving and men shouting. He decided to put the saddle on Big Billy today and ride him the rest of the distance to the Schendler Farm. It would be the first time he had ridden him since the bay had been shot, but he felt it was time. He had watched his horse through much of the day yesterday, and he did not seem to be giving to the soreness of his flank wound.

Putting the saddle on the big bay horse was not as easy as he thought it would be. Big Billy was bigger than the Union horse, and the cinch would not go around him without lengthening it considerably. Also, the leather stabilizer that fit around the Union horse's chest wouldn't fit Big Billy no matter what he did. In the end, he had no choice but to roll it up and tie it to the back of the saddle. Perhaps it would come in handy with another horse later, but it would never fit on Big Billy.

At last they were ready to leave. Matt put the rope around the Union horse's neck and climbed on the big bay. He guided them both out to the road and headed east toward Berryville.

Matt passed several wagons rolling toward Winchester. They looked to be full of supplies for the troops, and he reasoned that the drivers were probably farmers attempting to sell their goods to the army. No one else seemed to have any money. From time to time, he sighted men walking up in the woods on the ridge above the road. They, like Matt, were moving away from Winchester. Matt wondered how the army would be able to feed all of the men without the hundreds of wagons they had left north of the Potomac and how the farms could be of help if they had all been burned to the ground.

That last thought sent a chill down Matt's spine. It had never occurred to him before now, but what if the Schendler Farm had been destroyed like several he had already seen? What if the house and the barn had been burned? He spurred Big Billy on into a gallop, and the big horse responded immediately.

After a couple of hours, they passed through Berryville, and he knew there were just a couple of miles to go before he reached the farm. After passing another house and barn that had been burned to the ground, Matt began getting a really bad feeling about what he might find when he turned up the little lane that led to the Schendlers' place. As he approached the turn on the road that led to the lane, he strained his eyes to see the house and the barn. There were too many trees, and his line of sight was blocked. Just a few more seconds. Finally, he breathed a sigh of relief. The house and barn were standing! From this distance, everything looked just as he had left it. Everything would be all right.

He could hardly contain the feeling he had in his chest without whooping out loud. He was at his new home at last! He turned Big Billy down the lane and let the big horse have his head. They were in a full run toward the house when he heard gunshots. His enthusiasm turned into confusion. Where were the gunshots coming from? He saw the dust fly up from the road just in front of him. Someone was shooting at him!

Matt pulled Big Billy up, slid off the horse, and dove for the ditch at the side of the road. When he did, Big Billy turned and retreated back up the lane several steps. The Union horse kept on running. He ran all the way up to the gate at the front of the property, which Matt could see was closed. That gate had not been closed when Matt was there before; what was going on? There was the sound of another shot. Were the shots coming from the house? Who was firing at him?

Cautiously lifting his head, Matt checked the house and saw that two of the windows on the first floor and two on the second floor were open and had gun barrels extended out toward the lane. He was almost sure that the last shot fired at him had come from a second-floor window on the left. He slipped his shirt off and held it up in the air, waving it so the shooter would be attracted to the motion. He then began to yell, "I'm Matt Mason! I'm Matt Mason!"

There was silence inside the house. Then he heard a scream and a familiar female voice shrieking, "Matt, is it thee?"

It was Ami Ruth's voice. He couldn't tell exactly where it was coming from, but the voice continued to scream. "Matt, Matt! Is it really thee?"

He climbed up from the ditch and began to trot up the lane toward the house. He saw a figure bolt out of the front door onto the porch, but it wasn't Ami Ruth. It was a boy in bib overalls with a bandana around his neck who took the front steps in a hard run. Oddly enough, Matt continued to hear Ami Ruth's voice yelling as the boy ran across the yard. Matt reached the gate at the entrance of the yard, climbed over it, and landed on the other side. The boy met him in a full body hug, and the two of them fell into a heap beside the gate.

Matt was lying there in a state of confusion. The boy was still yelling, only it was Ami Ruth's voice. Then the realization hit him. The "boy" was Ami Ruth dressed in boy's clothing! Her hair was tied up in a blond bundle under a hat, which had come off when she hit him in full stride. He began to laugh. She leaned back and looked at him, and then she hit him right in the face with the palm of her hand. The shock of the slap stopped his laugh. She was crying and yelling at him at the same time. Matt reached cross her body and grabbed hold of her arms just below the shoulders.

"Ami Ruth, what is going on here?" he demanded. "Why are you dressed this way, and what was that slap all about?"

She collapsed into spasms of crying. Her shoulders were shaking, and she could not get any words out that were understandable. Matt pulled her close to him. "Hold on now, Ami Ruth. Let's get control here and talk about this," he said.

Finally, she slowed her crying and began to get out some words he could understand. "I have been so afraid," she said. "Four or five days ago, I've lost track now, some deserters showed up in front of the house asking for food. Papa went out to talk to them, to offer what help we could give them.

"We had a plan if such a thing happened. Mama was to hide in a closet under some blankets. I was to go to the attic and hide on the back side of a stack of boxes we have stored there. I could hear Papa was speaking to them on the front porch, but I couldn't hear what was said. Then there were two gunshots. I immediately thought the worst because Papa would never carry a gun."

Ami Ruth stopped talking for a few seconds, and the sobs began to come again. Matt waited patiently, patting her back. When she regained her composure, she began the story again.

"I then heard a voice that said, 'Find his wife.' I could hear the men searching through the house for Mama, and finally, I heard her scream. From that point on, all I could hear was her crying. It just went on and on. I stayed hidden in the attic. Later, I couldn't hear Mama crying anymore. I heard footsteps on the stairs to the attic, and someone came up there and looked around. I stopped breathing for the entire time he was here. He didn't find me.

"I stayed hidden for the rest of that day and into the night. Finally, when it had been silent for a very long time, several hours at least, I came out and walked down the stairs as quietly as I could. I found Mama in the bedroom. She was dead. Papa was on the front porch. He had been shot in the chest. For the last four or five days, I have been here by myself, expecting that either those or some other deserters would come again."

All the time she had been talking, Matt was holding her. At this point, he said softly, "I am so sorry, Ami Ruth. You have been dealt a cruel blow losing your parents like that. It's war, and bad things happen in war to those involved and anyone close by. You and your family were in the line of fire, and bad things sometimes happen to good people."

Matt held her for a few more minutes without talking. She cried softly into his shoulder. Then Matt said, "Let's see if we can get my horses in, and we will sit down and talk through what to do now."

She nodded and got to her feet, heading for the house.

He went back to the gate and opened it. Big Billy came toward him, and he climbed up on the big horse. In a few minutes, they had located the Union horse across the vineyard. They retrieved him, and Matt walked them both back to the front yard of the house and tied them to the hitching post at the porch. Matt thought if there were other deserters in the area, it would not be bad if they got the idea that there were several people in the house.

Ami Ruth was sitting on the porch, watching him secure the horses, and as he walked up to join her, he looked at the gun barrels sticking out of the windows from the first floor. It took a second look before he realized that the gun barrels were, in fact, broom handles painted black to look like gun barrels. He smiled inadvertently, and Ami Ruth saw his expression.

She said, "I didn't know what else to do. I knew that Pa kept three rifles in the barn that he used to hunt squirrels and rabbits. All are single-shot rifles. I thought if other deserters were going to come, I needed the house to look like it was well fortified with guns and people who knew how to use them. I put two lanterns out on the lane and lit them each night so I could see if anyone was coming toward the front of the house. There are no roads up to the back of the farm over the ridge, so I didn't worry about that.

"Twice someone came up the lane, once at night and once in the daylight. I had the three real rifles in the upstairs bedrooms. I was prepared to fire a shot from each bedroom but hoped I would need only one warning shot. That was the case the first night. The warning shot scared them off, and they didn't come back. The next day there were two men who approached up the lane on foot. They were obviously Confederate deserters. They were wearing gray jackets and caps. I fired a warning shot at them, and they stopped for a minute. Then they came on, so by then, I had gone to the other room, and I fired a second warning shot. That time they turned around and ran back up the lane."

At that point, Matt began to smile.

She slapped him again, this time on the shoulder. "What are thou smiling about?" she asked.

"Ami Ruth, I have been traveling with the Confederate Army for three weeks and have been in the major battle of the war. I have watched hundreds of men getting shot. You have fired more musket balls in anger than I have, and you did it right from your front porch. How on earth did you learn to shoot a gun so well?"

She lifted her chin. "My Papa wanted to be sure I knew how to use a rifle," she said. "He used to take me hunting for squirrels and rabbits when I was younger. After the war began, he wanted to be sure I could load and shoot, in case he was not around to defend my mother.

But he also wanted to be sure I could aim to frighten someone without accidentally hurting or killing them. He set up a shooting gallery with tin cans over at the winery where I practiced, and I even hit a running rabbit a time or two. I don't want to boast, but I am a pretty good shot."

"Ami Ruth Schendler, there is sure more to you than meets the eye," Matt said admiringly. "I think you will be interested in something I found on the way home from Gettysburg." He retrieved the Henry rifle from Big Billy's scabbard and brought it to show her. "Look at this."

She regarded the rifle curiously and said, "I've never seen anything like that. What is it?"

"It is a repeating rifle. You can put as many as sixteen shells in it, and it will keep firing until you run out. Then you can put in sixteen more. In terms of firepower, it is like having five men on your side."

Her eyebrows shot up. "Where did thee get it?" she asked.

"There is time for lots of talk later," Matt said. "Right now I think we need to get a plan ready to defend ourselves. If your experience and mine over the last several days is a predictor of the future, I think we are not done with the intruders who want to take advantage of our Quaker background.

"My Pa always said, 'The way to avoid a fight is to be ready to fight if you need to.' I think we need to get ready, and maybe more important, we need to say to the outside world that we are ready to defend ourselves if we need to."

The rest of that day, Matt and Ami Ruth put together their plan. The broomsticks painted black to look like gun barrels were a good idea, as were the two rifles sticking out of the upstairs windows. However, any Confederate deserters who came their way needed a bit more warning than just what they could see from the road.

Ami Ruth told Matt where to find the black paint she had used to paint the broomsticks. He took a couple of the big paste board boxes from the attic and cut them into large pieces. Then he painted signs on both of them. One was to be placed at the end of the lane out by the road, and the other was placed about halfway up the lane toward the house. The first said:

This is the Schendler Farm. Sorry, but we have nothing left to give you. Others have come before and taken everything.

We have six rifles and a pistol available on our property. Five of the rifles are Smith & Wesson single-shot rifles, and the sixth is a Henry Model 60 Repeating Rifle. We have men here who know how to use them.

Please stay away. If you approach the house, you will be fired on when you reach the second sign halfway up the lane.

The second sign said:

If you have made it this far, it is likely you have a rifle trained on you right now.

You may not pass this point without being shot. Please see the picture below.

It will tell you what is about to happen.

Below the last sentence, Matt had drawn a picture of a rifle aimed at a stick figure with a Confederate cap on. The stick man has doubled over as if he had been shot.

When Matt finished his handiwork, he showed it to Ami Ruth. She began to laugh. "Do thee think that will keep anyone away?" she asked.

"I don't know, but it can't hurt," Matt responded with an answering laugh.

Matt rode Big Billy up the lane and placed the signs. When he came back, he looked again at the front of the house and thought about how to further fortify the place. He went to the barn and hitched up the one farm horse left in the back paddock to the small wagon. He carried several hay bales out to the wagon and stacked them in the bed. He then drove the wagon around to the front of the house and carried the hay bales up on the front porch, stacking several in front of the front door and in front of two of the windows. There would be some advantage in a fire fight to being able to move back and forth on the porch and not being restricted just to the windows. The bales of hay would provide cover as he moved around. The Henry rifle would give him a major advantage over any Confederate soldier. No Confederate had a Henry.

Matt and Ami Ruth set up a schedule for keeping watch, primarily using the lanterns out on the lane for light. Matt knew that the lanterns would help anyone who happened by that way to read the signs. Though he and Ami Ruth couldn't see very well in the dark, neither could anyone who decided to try to attack the farm. If someone was serious about attacking the farm, they would put out the lanterns and use the dark as an ally. So the person keeping watch had to stay in the dark away from the light so their eyes would be adjusted to the dark in case trouble came.

As dusk approached, Matt sat down on the front porch to talk with Ami Ruth. He asked about the men at the winery and why they had abandoned her. She told him that they helped as much as they could.

"They couldn't be blamed," she said. "They are Quaker farmers and not soldiers. They have their own families to worry about. I knew we couldn't count on them to defend the farm."

Matt didn't like that response. What they had done by disappearing was to leave a sixteen-year-old girl all alone to fend for herself when danger was everywhere with the war so close by. If they got through this over the next several days, he would have some serious words to say to them if they wanted to come back to work again on the Schendler Farm.

Ami Ruth continued, "Before the men left, two of them came and helped me bury my folks. I sent one of them up to Charlestown to mail a letter to David. I don't know where he is, but the Union mail service ought to be able to find his unit. I thought he needed to know that our folks were dead and to come home if he could. I sent the letter to be mailed at Charlestown instead of to Berryville because it is Union territory, and I thought the letter had a better chance of reaching him if it was mailed there."

"That was good thinking," Matt said. "What about changing into the boy's clothing?" She had not exchanged the bib overalls for a dress, though she had let her hair down and had cleaned herself up somewhat. Matt noticed how pretty she looked, even in the faded overalls.

"I knew that any chance I had of making it through by myself would be gone if men traveling by on the road thought I was a girl here all alone," she said simply. "These are some of David's old clothes."

"Ami Ruth, what would you have done if the men kept on coming after you fired your second rifle?" he asked.

She said, "I had the one remaining horse on the place saddled and hitched just outside the back door. I intended to go down the back steps and take that horse down the road to the winery and out the back road into the hills. There are some Quakers who live about five miles up the old hill road. I intended to ask them to help me, maybe put me up for a while until the war moved on."

Matt thought that sounded like a good plan and one that was workable and told her so. "I suggest that we saddle Big Billy and the Union horse and leave them there for the next several days. If we get more deserters than we can handle at one time, we can both head for the hills and your Quaker friends.

"There is one thing we can count on," Matt said. "The war will not last forever, and even if it goes on and on, the Army of Northern Virginia is on the move and won't be close by at Winchester for very much longer."

Matt was doing his best to sound positive for Ami Ruth. She had been in fear for several days, and his presence obviously gave her some confidence that they could make it through this crisis. Matt wasn't so sure everything would turn out well, but having a plan A and a plan B made him feel better. He felt very good about being there at the farm, and he especially liked being there with Ami Ruth.

THE MUTUAL DEFENSE AGREEMENT

Several times over the next week, Matt and Ami Ruth saw one or two men who were dressed like soldiers walk down the road and stop to read the sign at the end of the lane. In each case, they kept on walking. Matt was pleased that his plan seemed to be working. They had not had much sleep, and the farm was no longer what Matt could identify as a working farm, but they were safe, and there had been no incidents that required him to fire his gun.

On the eighth day, Ami Ruth called Matt to the front porch. She pointed out that there were five men standing on the road near the sign. Two were on horseback, and three were on foot. They seemed to be looking at the farm. Even from that distance, Matt could tell that several of the men had rifles. In a few minutes, the men began to move purposefully down the lane toward the house.

Matt told Ami Ruth to go to the second floor and to be sure the rifles were ready to fire. She stopped at the front door and looked hard at Matt. She said, "Matt, this is a Quaker house. We shall not kill or injure anyone on our land."

"We may not have the choice if they continue to come up the lane," Matt responded. "They have already taken your parents. We don't want to be the next casualties on the list."

Ami Ruth said again, "Matt, we do not want anyone killed or injured on our land. Does thee understand?" Her use of the words "does thee understand?" emphasized her Quaker upbringing.

Matt felt immediately as if she had just tied one hand behind his back. He could see the possibilities of slowing the attackers down by scaring them with his Henry repeating rifle, but eventually, they were going to come across the fence that bordered the front yard. He was not going to let them approach the house, and he was going to protect Ami Ruth no matter what; the question was how to do it without actually shooting anyone. He wasn't sure he knew how to accomplish that.

He stayed on the front porch, taking advantage of the cover provided by the bales of hay he had placed there. The men on horseback reached the halfway point of the lane, where Matt had placed the second sign, and it was obvious that they were intent on coming on down to the house. Matt took the Henry and fired a warning shot that landed a few feet in front of the first horseman. That stopped their forward movement briefly, but then they dismounted and began to come on foot, using their horses as shields.

Matt then placed a shot at the feet of the horse in front of the group, which was shielding the man who appeared to be their leader. The horse shied, pulled his reins out of the leader's hand, and headed back toward the road at a gallop. The second horse hightailed it after the first one. The men who were hiding behind the horses dove for cover on both sides of the lane, some hiding in the wheat field, some in the vineyard. Matt yelled to Ami Ruth upstairs, "Ami Ruth, get out of there! They're coming!"

He looked down the rifle sight for the renegades. The wheat field was high with winter wheat, and it was hard to make out where the three renegades were hiding. The vineyard was more open, and he could see where the two men who had scattered to that side were crouched among the grape vine trellises.

Matt fired several more shots just in front of the men on each side of the lane. He knew that the shots would eventually be seen as just a bluff. They probably knew this was a Quaker farm, and anyone here would be reluctant to actually shoot anyone. He knew his shots would only hold them off for a few minutes. He hoped that by showing off the rapid-fire capabilities of his Henry Rifle he might scare them away, but his hopes were short-lived. He saw them getting ready to charge the gate.

Matt was in a quandary. Did he shoot to kill, or continue to miss the men and hope they decided the Schendler Farm would be too tough to take? How long could he wait to decide? Ami Ruth's words were still in his ears.

Just at that instant, Matt heard the loud ringing of a bell. It seemed to be coming from the barn! The ringing filled the air, and when Matt looked out over the fields, he realized it seemed to be confusing the renegades. They were still down on the ground and seemed to be talking to each other back and forth across the lane. Matt didn't know who was ringing the bell or why, but he didn't much care since the sound seemed to be keeping the renegades from charging the gate. That delayed the inevitable decision Matt would have to make, whether to heed Ami Ruth's words or do what he had to do to protect her and the house.

His respite was a brief one. Matt heard the report of the rifles coming from the fields in front of the house and sensed the renegades' preparation to charge. Several of the rifle balls hit close to Matt, and he was glad he had taken the time to put the hay bales in place around the front porch. He stayed close to the stacked bales nearest the front door so he could dive behind them if necessary. They might have to patch some bullet holes in the front porch, but so far, the rifle balls were doing little damage.

As the bell continued to ring, Matt's mind quickly calculated the capabilities of the men and their weaponry. He knew that the group of men probably had only about five shots in their rifles without reloading. He figured that when their single-shot rifles had been fired, they would want to get closer so they could use their pistols. He figured each of them had six shots in the pistol chambers if they were revolvers, but they were easy to reload, and they could do it on the move. The closer the intruders came to the house, the more impossible the situation for Matt and Ruth would become.

Matt wasn't sure where Ami Ruth was now. She could be gone, or she could be the one ringing the bell in the barn. He yelled again as loud as he could, "Ami Ruth, get out of there now!"

Matt visualized Ami Ruth escaping down the back stairs and taking the horse down the lane toward the vineyard, riding to that Quaker neighbor's house for safety. The bell kept ringing while Matt continued to pepper the fields where the men were hiding. He ran out of ammunition and reached for the box of shells and reloaded. Now he had another sixteen shots, but during the brief pause, the men in the field again began moving forward. Before long, they would be rushing the gate!

Suddenly, a movement up by the road caught Matt's eye. Peering through the trees, he saw a black buggy with several men inside. Behind them was another wagon with several men in the wagon bed. When they reached the entrance to the lane leading to the house, the men—Matt counted a dozen or more—moved out onto the road and down the lane like a small army. Another wagon arrived, and there were several people inside it as well. Before another minute had passed, the fields up by the road seemed full of people, men and women both, and many were carrying pitchforks and axes. Some followed the first group down the lane, and others crossed the fence and moved through the fields.

As the group wielding their farm tools approached the renegades, the five men stood up and put their hands in the air, rifles abandoned at their feet. Matt's heart leapt in his chest. The crisis was over!

The bell continued to ring, and Matt moved off the porch toward the barn. Who had sounded the alarm? With his rifle still in hand, Matt approached the barn and looked into the loft. There was Ami Ruth, blonde hair flying, pulling on the bell rope as hard as she could. Matt yelled up to her that she could stop.

Ami Ruth climbed down from the loft, her face still red with the effort of pulling the bell rope. Matt hugged her tight. He then held her at arm's length and demanded, "Ami Ruth, what just happened?"

She had a big smile on her face. "Pa and the other farmers in the area decided more than a year ago, following the first battle of Winchester, that they would band together to help protect each other. There were some problems with deserters afterward, and they realized that if a major battle happened near here again, deserters and renegades would swarm the area. Our farms were in greater jeopardy from the deserters than from the two armies, so they decided that a mutual defense agreement was in everyone's best interest. They needed an alarm system, so they ordered twenty bells together from a foundry in Philadelphia."

Ami Ruth was talking with great excitement at this point, almost talking faster than Matt could listen. She went on. "They chose the Mt. Holly Iron Foundry Works, the same one that had recast the Liberty Bell back in 1776. When the bells were ready, they sent David to Philadelphia with a wagon to retrieve them.

"Everybody hung their bells in their barns, and on one day they all rang them at the same time, as sort of a drill. The bells were crafted so the ring of each bell would be as close as possible to the sound of the other bells. They wanted to be able to distinguish the sound of distress from every other sound of metal on metal. The signal was to tell them where the trouble was and for each of them, as quickly as possible, to find the ringing bell.

"I watched Pa ring the bell he hung in our loft months ago, but to be honest, I didn't even think about the bell again until thee yelled at me to get out of the house. He was always very particular about the bell and told Mama and me that no one was ever to ring it but him. When I heard thy voice, the memory of the bell hit me, and I knew that was the answer to our problem. So I did get out of the house just like thee said, but instead of running off up the winery road, I went to the barn loft and began pulling on the rope."

She had just finished explaining about the bell when they reached the front yard. By then the yard was beginning to fill with the neighbors who were bringing the five renegades through the front gate.

Matt was overjoyed with what had just happened. He had been living with an overwhelming feeling of pending disaster, and now he felt nothing but relief. He also felt a newfound respect for these Amish and Quaker farmers who rejected violence in any form but could band together to bring about a peaceful solution to a violent problem just by sheer weight of numbers.

Ami Ruth introduced Matt to several of their benefactors, and Matt was soon shaking hands and thanking them one after the other. In his isolated farm in North Carolina, living with his Ma and Pa, he had never felt a part of a community, but he was certainly feeling a part of this group today.

One member of the little Quaker army approached Matt. He said, "Matt, I believe that all of these men are deserters from the Confederate Army. I would be pleased to escort them back to Winchester and turn them over to the authorities."

Matt nodded his pleasure at the offer. The quicker these renegades were off Schendler Farm property, the better he would like it. "Thank you, sir, that would be wonderful!" he said.

He was about to say something else to Ami Ruth when he realized she had left his side. She was running across the yard, screaming at the top of her lungs, toward a man who had just come down the lane. She was yelling, "David! David! David!"

Matt watched as she grabbed her older brother in a bear hug and saw the tears begin to flow. Matt's face split in a big grin. Earlier he had thought about good luck piling on top of good luck. Here was another example. In the midst of all of the tumult, he heard his Ma's voice again. She said, clear as a bell, "His wonders never cease." She was right again. How else could he account for everything that had happened?

Ami Ruth finally brought her brother over to where Matt was still shaking hands and thanking his new friends. "Matt, this is my brother David, all the way from Pennsylvania. David, this is Matt Mason, who has been protecting me and our farm."

The two shook hands, and before they knew it, they were hugging each other too. Ami Ruth put her arms around both of them. When they finally broke apart, Matt asked the obvious question. "Where did you come from?"

"We were camped just south of Gettysburg when I got the letter from Ami Ruth about our folks," David said. "I asked for leave and was on the road the next morning. I have been riding south ever since. I crossed the Potomac at Harper's Ferry and came on as fast as I could."

"I was at Gettysburg too," Matt said. "How did you avoid the Confederate patrols?"

David responded, "Well, first I took off my uniform as soon as I left my unit. I put on the dress of a Quaker man, the white shirt, black pants, and most importantly, the hat. I was in the heart of Quaker and Amish territory. Dressed as a Quaker, I would attract less attention than I would have as a Union soldier. Both sides view Quakers and the

Amish as neutral in the war, but I did the best I could to stay away from any military personnel, Union or Confederate. That worked pretty well until I was about five miles away from here. I never saw so many renegades, deserters, derelicts, and good-for-nothings on the road! I could easily understand what happened to my folks. I was pleased that Ami Ruth got word to me so quickly and that I was close enough to get home, but it looks like I just missed all the excitement!"

Matt, Ami Ruth, and David stayed in the front yard until all the neighbors dispersed. The words "Thank you" were uttered over and over to the many friends who had come so quickly to answer their distress call. Matt knew that he would certainly answer anyone else's bell in the future, though he hoped there was never another such occasion.

When everyone was gone, the three young people went up on the porch. Ami Ruth said she was going to see what they might have for supper. Matt and David sat down to begin to get acquainted, and Matt told David about what had happened before he arrived. "Your sister is really something," Matt concluded. "Your homecoming would have been very different if she hadn't remembered that bell."

A little later, Ami Ruth came to the door and announced, "Supper will soon be ready. I want thee both to know that this is the first time I have fixed a meal in our kitchen since we lost Mama, so it will not be a normal Schendler supper. The earlier renegades took all of our meat, but we still have vegetables. So supper tonight is all vegetables with green beans, pinto beans, mashed potatoes, stewed crab apples, and grapes. I do need someone to milk our cow so we can have some milk to go with the vegetables."

"I'll volunteer," David said.

After supper, Matt went to the barn to settle his horses in for the night. When he returned, he walked into the back door of the house and was struck by the silence. He walked all the way through the house and did not find Ami Ruth or David. Finally, he went to the front porch. He stood at the front steps looking out at the little family cemetery in the distance. Ami Ruth and David were standing there together just inside the picket fence. She kept putting her handkerchief to her face, and Matt could tell that she was crying. David put his arm around her, and they stood there together for several minutes. Finally, they started back toward the house, walking arm in arm.

Later that night, the three of them sat down together on the porch to talk about the future. David was approaching twenty years of age and was obviously the senior member of the threesome. He carried the conversation while Matt and Ami Ruth listened. David said that he knew by the laws of the state of Virginia that he was now the owner of the farm. He would need to file the necessary papers at the county seat to move the process of inheritance forward. Ami Ruth, as a female member of the family, could not own property by herself, but she could be a part owner with a husband. David pointed out that he was committed to the ministry, and by the rules of that profession, he could not have two professions, minister and farmer. That complicated the situation with the farm.

Ami Ruth told David about their parents inviting Matt to become a part of their family and to come back to the farm after he found his father. David seemed comfortable with that arrangement and thought a moment before speaking.

"Here are the options open to us," said David. "One, we can sell the farm to Matt. How much money do you have, Matt?"

Matt thought of what was left of the Yankee soldier's money. "Nine dollars, Union," he said.

"That sounds like a fair price," David said, smiling. "Or two, when Ami Ruth gets married, she can share ownership of the farm with her husband."

Matt interjected, "Neither of those options takes care of your future, David."

"Don't worry about me. The Lord will be taking care of me," he responded.

They talked into the evening. Matt carried the lanterns out to the lane so their night defenses would be set up. They decided to go to bed and wake up in the morning to get a fresh start on their discussions.

David took the first watch on the porch, and Ami Ruth went upstairs to her room. Matt went to his makeshift room in the barn to get a few hours of sleep until he relieved David at midnight. He was sound asleep when he felt a hand on his shoulder. It was Ami Ruth.

"Matt," she whispered, "we could get married and live here on the farm as husband and wife. I am already sixteen, and you will be sixteen next month. That is legal age in Virginia. We would then be joint owners of the farm. That would solve all of the inheritance problems. What do you think?"

Matt wasn't sure he had heard her right. Get married? Matt knew he would have to be careful how he responded to her proposal.

He spoke slowly, choosing his words carefully. "Getting married is a pretty permanent solution to this problem for two people who are just sixteen years old," he said. "I'm not sure we are ready yet. We need some time. Let's think about it and talk more in the morning."

Without a word, Ami Ruth left him in the barn and went back to the house. Matt did not sleep anymore that night. He took over the watch at midnight and stayed wide awake, thinking about the prospect of being married to Ami Ruth and becoming part owner of a farm, and not just any farm—this wonderful farm! He had to admit that he liked the idea, but he didn't feel ready to be a married man yet. After all, he was just fifteen years old. Well, sixteen in just a couple of weeks.

New ideas and second thoughts were explored with each conversation with David over the next two weeks until his leave ended, and conversations with Ami Ruth extended for months after that. It became obvious that no permanent solution could be arrived at right away. There were major milestones coming in their future, especially for David. He would be free of his military obligation when the war ended—whenever that happened. They decided the issue of the farm's ownership would be resolved with the completion of his studies at the seminary after the war.

Matt and Ami Ruth were young yet and had much to look forward to. They had time on their side, as youth always does.

EPILOGUE

David Picks Up the Story

When I came home from Gettysburg to that amazing scene at my family farm, the world I left had changed significantly. My parents were gone, and Ami Ruth, the little girl I left behind, was now very much the young lady. Still, she and Matt at sixteen were just growing into adulthood. While both were very mature for their ages, it did not seem prudent to leave them alone on the farm with an overwhelming load of new responsibility. Ami Ruth and Matt had talked about marriage, and I could see the desire of both of them to get the matter of their future together settled. However, with some reasoning, they both agreed that it would be best to wait at least until a couple of years, perhaps until they were eighteen.

The Civil War ended in April 1865, and I completed my seminary studies a few months later. That July, I returned home and performed the wedding ceremony for Matt and Ami Ruth in the little Meeting House of the Society of Friends near Berryville. All of the Amish and Quaker friends Matt had met during the renegade crisis were there to be a part of the celebration. It was a joyous summer day. Ami Ruth made a beautiful bride wearing our mother's wedding dress, and Matt was a handsome groom. He was proud to finally be wearing a pair of size 14 shoes!

If you wonder how Matt and Ami Ruth managed to live and work together through that two-year period without being married, without emotions taking control, and without the neighbors talking, it was a valid concern. I solved this problem by inviting Aunt Elizabeth, our mother's maiden sister, to come and live with them. She provided help and support for Ami Ruth, who missed our mother terribly, while serving as an excellent chaperone. Matt maintained his residence in the barn.

Our farm had always been a working farm, and Matt quickly got it in shape again. His experience on the little farm in North Carolina was obvious. When I came back after two years, it was hard not to be impressed with what he had done, especially with the vineyard and the winery. The vineyard extended back across another valley and up the ridge on the other side. An addition had been added to the winery so he could bottle more wine. He and his winery foreman were experimenting with some new grape varieties, seeing if they will thrive in Virginia. Indeed, under his management, the winery was becoming famous beyond the region. After the war ended, it became possible for Matt to sell Schendler wines in the major cities of the north, including Washington, DC, Baltimore, and Philadelphia. As I write this, he has begun exploring the possibility of shipping Schendler wine through the port of Baltimore to England and Europe as well.

Big Billy, Matt's big bay horse, became a popular stud in the region with horse breeders bringing their mares to the Schendler Farm on a regular basis. One could say life was good on the Schendler Farm, but for no resident was that more true than for Big Billy!

At the time of the wedding, the major unresolved issue that still weighed heavily on Matt's heart was whether his Pa had survived the war in one of the Union prisoner-of-war camps. By the time I returned to perform the wedding ceremony, the war had been over for three months. Matt told me he had purchased advertisements in a number of newspapers in major cities across the South, seeking information about Zeke Mason. I was coming from Philadelphia and knew from our local newspapers there that his advertisements were just one among thousands placed by the families of both Southern and Northern soldiers looking for their sons and fathers after the opening of the prisoner-of-war camps all across the battling states. Because there were no prisoner-of-war exchanges the last two years of the war, most did not even know if their loved ones were alive or dead.

One of the advertisements Matt placed was in the little weekly newspaper called *The Mt. Airy News* back in his hometown in North Carolina. He felt that if his father was alive, he might try to make it back to Mt. Airy, a place with which he was familiar and where he would want to visit his wife's grave. Matt shared with me that a letter came in the mail just the other day in response to his Mt. Airy advertisement. It read as follows:

Dear Matt,

It was great to read your advertisement in the local newspaper and to know where you are. I was captured on Cemetery Ridge at the end of Pickett's Charge. I was injured with a leg wound, which is all healed up now. They put several of us in the prisoner-of-war camp on Point Lookout just below St. Mary's City, Maryland. I will tell you all about it when we are together again. I am going to begin walking in your direction tomorrow. I think it will take me about three weeks to get there. Look for me in late July. As your sainted Ma would say, "My cup runneth over."

Your Pa,
Isaac Mason

AUTHOR'S NOTES

The History Behind Journey to Gettysburg

Journey to Gettysburg is a fiction-based-on-fact story. The Battle of Gettysburg was a pivotal turning point in the Civil War that sealed the fate of the South in its battle for independence from the Union. Matt Mason is a fictional character who was a bystander, observer, and then a participant in one of the major milestones in the history of the United States. His story begins with the tragic loss of his mother at their farm near the little town of Mt. Airy, North Carolina. It continues as he travels town to town and city to city in his search for his Pa, who was serving in the Army of Northern Virginia. That army was on its way to Gettysburg. Along the way he meets a number of people who make his trek noteworthy. These encounters give the reader a feel for the stress of war times and the constant preoccupation of the people with tragedy and threat in places near and far to them. It also shows the natural kindness of people as Matt Mason finds many new friends and benevolent relationships with strangers. Here is some historical background that will enrich your understanding of the book.

The Amish and Quaker Groups

It is easy to confuse the Amish and Quaker religious groups. Both are denominations of conservative Christians, and both are found in large numbers in Pennsylvania, Maryland, and northern Virginia. In many ways they live similar lives. Both are known to use the words *thee* and *thou* when referring to themselves and others. Both tend toward simple living and plain dress and are reluctant to adopt the conveniences of modern technology. Neither group believes in slavery or in war.

Major differences began to occur between the two groups during the mid-nineteenth century. The Amish tended to stay on their farms and to relate primarily to others within their own group, as had been their history. The Quakers, in contrast, began to open businesses and to relate to the rest of the population, whom they referred to as the "English."

It is logical that in the early 1860s, living in close proximity to each other, these similar religious groups with strong conservative values should band together for mutual protection and to promote their business interests both within and outside of their communities.

Cities and Towns

All of the places mentioned in the story are real, though some of the towns have changed their names since the mid-1800s. For instance, the towns of Jacksonville and Big Lick in Virginia are now called Floyd and Roanoke respectively. If you wondered, there really is a place named Paw Paw, West Virginia. It is located on the most southern bend of the Potomac River west of Williamsport. It got its name from the pawpaw tree that has a fruit of that same name, so that old children's song about the pawpaw was about a real commodity. In case you don't remember the song, the chorus went as follows:

> *Picking up pawpaws putting them in a basket,*
> *Picking up pawpaws putting them in a basket,*
> *Picking up pawpaws putting them in a basket,*
>   *Way down yonder in the pawpaw patch.*

Hospitals

The tragic occurrence in chapter 3 changed the route of travel for young Matt Mason. He had intended to travel through Big Lick and then go the rest of the way north up the Shenandoah Valley on level ground. Having his eye injured in the confrontation with the renegades made it imperative that he go to a military hospital in Lynchburg for treatment. That city became a medical center for the South during the Civil War. More than 190 battles were fought in the state of Virginia during the war, and casualties were heavy on both sides. The fact that Lynchburg was well off the beaten path yet still had three railroads that ended there as well as the James River for transportation made it a logical place for the location of major military hospitals. There were thirty-two hospitals in Lynchburg during the 1860s. The Ladies' Aid Hospital, so named because it was staffed and managed by women, had the best survival statistics. Thus, it was the one recommended for Matt Mason when he needed treatment for his injured eye.

Horses

During the Civil War, the Union Army issued horses to its cavalry while the Confederate Army required its horse soldiers to furnish their own mounts.

Hearing about the surprise attack on the Confederate cavalry at Brandy Station from the two renegades in chapter 3 proved to be a major positive for young Matt. When he arrived in that vicinity on his journey, he spent a night on the Brandy Station campsite, hoping that a horse would still be hanging around. That is how he came to find the big bay horse that he called Big Billy. Mr. Schendler suggested to him that such a fine horse must have belonged to an officer. Indeed, there was a big bay horse that was the property of cavalry officer Wade Hampton, who was second in command of General Lee's cavalry under the leadership of General JEB Stuart. Wade Hampton was from Charleston, South Carolina, and his horse, Butler, was raised on a plantation just outside the city. Hampton was injured in the battle at Brandy Station, cut on the back of the head by a saber, and was knocked unconscious. He lost his big bay horse and did not find him again for the remainder of the war.

Hampton was injured again at Gettysburg and survived yet another saber cut, this time to the front of his head. He carried a visible scar there for the rest of his life. Wade Hampton was later promoted to general in charge of the cavalry when JEB Stuart was killed late in the war. After the war, he was elected governor of South Carolina and later US Senator.

Shoes

It is estimated that up to 25 percent of Confederate soldiers and 15 percent of Union soldiers spent much of the war without shoes. That was not too bad during the summer months as many were used to living and working without shoes, except in the dead of winter. Southerners, especially, walked barefoot much of the year. However, it was a serious problem when marching long distances between engagements and trying to carry on the war during the winter months.

It should come as no surprise that Gettysburg was not the target for the Confederate Army when it invaded Pennsylvania. The initial target was Harrisburg, the capital city in Pennsylvania. The attraction of Harrisburg was not only that it was the capital of a state but that it had been the capital of the United States during a part of the Revolutionary War. The revolutionaries had moved the seat of government there to create more distance between the US government and the British forces. Thus, Harrisburg was well known in France, and that was the country General Robert E. Lee was trying to impress with his first major conquest north of the Mason-Dixon Line. If he could take Harrisburg, he felt France might have been persuaded to lend a hand in the war. It might have, at least, sent its fleet to help break the blockade of the South's ports so they could trade internationally and ship supplies to their armies. Unfortunately for the South, it was not to be.

The detour to Gettysburg had to do with the shoe factory that was located in that little county-seat town. That the Battle of Gettysburg began between two groups of soldiers who were in town to find shoes should not be a surprise considering the lack of shoes among their troops. That situation was used as a plot ploy in chapter 14 to involve young Matt and his Pa directly in the beginnings of this major battle of the Civil War.

Incidentally, Matt never did get his shoes during the war. The fact that he and Zeke were attacked near the shoe factory in Gettysburg and that Matt had size 14 feet, an unusually large size, proved to be major factors in keeping our young hero barefoot throughout the story.

The Significance of the Battle of Gettysburg

The Battle of Gettysburg is quite simply the most important battle in US history. It was the turning point of the Civil War, and had it not ended as it did, the United States might be three or even four separate countries today. Here are some important points that underpin *Journey to Gettysburg*.

Leadership. General Robert E. Lee said in his memoirs that had he not lost General Thomas "Stonewall" Jackson at the Battle of Chancellorsville, he would have won at Gettysburg. He entered that crucial battle with an undefeated record in major battles after two years of the war. But, at Chancellorsville he lost his best battle tactician and closest friend. The replacement chosen for Jackson to lead the Army of Northern Virginia's Second Corps was General Richard Ewell. He was not a seasoned military officer and was not as aggressive a general as Jackson had proven to be.

At the end of the first day of the Battle at Gettysburg, General Ewell's troops had pushed the Union Army back through the town of Gettysburg and had numerical superiority of soldiers on the field. General Lee ordered General Ewell to continue to push the Union Army and to capitalize on the numerical advantage. Instead, General Ewell went against those orders and decided to rest his troops through the rest of that night. By morning, the Union Army had received reinforcements, and the South never again had superior numbers on the field. Some have pointed to Ewell's reluctance to push his advantage as one of three major reasons why the South lost the battle.

Battle tactics. Normal battle tactics of the time directed that an army that had smaller numbers should choose well its location on the battlefield. Occupying the high ground was advantageous. And it was advised that the smaller-numbered army should set up in a defensive formation and force the opposition to attempt to push them off their high ground and from their defensive fortifications. More casualties occur during attack than while defending.

At Gettysburg, the opposite occurred. The Union had ninety thousand troops compared to approximately seventy thousand for the South. In addition, about 20 percent of the Union troops had Henry repeating rifles that could shoot as many as five rounds per minute. The Confederate troops were equipped with Smith & Wesson single-shot rifles that could shoot at most one shot per minute. The fifteen thousand Union troops with Henrys made the value of those troops roughly five times the value of a single Southern soldier in terms of firepower. Thus, the advantage of the Union was closer to double the number of Southern soldiers on the field. Despite this situation, Union General George Meade deployed his troops on the high ground in a defensive formation and left it to the Confederate troops to try to dislodge them. The South just didn't have enough firepower to defeat the Union soldiers deployed in defensive fortifications and occupying the high ground. They would have been wiser not to have tried.

Casualties. When one looks at casualties, it is hard to know which side won the Battle of Gettysburg. The Union suffered 30,000 killed and wounded, the South 27,000. One of the major differences was the fact that of the 27,000 Southern casualties, 8,000 were wounded. Those wounded were transported from the battlefield in more than 700 wagons. Between the battlefield and the town of Williamsport, a four-day ride by wagon, the South lost 580 of the wagons carrying their wounded. Wagons broke down, and the wagon train was not defended. The Union Army and the surrounding civilian population made a major effort to disable the wagons so the wounded could not be taken back South. Thus, a large number of the Southern wounded were left on the side of the road to fend for themselves. Many died along the road, and many others ended up in Union prisoner-of-war camps. In the end, only 1,200 of the 8,000 wounded continued to be potential fighting men through the next two years of the war.

The Union also had approximately 8,000 wounded. By contrast, the Union was able to rehabilitate almost 6,000 of their casualties from the battlefield at Gettysburg. The losses of their wounded were mostly to disease and infection.

Cannons. One of the major focal points in the *Journey to Gettysburg* story is the cannons under the leadership of Colonel Edward Porter Alexander, who served under General Henry Heth. Matt Mason's Pa was a soldier in Alexander's command. The South went into Gettysburg with approximately 170 cannons. They came out of the battle with around seventy. Because of the high water at Williamsport and the lack of a bridge over the Potomac, the South had to destroy their remaining cannons because they could not get them back across the river. At that time in history, the North had more than twenty foundries where cannons could be built. Unfortunately, the South had only one. It was in Richmond, Virginia, and it was largely nonfunctional because of the Union blockade at the mouth of the Chesapeake. General Lee knew that without cannons, he would never again be able to face off with the Union in a major battle because he had no artillery. Losing the cannons was a major blow to the Southern cause.

The Chesapeake and Ohio Canal

When Matt Mason was attempting to make his way from Williamsport, Maryland, back to the Schendler Farm near Berryville, Virginia, he chose to travel up the Potomac River, hoping to find a place where he could ford the river with his injured horse, Big Billy. He did not realize that the Chesapeake and Ohio Canal was built close to the Potomac River on the south side and ran all the way from Cumberland, Maryland, to Washington, DC. It was operated from 1831 to 1924 and was in full use in 1863, when this story takes place. Matt chose to cross the two bodies of water at Paw Paw, West Virginia, because the river was narrow at that point, and the canal ran through the Paw Paw Tunnel. That gave him an overpass where he could walk the horse across the canal without difficulty.

Virginia Wine Country

The area around Berryville, Virginia, is known as Virginia's Wine Country. There are numerous vineyards, and several of them have their own labels. The Schendler Farm is a fictional name, but it could have been any of a dozen or more vineyards that were active in the 1860s that are still productive today. For all of its history, the major cash crop of the state of Virginia has been tobacco. However, in the vicinity of Berryville both then and now, grapes are the dominant crop, and wine is the most important agricultural cash crop.

AFTERWORD

Several issues remain unresolved as the story concludes. As is always the case, sometimes the unresolved parts of a story are as interesting as the parts that are resolved. Speculation on the possibilities keeps the story alive into the future. That is my intent with the story of Matt Mason and his *Journey to Gettysburg*. If you enjoyed this story, I expect that you may read a sequel at some point in the not-too-distant future that relates to Reconstruction in the South and its effect on the Amish and Quaker communities of northern Virginia. There you will be able to rejoin Matt Mason, his wife Ami Ruth, their children, and the Schendler Farm. And you can expect to find the big bay horse, Big Billy, there and still popular among the mares in the region.

ABOUT THE AUTHOR

Dr. Mark L. Hopkins is a mid-westerner by birth and a southerner by choice. He holds three degrees from Missouri universities. He taught history for several years and is past president of four colleges, one each in the states of Iowa, Illinois, South Carolina, and California. Dr. Hopkins writes a weekly column that is syndicated by GateHouse Media and is regularly published across 26 states in more than 400 newspapers. He likes history and humor, and both are reflected in his columns. Dr. Hopkins has written academic papers, magazine articles, chapters for books, and many articles for newspapers. He is enjoying his first effort at writing fiction and hopes to continue writing in the field of fiction in future years.

Dr. Hopkins' wife Ruth is a professional artist and they have three grown children, Sara, an Optometrist, Amy, a college administrator, and Steven, an attorney and insurance executive. They also have six grandchildren that range in age from 21 to 6.

CPSIA information can be obtained
at www.ICGtesting.com
Printed in the USA
FSHW011540080420
68957FS